EYES *to* SEE

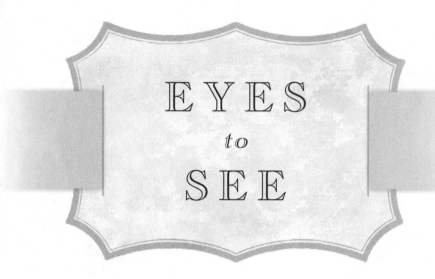

EYES
to
SEE

Edited by

BRET LOTT

THOMAS NELSON
Since 1798

NASHVILLE   DALLAS   MEXICO CITY   RIO DE JANEIRO   BEIJING

Published in Nashville, Tennessee, by Thomas Nelson. Thomas Nelson is a registered trademark of Thomas Nelson, Inc.

Thomas Nelson, Inc., titles may be purchased in bulk for educational, business, fund-raising, or sales promotional use. For information, please e-mail SpecialMarkets@ThomasNelson.com.

Library of Congress Cataloging-in-Publication Data

Eyes to see / edited by Bret Lott.
    p. cm.
  ISBN 1-59554-319-8 (hardcover)
  1. Short stories. I. Lott, Bret.
PN6120.2.E96 2077
808.83'1—dc22   20077036676

Printed in the United States of America
08 09 10 11 QW 6 5 4 3 2 1

CONTENTS

CONTENTS

INTRODUCTION

WHEN I FIRST BEGAN WRITING SERIOUSLY, WHEN I FIRST gave thought to the idea of actually trying to be a *writer*, the only form I ever imagined myself writing in was the short story. The entire time I was in graduate school, learning to write and write and write, all I ever talked about, thought about, dreamed about were short stories.

My favorite author was Raymond Carver, a man who never published a novel and whose stories were so exquisitely rendered, so beautifully crafted and spare and rock-hard, not to mention meaningful in their portrayal of the working class I came from and about which I wanted to write, that I simply never gave thought to trying any other form. He was the writer I most wanted to write like, the one whose voice and vision and artistry I hoped most to emulate for the quality of that work, and because novels never figured in to his writing life, neither would they to mine. I knew, I just *knew*, I would never write anything but short stories.

There was and remains something pure not only to his stories but to the form at large, something beautiful and moving about holding in one's hand a narrative, gem-like and perfect, that could be read in one sitting, opening its world before my very eyes and revealing its secrets in a small pocket of time that allowed me to go somewhere else and know something new.

But I find myself at this point in my life being primarily a novelist. This isn't because I ceased to enjoy the short story, or because I think less of the form now than I did when I first started writing. Not at all. Allow me a moment to tell a tale, one I can't tell without sounding as though I am boasting, but trust me, I tell it in humility (though even assigning myself the trait of humility means, of course, I am no longer being humble): The first two books I published were novels, the third a collection of short stories, and when the review of that collection appeared in the *New York Times Book Review*, the first line began, "Novelist Bret Lott's first collection of short stories . . ."

Novelist Bret Lott.

The review was a good one, a review anyone would have been proud to have garnered (if one puts any stock at all in reviews to begin with), and yet I was disappointed—really—in that I was known as a novelist, when for so many years I had wanted only to write short stories.

And so it is with fear and trembling that I come to writing this introduction to the stories collected here. These are great short stories by great writers, timeless classics rendered in a form I had hoped to master on my own at some point in my writing life, and yet here I am, a novelist.

So who am I, I want to know, to gather them together and present them to you?

The answer, of course, is that I am a reader, indeed one who has loved stories since before I could even read them, and it is my hope that this gathering of them will delight and move and challenge and humble you as much as it does me.

A good story will do all of these things, and more. A good story can change the way we think, the way we live and love and make our way through this world. And because of the importance of *story*, and the way it can change our lives, it is with even deeper humility, even deeper fear and trembling, that I try to write this introduction.

Because with this collection there is everywhere evident the fact there is much more at stake than simply a good story. There is more at stake than artistry, than the beauty of the form. Gathered here is an array of stories that seek to speak to and of the greatest story ever told: the love of God for us, a love so deep He gave His only begotten Son that we might have life everlasting.

Inherent to that Story of all stories—a true story, not like the fictive tales here—is conflict. Christ's presence among us wrought the greatest conflict ever known: that of man as a creation of God against that same man felled by the sin of believing himself to be god of his own life. It is only through the revelation of love from God through Christ's life, a love so vast and a sacrifice so beyond our comprehension, that we human beings can see, finally, that only through forsaking ourselves as believers in our own divinity can we come to understand true meaning and true love. It is only by giving up ourselves that we can come to solve the conflict inherent to the story of all our lives.

The stories gathered here have in common that struggle of self with self, and though such a summary statement as that would seem to say that all the stories here are the same, they are not, just as the struggle each of us must suffer through in coming to Christ is only and always the particular struggle of a particular creation of God.

What informs that struggle common to all these characters is the brutal fact that we all falter, and must find our own way to hold hard to our knowledge of a transcendent God. Our struggles may manifest themselves in such diverse ways as the seeming cowardice of Kisuke in Shusako Endo's "The Final Martyrs," or the moment of absolute clarity Grace affords the bewildered and terrified grandmother in Flannery O'Connor's "A Good Man Is Hard to Find," or in such apparent happenstance as the repeated obstacles Henry Van Dyke's Other Wise Man encounters again and again. This struggle with self may be displayed in harmlessly selfish motives such as the widower Tanner's desire for company in Helen Norris's "The Christmas Wife," Tanner himself "a reasonable man in his early sixties, desiring peace, a measure of joy, and reassurance," his actions nowhere near as sinful and deserving of condemnation as Fyodor Dostoevsky's "devilishly cunning" honest thief, or as actively—and mournfully—implicit in another's crime as Luke Ripley in Andre Dubus's "A Father's Story."

Yet in every story collected here is found the unifying element of the embracing of God, a principle and an action that yields the cornucopia of stories this collection presents.

Finally, while writing this introduction, I came across a quote by Ingmar Bergman, the internationally renowned and respected filmmaker who just this week passed away. Mr. Bergman was raised in a devoutly religious family, though as far as we can know from this side of heaven he was not a believer. But the following observation he made about contemporary art and its relationship to God is one worthy, I believe, of appending here at the end of an introduction I have felt myself unworthy to write from first word to last.

"It is my opinion" Bergman wrote, "that art lost its creative urge the moment it was separated from worship."

I agree with him when it comes to most all of our secular writing today. Too often stories are simply woeful maunderings through the lives of people whose only hope is in themselves as the gods of their lives. Such is the pitiful return on making ourselves into that god Satan continues to tempt us into believing we all can be.

But the works gathered here, these classic Christian stories, have set at their hearts the true worship of God, and therefore yield a return beyond our imagination; these stories, because they are made in humility and in recognition of the one true God, yield for us ways of seeing the eternal importance of God's mercy and grace, and, most importantly, His infinite love for us, and I am thankful and humbled to be allowed here to offer them to you.

Bret Lott
August 2007
Charleston, South Carolina

EYES *to* SEE

G. K. CHESTERTON

BORN IN LONDON IN 1874 TO A MIDDLE-CLASS FAMILY, Gilbert Keith Chesterton was a journalist, poet, and biographer but was most famous for his beloved "Father Brown" mystery stories, which he wrote between 1911 and 1936. An influential Christian writer and thinker, he was the author of, among other important works, *The Everlasting Man*, *Heretics*, and *Orthodoxy*.

While a student at University College and the Slade School of Art from 1893 to 1896, Chesterton experienced a crisis of uncertainty and depression, and left the university without a degree. He then worked for London publishers and later renewed his Christian faith, due in no small part to Frances Blogg, the woman he courted and then married in 1901.

In 1909 Chesterton and his wife moved twenty-five miles west of London to the village of Beaconsfield, where he continued his writing life, and from which he traveled widely. In 1922 he converted from Anglicanism to Roman Catholicism.

During his lifetime he published sixty-nine books, and received honorary degrees from Edinburgh, Dublin, and Notre Dame universities. Chesterton died on June 14, 1936, at his home in Beaconsfield.

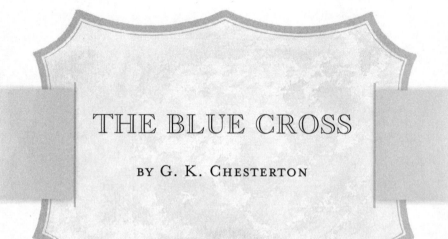

THE BLUE CROSS

BY G. K. CHESTERTON

Between the silver ribbon of morning and the green glittering ribbon of sea, the boat touched Harwich and let loose a swarm of folk like flies, among whom the man we must follow was by no means conspicuous—nor wished to be. There was nothing notable about him, except a slight contrast between the holiday gaiety of his clothes and the official gravity of his face. His clothes included a slight, pale grey jacket, a white waistcoat, and a silver straw hat with a grey-blue ribbon. His lean face was dark by contrast, and ended in a curt black beard that looked Spanish and suggested an Elizabethan ruff. He was smoking a cigarette with the seriousness of an idler. There was nothing about him to indicate the fact that the grey jacket covered a loaded revolver, that the white waistcoat covered a police card, or that the straw hat covered one of the most powerful intellects in Europe. For this was Valentin himself, the head of the Paris police and the most famous investigator of the world; and he was coming from Brussels to London to make the greatest arrest of the century.

Flambeau was in England. The police of three countries had tracked the great criminal at last from Ghent to Brussels, from Brussels to the Hook of Holland; and it was conjectured that he would take some advantage of the unfamiliarity and confusion of the Eucharistic Congress, then taking place in London. Probably he would travel as some minor clerk or secretary connected with it; but, of course, Valentin could not be certain; nobody could be certain about Flambeau.

It is many years now since this colossus of crime suddenly ceased keeping the world in a turmoil; and when he ceased, as they said after the death of Roland, there was a great quiet upon the earth. But in his best days (I mean, of course, his worst) Flambeau was a figure as statuesque and international as the Kaiser. Almost every morning the daily paper announced that he had escaped the consequences of one extraordinary crime by committing another. He was a Gascon of gigantic stature and bodily daring; and the wildest tales were told of his outbursts of athletic humour; how he turned the juge d'instruction upside down and stood him on his head, "to clear his mind"; how he ran down the Rue de Rivoli with a policeman under each arm. It is due to him to say that his fantastic physical strength was generally employed in such bloodless though undignified scenes; his real crimes were chiefly those of ingenious and wholesale robbery. But each of his thefts was almost a new sin, and would make a story by itself. It was he who ran the great Tyrolean Dairy Company in London, with no dairies, no cows, no carts, no milk, but with some thousand subscribers. These he served by the simple operation of moving the little milk cans outside people's doors to the doors of his own customers. It was he who had kept up an unaccountable and close correspondence with a young lady whose whole letter-bag was intercepted, by the extraordinary trick of photographing his messages infinitesimally small upon the slides of a microscope. A sweeping simplicity, however, marked many of his experiments. It is said that he once repainted all the numbers in a street in the dead of night merely to divert one traveler into a trap. It is quite certain that he invented a portable pillar-box, which he put up at corners in quiet suburbs on the chance of strangers dropping postal orders into it. Lastly, he was known to be a startling acrobat; despite his huge figure, he could leap like a grasshopper and melt into the tree-tops like a monkey. Hence the great Valentin, when he set out to find Flambeau, was perfectly aware that his adventures would not end when he had found him.

But how was he to find him? On this the great Valentin's ideas were still in process of settlement.

There was one thing which Flambeau, with all his dexterity of disguise, could not cover, and that was his singular height. If Valentin's quick eye had caught a tall apple-woman, a tall grenadier, or even a tolerably tall duchess, he might have arrested them on the spot. But all along his train there was nobody that could be a disguised Flambeau, any more than a cat could be a disguised giraffe. About the people on the boat he had already satisfied himself; and the people picked up at Harwich or on the journey limited themselves with certainty to six. There was a short railway official traveling up to the terminus, three fairly short market gardeners picked up two stations afterwards, one very short widow lady going up from a small Essex town, and a very short Roman Catholic priest going up from a small Essex village. When it came to the last case, Valentin gave it up and almost laughed. The little priest was so much the essence of those Eastern flats; he had a face as round and dull as a Norfolk dumpling; he had eyes as empty as the North Sea; he had several brown paper parcels, which he was quite incapable of collecting. The Eucharistic Congress had doubtless sucked out of their local stagnation many such creatures, blind and helpless, like moles disinterred. Valentin was a sceptic in the severe style of France, and could have no love for priests. But he could have pity for them, and this one might have provoked pity in anybody. He had a large, shabby umbrella, which constantly fell on the floor. He did not seem to know which was the right end of his return ticket. He

explained with a moon-calf simplicity to everybody in the carriage that
he had to be careful, because he had something made of real silver "with
blue stones" in one of his brown-paper parcels. His quaint blending of
Essex flatness with saintly simplicity continuously amused the French-
man till the priest arrived (somehow) at Tottenham with all his parcels,
and came back for his umbrella. When he did the last, Valentin even
had the good nature to warn him not to take care of the silver by
telling everybody about it. But to whomever he talked, Valentin kept
his eye open for someone else; he looked out steadily for anyone, rich
or poor, male or female, who was well up to six feet; for Flambeau was
four inches above it.

He alighted at Liverpool Street, however, quite conscientiously
secure that he had not missed the criminal so far. He then went to
Scotland Yard to regularise his position and arrange for help in case of
need; he then lit another cigarette and went for a long stroll in the
streets of London. As he was walking in the streets and squares beyond
Victoria, he paused suddenly and stood. It was a quaint, quiet square,
very typical of London, full of an accidental stillness. The tall, flat
houses round looked at once prosperous and uninhabited; the square
of shrubbery in the centre looked as deserted as a green Pacific islet.
One of the four sides was much higher than the rest, like a dais; and
the line of this side was broken by one of London's admirable acci-
dents—a restaurant that looked as if it had strayed from Soho. It was
an unreasonably attractive object, with dwarf plants in pots and long,
striped blinds of lemon yellow and white. It stood specially high above
the street, and in the usual patchwork way of London, a flight of steps
from the street ran up to meet the front door almost as a fire-escape

might run up to a first-floor window. Valentin stood and smoked in front of the yellow-white blinds and considered them long.

The most incredible thing about miracles is that they happen. A few clouds in heaven do come together into the staring shape of one human eye. A tree does stand up in the landscape of a doubtful journey in the exact and elaborate shape of a note of interrogation. I have seen both these things myself within the last few days. Nelson does die in the instant of victory; and a man named Williams does quite accidentally murder a man named Williamson; it sounds like a sort of infanticide. In short, there is in life an element of elfin coincidence which people reckoning on the prosaic may perpetually miss. As it has been well expressed in the paradox of Poe, wisdom should reckon on the unforeseen.

Aristide Valentin was unfathomably French; and the French intelligence is intelligence specially and solely. He was not "a thinking machine"; for that is a brainless phrase of modern fatalism and materialism. A machine only is a machine because it cannot think. But he was a thinking man, and a plain man at the same time. All his wonderful successes, that looked like conjuring, had been gained by plodding logic, by clear and commonplace French thought. The French electrify the world not by starting any paradox, they electrify it by carrying out a truism. They carry a truism so far—as in the French Revolution. But exactly because Valentin understood reason, he understood the limits of reason. Only a man who knows nothing of motors talks of motoring without petrol; only a man who knows nothing of reason talks of reasoning without strong, undisputed first principles. Here he had no strong first principles. Flambeau had been missed at Harwich; and if he was in London at all, he might be anything from a tall tramp on Wimbledon Common to a tall toast-master at the Hotel Metropole. In such a naked state of nescience, Valentin had a view and a method of his own.

In such cases he reckoned on the unforeseen. In such cases, when he could not follow the train of the reasonable, he coldly and carefully followed the train of the unreasonable. Instead of going to the right places—banks, police stations, rendezvous—he systematically went to the wrong places; knocked at every empty house, turned down every cul de sac, went up every lane blocked with rubbish, went round every crescent that led him uselessly out of the way. He defended this crazy course quite logically. He said that if one had a clue this was the worst way; but if one had no clue at all it was the best, because there was just the chance that any oddity that caught the eye of the pursuer might be the same that had caught the eye of the pursued. Somewhere a man must begin, and it had better be just where another man might stop. Something about that flight of steps up to the shop, something about the quietude and quaintness of the restaurant, roused all the detective's rare romantic fancy and made him resolve to strike at random. He went up the steps, and sitting down at a table by the window, asked for a cup of black coffee.

It was half-way through the morning, and he had not breakfasted; the slight litter of other breakfasts stood about on the table to remind him of his hunger; and adding a poached egg to his order, he proceeded musingly to shake some white sugar into his coffee, thinking all the time about Flambeau. He remembered how Flambeau had escaped, once by a pair of nail scissors, and once by a house on fire; once by having to pay for an unstamped letter, and once by getting people to look through a telescope at a comet that might destroy the world. He thought his detective brain as good as the criminal's, which was true. But he fully realised the disadvantage. "The criminal is the creative artist; the detective only the critic," he said with a sour smile, and lifted his coffee cup to his lips slowly, and put it down very quickly. He had put salt in it.

He looked at the vessel from which the silvery powder had come; it was certainly a sugar-basin; as unmistakably meant for sugar as a champagne-bottle for champagne. He wondered why they should keep salt in it. He looked to see if there were any more orthodox vessels. Yes; there were two salt-cellars quite full. Perhaps there was some speciality in the condiment in the salt-cellars. He tasted it; it was sugar. Then he looked round at the restaurant with a refreshed air of interest, to see if there were any other traces of that singular artistic taste which puts the sugar in the salt-cellars and the salt in the sugar-basin. Except for an odd splash of some dark fluid on one of the white-papered walls, the whole place appeared neat, cheerful and ordinary. He rang the bell for the waiter.

When that official hurried up, fuzzy-haired and somewhat bleareyed at that early hour, the detective (who was not without an appreciation of the simpler forms of humour) asked him to taste the sugar and see if it was up to the high reputation of the hotel. The result was that the waiter yawned suddenly and woke up.

"Do you play this delicate joke on your customers every morning?" inquired Valentin. "Does changing the salt and sugar never pall on you as a jest?"

The waiter, when this irony grew clearer, stammeringly assured him that the establishment had certainly no such intention; it must be a most curious mistake. He picked up the sugar-basin and looked at it; he picked up the salt-cellar and looked at that, his face growing more and more bewildered. At last he abruptly excused himself, and hurrying away, returned in a few seconds with the proprietor. The proprietor also examined the sugar-basin and then the salt-cellar; the proprietor also looked bewildered.

Suddenly the waiter seemed to grow inarticulate with a rush of words.

"I zink," he stuttered eagerly, "I zink it is those two clergy-men."

"What two clergymen?"

"The two clergymen," said the waiter, "that threw soup at the wall."

"Threw soup at the wall?" repeated Valentin, feeling sure this must be some singular Italian metaphor.

"Yes, yes," said the attendant excitedly, and pointed at the dark splash on the white paper; "threw it over there on the wall."

Valentin looked his query at the proprietor, who came to his rescue with fuller reports.

"Yes, sir," he said, "it's quite true, though I don't suppose it has anything to do with the sugar and salt. Two clergymen came in and drank soup here very early, as soon as the shutters were taken down. They were both very quiet, respectable people; one of them paid the bill and went out; the other, who seemed a slower coach altogether, was some minutes longer getting his things together. But he went at last. Only, the instant before he stepped into the street he deliberately picked up his cup, which he had only half emptied, and threw the soup slap on the wall. I was in the back room myself, and so was the waiter; so I could only rush out in time to find the wall splashed and the shop empty. It don't do any particular damage, but it was confounded cheek; and I tried to catch the men in the street. They were too far off though; I only noticed they went round the next corner into Carstairs Street."

The detective was on his feet, hat settled and stick in hand. He had already decided that in the universal darkness of his mind he could only follow the first odd finger that pointed; and this finger was odd enough. Paying his bill and clashing the glass doors behind him, he was soon swinging round into the other street.

It was fortunate that even in such fevered moments his eye was cool and quick. Something in a shop-front went by him like a mere flash; yet he went back to look at it. The shop was a popular green-grocer and fruiterer's, an array of goods set out in the open air and plainly ticketed with their names and prices. In the two most prominent compartments were two heaps, of oranges and of nuts respectively. On the heap of nuts lay a scrap of cardboard, on which was written in bold, blue chalk, "Best tangerine oranges, two a penny." On the oranges was the equally clear and exact description, "Finest Brazil nuts, 4d. a lb." M. Valentin looked at these two placards and fancied he had met this highly subtle form of humour before, and that somewhat recently. He drew the attention of the red-faced fruiterer, who was looking rather sullenly up and down the street, to this inaccuracy in his advertisements. The fruiterer said nothing, but sharply put each card into its proper place. The detective, leaning elegantly on his walking-cane, continued to scrutinise the shop. At last he said, "Pray excuse my apparent irrelevance, my good sir, but I should like to ask you a question in experimental psychology and the association of ideas."

The red-faced shopman regarded him with an eye of menace; but he continued gaily, swinging his cane, "Why," he pursued, "why are two tickets wrongly placed in a greengrocer's shop like a shovel hat that has come to London for a holiday? Or, in case I do not make myself clear, what is the mystical association which connects the idea of nuts marked as oranges with the idea of two clergymen, one tall and the other short?"

The eyes of the tradesman stood out of his head like a snail's; he really seemed for an instant likely to fling himself upon the stranger. At last he stammered angrily: "I don't know what you 'ave to do with it, but if you're one of their friends, you can tell 'em from me that I'll knock their silly 'eads off, parsons or no parsons, if they upset my apples again."

"Indeed?" asked the detective, with great sympathy. "Did they upset your apples?"

"One of 'em did," said the heated shopman; "rolled 'em all over the street. I'd 'ave caught the fool but for havin' to pick 'em up."

"Which way did these parsons go?" asked Valentin.

"Up that second road on the left-hand side, and then across the square," said the other promptly.

"Thanks," replied Valentin, and vanished like a fairy. On the other side of the second square he found a policeman, and said: "This is urgent, constable; have you seen two clergymen in shovel hats?"

The policeman began to chuckle heavily. "I 'ave, sir; and if you arst me, one of 'em was drunk. He stood in the middle of the road that bewildered that—"

"Which way did they go?" snapped Valentin.

"They took one of them yellow buses over there," answered the man; "them that go to Hampstead."

Valentin produced his official card and said very rapidly: "Call up two of your men to come with me in pursuit," and crossed the road with such contagious energy that the ponderous policeman was moved to almost agile obedience. In a minute and a half the French detective was joined on the opposite pavement by an inspector and a man in plain clothes.

"Well, sir," began the former, with smiling importance, "and what may—?"

Valentin pointed suddenly with his cane. "I'll tell you on the top of that omnibus," he said, and was darting and dodging across the tangle of the traffic. When all three sank panting on the top seats of the yellow vehicle, the inspector said: "We could go four times as quick in a taxi."

"Quite true," replied their leader placidly, "if we only had an idea of where we were going."

"Well, where are you going?" asked the other, staring.

Valentin smoked frowningly for a few seconds; then, removing his cigarette, he said: "If you know what a man's doing, get in front of him; but if you want to guess what he's doing, keep behind him. Stray when he strays; stop when he stops; travel as slowly as he. Then you may see what he saw and may act as he acted. All we can do is to keep our eyes skinned for a queer thing."

"What sort of queer thing do you mean?" asked the inspector.

"Any sort of queer thing," answered Valentin, and relapsed into obstinate silence.

The yellow omnibus crawled up the northern roads for what seemed like hours on end; the great detective would not explain further, and perhaps his assistants felt a silent and growing doubt of his errand. Perhaps, also, they felt a silent and growing desire for lunch, for the hours crept long past the normal luncheon hour, and the long roads of the North London suburbs seemed to shoot out into length after length like an infernal telescope. It was one of those journeys on which a man perpetually feels that now at last he must have come to the end of the universe, and then finds he has only come to the beginning of Tufnell Park. London died away in draggled taverns and dreary scrubs, and then was unaccountably born again in blazing high streets and blatant hotels. It was like passing through thirteen separate vulgar cities all just touching each other. But though the winter twilight was already threatening the road ahead of them, the Parisian detective still sat silent and watchful, eyeing the frontage of the streets that slid by on either side. By the time they had left Camden Town behind, the policemen were nearly asleep; at least, they gave something like a jump as Valentin leapt erect, struck a hand on each man's shoulder, and shouted to the driver to stop.

They tumbled down the steps into the road without realising why they had been dislodged; when they looked round for enlightenment they found Valentin triumphantly pointing his finger towards a window on the left side of the road. It was a large window, forming part of the long facade of a gilt and palatial public-house; it was the part reserved for respectable dining, and labeled "Restaurant." This window, like all the rest along the frontage of the hotel, was of frosted and figured glass; but in the middle of it was a big, black smash, like a star in the ice.

"Our cue at last," cried Valentin, waving his stick; "the place with the broken window."

"What window? What cue?" asked his principal assistant. "Why, what proof is there that this has anything to do with them?"

Valentin almost broke his bamboo stick with rage.

"Proof!" he cried. "Good God! the man is looking for proof! Why, of course, the chances are twenty to one that it has nothing to do with them. But what else can we do? Don't you see we must either follow one wild possibility or else go home to bed?" He banged his way into the restaurant, followed by his companions, and they were soon seated at a late luncheon at a little table, and looked at the star of smashed glass from the inside. Not that it was very informative to them even then.

"Got your window broken, I see," said Valentin to the waiter as he paid the bill.

"Yes, sir," answered the attendant, bending busily over the change, to which Valentin silently added an enormous tip. The waiter straightened himself with mild but unmistakable animation.

"Ah, yes, sir," he said. "Very odd thing, that, sir."

"Indeed? Tell us about it," said the detective with careless curiosity.

"Well, two gents in black came in," said the waiter; "two of those foreign parsons that are running about. They had a cheap and quiet little lunch, and one of them paid for it and went out. The other was just going out to join him when I looked at my change again and found he'd paid me more than three times too much. 'Here,' I says to the chap who was nearly out of the door, 'you've paid too much.' 'Oh,' he says, very cool, 'have we?' 'Yes,' I says, and picks up the bill to show him. Well, that was a knock-out."

"What do you mean?" asked his interlocutor.

"Well, I'd have sworn on seven Bibles that I'd put 4s. on that bill. But now I saw I'd put 14s., as plain as paint."

"Well?" cried Valentin, moving slowly, but with burning eyes, "and then?"

"The parson at the door he says all serene, 'Sorry to confuse your accounts, but it'll pay for the window.' 'What window?' I says. 'The one I'm going to break,' he says, and smashed that blessed pane with his umbrella."

All three inquirers made an exclamation; and the inspector said under his breath, "Are we after escaped lunatics?" The waiter went on with some relish for the ridiculous story:

"I was so knocked silly for a second, I couldn't do anything. The man marched out of the place and joined his friend just round the corner. Then they went so quick up Bullock Street that I couldn't catch them, though I ran round the bars to do it."

"Bullock Street," said the detective, and shot up that thoroughfare as quickly as the strange couple he pursued.

Their journey now took them through bare brick ways like tunnels; streets with few lights and even with few windows; streets that seemed built out of the blank backs of everything and everywhere. Dusk was deepening, and it was not easy even for the London policemen to guess in what exact direction they were treading. The inspector, however, was pretty certain that they would eventually strike some part of Hampstead Heath. Abruptly one bulging gas-lit window broke the blue twilight like a bull's-eye lantern; and Valentin stopped an instant before a little garish sweetstuff shop. After an instant's hesitation he went in; he stood amid the gaudy colours of the confectionery with entire gravity and bought thirteen chocolate cigars with a certain care. He was clearly preparing an opening; but he did not need one.

An angular, elderly young woman in the shop had regarded his elegant appearance with a merely automatic inquiry; but when she saw the door behind him blocked with the blue uniform of the inspector, her eyes seemed to wake up.

"Oh," she said, "if you've come about that parcel, I've sent it off already."

"Parcel?" repeated Valentin; and it was his turn to look inquiring.

"I mean the parcel the gentleman left—the clergyman gentleman."

"For goodness' sake," said Valentin, leaning forward with his first real confession of eagerness, "for Heaven's sake tell us what happened exactly."

"Well," said the woman a little doubtfully, "the clergymen came in about half an hour ago and bought some peppermints and talked a bit, and then went off towards the Heath. But a second after, one of them runs back into the shop and says, 'Have I left a parcel?' Well, I looked everywhere and couldn't see one; so he says, 'Never mind; but if it should turn up, please post it to this address,' and he left me the address and a shilling for my trouble. And sure enough, though I thought I'd looked everywhere, I found he'd left a brown paper parcel, so I posted it to the place he said. I can't remember the address now; it was somewhere in Westminster. But as the thing seemed so important, I thought perhaps the police had come about it."

"So they have," said Valentin shortly. "Is Hampstead Heath near here?"

"Straight on for fifteen minutes," said the woman, "and you'll come right out on the open." Valentin sprang out of the shop and began to run. The other detectives followed him at a reluctant trot.

The street they threaded was so narrow and shut in by shadows that when they came out unexpectedly into the void common and vast sky they were startled to find the evening still so light and clear. A perfect dome of peacock-green sank into gold amid the blackening trees and the dark violet distances. The glowing green tint was just deep enough to pick out in points of crystal one or two stars. All that was left of the daylight lay in a golden glitter across the edge of Hampstead and that popular hollow which is called the Vale of Health. The holiday makers who roam this region had not wholly dispersed; a few couples sat shapelessly on benches; and here and there a distant girl still shrieked in one of the swings. The glory of heaven deepened and darkened around the sublime vulgarity of man; and standing on the slope and looking across the valley, Valentin beheld the thing which he sought.

Among the black and breaking groups in that distance was one especially black which did not break—a group of two figures clerically clad. Though they seemed as small as insects, Valentin could see that one of them was much smaller than the other. Though the other had a student's stoop and an inconspicuous manner, he could see that the man was well over six feet high. He shut his teeth and went forward, whirling his stick impatiently. By the time he had substantially diminished the distance and magnified the two black figures as in a vast microscope, he had perceived something else; something which startled him, and yet which he had somehow expected. Whoever was the tall priest, there could be no doubt about the identity of the short one. It was his friend of the Harwich train, the stumpy little cure of Essex whom he had warned about his brown paper parcels.

Now, so far as this went, everything fitted in finally and rationally enough. Valentin had learned by his inquiries that morning that a Father Brown from Essex was bringing up a silver cross with sapphires, a relic of considerable value, to show some of the foreign priests at the congress. This undoubtedly was the "silver with blue stones"; and Father Brown undoubtedly was the little greenhorn in the train. Now there was nothing wonderful about the fact that what Valentin had found out Flambeau had also found out; Flambeau found out everything. Also there was nothing wonderful in the fact that when Flambeau heard of a sapphire cross he should try to steal it; that was the most natural thing in all natural history. And most certainly there was nothing wonderful about the fact that Flambeau should have it all his own way with such a silly sheep as the man with the umbrella and the parcels. He was the sort of man whom anybody could lead on a string to the North Pole; it was not surprising that an actor like Flambeau, dressed as another priest, could lead him to Hampstead Heath. So far the crime seemed clear enough; and while the detective pitied the priest for his helplessness, he almost despised Flambeau for condescending to so gullible a victim. But when Valentin thought of all that had happened in between, of all that had led him to his triumph, he racked his brains for the smallest rhyme or reason in it. What had the stealing of a blue-and-silver cross from a priest from Essex to do with chucking soup at wall paper? What had it to do with calling nuts oranges, or with paying for windows first and breaking them afterwards? He had come to the end of his chase; yet somehow he had missed the middle of it. When he failed (which was seldom), he had usually grasped the clue, but nevertheless missed the criminal. Here he had grasped the criminal, but still he could not grasp the clue.

The two figures that they followed were crawling like black flies across the huge green contour of a hill. They were evidently sunk in conversation, and perhaps did not notice where they were going; but they were certainly going to the wilder and more silent heights of the Heath. As their pursuers gained on them, the latter had to use the undignified attitudes of the deer-stalker, to crouch behind clumps of trees and even to crawl prostrate in deep grass. By these ungainly ingenuities the hunters even came close enough to the quarry to hear the murmur of the discussion, but no word could be distinguished except the word "reason" recurring frequently in a high and almost childish voice. Once over an abrupt dip of land and a dense tangle of thickets, the detectives actually lost the two figures they were following. They did not find the trail again for an agonising ten minutes, and then it led round the brow of a great dome of hill overlooking an amphitheatre of rich and desolate sunset scenery. Under a tree in this commanding yet neglected spot was an old ramshackle wooden seat. On this seat sat the two priests still in serious speech together. The gorgeous green and gold still clung to the darkening horizon; but the dome above was turning slowly from peacock-green to peacock-blue, and the stars detached themselves more and more like solid jewels. Mutely motioning to his followers, Valentin contrived to creep up behind the big branching tree, and, standing there in deathly silence, heard the words of the strange priests for the first time.

After he had listened for a minute and a half, he was gripped by a devilish doubt. Perhaps he had dragged the two English policemen to the wastes of a nocturnal heath on an errand no saner than seeking figs on its thistles. For the two priests were talking exactly like priests, piously, with learning and leisure, about the most aerial enigmas of theology. The little Essex priest spoke the more simply, with his round face turned to the strengthening stars; the other talked with his head bowed, as if he were not even worthy to look at them. But no more innocently clerical conversation could have been heard in any white Italian cloister or black Spanish cathedral.

The first he heard was the tail of one of Father Brown's sentences, which ended: ". . . what they really meant in the Middle Ages by the heavens being incorruptible."

The taller priest nodded his bowed head and said:

"Ah, yes, these modern infidels appeal to their reason; but who can look at those millions of worlds and not feel that there may well be wonderful universes above us where reason is utterly unreasonable?"

"No," said the other priest; "reason is always reasonable, even in the last limbo, in the lost borderland of things. I know that people charge the Church with lowering reason, but it is just the other way. Alone on earth, the Church makes reason really supreme. Alone on earth, the Church affirms that God himself is bound by reason."

The other priest raised his austere face to the spangled sky and said:

"Yet who knows if in that infinite universe—?"

"Only infinite physically," said the little priest, turning sharply in his seat, "not infinite in the sense of escaping from the laws of truth."

Valentin behind his tree was tearing his fingernails with silent fury. He seemed almost to hear the sniggers of the English detectives whom he had brought so far on a fantastic guess only to listen to the metaphysical gossip of two mild old parsons. In his impatience he lost the equally elaborate answer of the tall cleric, and when he listened again it was again Father Brown who was speaking:

"Reason and justice grip the remotest and the loneliest star. Look at those stars. Don't they look as if they were single diamonds and sapphires? Well, you can imagine any mad botany or geology you please. Think of forests of adamant with leaves of brilliants. Think the moon is a blue moon, a single elephantine sapphire. But don't fancy that all that frantic astronomy would make the smallest difference to the reason and justice of conduct. On plains of opal, under cliffs cut out of pearl, you would still find a notice-board, 'Thou shalt not steal.'"

Valentin was just in the act of rising from his rigid and crouching attitude and creeping away as softly as might be, felled by the one great folly of his life. But something in the very silence of the tall priest made him stop until the latter spoke. When at last he did speak, he said simply, his head bowed and his hands on his knees:

"Well, I think that other worlds may perhaps rise higher than our reason. The mystery of heaven is unfathomable, and I for one can only bow my head."

Then, with brow yet bent and without changing by the faintest shade his attitude or voice, he added:

"Just hand over that sapphire cross of yours, will you? We're all alone here, and I could pull you to pieces like a straw doll."

The utterly unaltered voice and attitude added a strange violence to that shocking change of speech. But the guarder of the relic only seemed to turn his head by the smallest section of the compass. He seemed still to have a somewhat foolish face turned to the stars. Perhaps he had not understood. Or, perhaps, he had understood and sat rigid with terror.

"Yes," said the tall priest, in the same low voice and in the same still posture, "yes, I am Flambeau."

Then, after a pause, he said:

"Come, will you give me that cross?"

"No," said the other, and the monosyllable had an odd sound.

Flambeau suddenly flung off all his pontifical pretensions. The great robber leaned back in his seat and laughed low but long.

"No," he cried, "you won't give it me, you proud prelate. You won't give it me, you little celibate simpleton. Shall I tell you why you won't give it me? Because I've got it already in my own breast-pocket."

The small man from Essex turned what seemed to be a dazed face in the dusk, and said, with the timid eagerness of "The Private Secretary":

"Are—are you sure?"

Flambeau yelled with delight.

"Really, you're as good as a three-act farce," he cried. "Yes, you turnip, I am quite sure. I had the sense to make a duplicate of the right parcel, and now, my friend, you've got the duplicate and I've got the jewels. An old dodge, Father Brown—a very old dodge."

"Yes," said Father Brown, and passed his hand through his hair with the same strange vagueness of manner. "Yes, I've heard of it before."

The colossus of crime leaned over to the little rustic priest with a sort of sudden interest.

"You have heard of it?" he asked. "Where have you heard of it?"

"Well, I mustn't tell you his name, of course," said the little man simply. "He was a penitent, you know. He had lived prosperously for about twenty years entirely on duplicate brown paper parcels. And so, you see, when I began to suspect you, I thought of this poor chap's way of doing it at once."

"Began to suspect me?" repeated the outlaw with increased intensity. "Did you really have the gumption to suspect me just because I brought you up to this bare part of the heath?"

"No, no," said Brown with an air of apology. "You see, I suspected you when we first met. It's that little bulge up the sleeve where you people have the spiked bracelet."

"How in Tartarus," cried Flambeau, "did you ever hear of the spiked bracelet?"

"Oh, one's little flock, you know!" said Father Brown, arching his eyebrows rather blankly. "When I was a curate in Hartlepool, there were three of them with spiked bracelets. So, as I suspected you from the first, don't you see, I made sure that the cross should go safe, anyhow. I'm afraid I watched you, you know. So at last I saw you change the parcels. Then, don't you see, I changed them back again. And then I left the right one behind."

"Left it behind?" repeated Flambeau, and for the first time there was another note in his voice beside his triumph.

"Well, it was like this," said the little priest, speaking in the same unaffected way. "I went back to that sweet-shop and asked if I'd left a parcel, and gave them a particular address if it turned up. Well, I knew I hadn't; but when I went away again I did. So, instead of running after me with that valuable parcel, they have sent it flying to a friend of mine in Westminster." Then he added rather sadly: "I learnt that, too, from a poor fellow in Hartlepool. He used to do it with handbags he stole at railway stations, but he's in a monastery now. Oh, one gets to know, you know," he added, rubbing his head again with the same sort of desperate apology. "We can't help being priests. People come and tell us these things."

Flambeau tore a brown paper parcel out of his inner pocket and rent it in pieces. There was nothing but paper and sticks of lead inside it. He sprang to his feet with a gigantic gesture, and cried:

"I don't believe you. I don't believe a bumpkin like you could manage all that. I believe you've still got the stuff on you, and if you don't give it up—why, we're all alone, and I'll take it by force!"

"No," said Father Brown simply, and stood up also, "you won't take it by force. First, because I really haven't still got it. And, second, because we are not alone."

Flambeau stopped in his stride forward.

"Behind that tree," said Father Brown, pointing, "are two strong policemen and the greatest detective alive. How did they come here, do you ask? Why, I brought them, of course! How did I do it? Why, I'll tell you if you like! Lord bless you, we have to know twenty such things when we work among the criminal classes! Well, I wasn't sure you were a thief, and it would never do to make a scandal against one of our own clergy. So I just tested you to see if anything would make you show yourself. A man generally makes a small scene if he finds salt in his coffee; if he doesn't, he has some reason for keeping quiet. I changed the salt and sugar, and you kept quiet. A man generally objects if his bill is three times too big. If he pays it, he has some motive for passing unnoticed. I altered your bill, and you paid it."

The world seemed waiting for Flambeau to leap like a tiger. But he was held back as by a spell; he was stunned with the utmost curiosity.

"Well," went on Father Brown, with lumbering lucidity, "as you wouldn't leave any tracks for the police, of course somebody had to. At every place we went to, I took care to do something that would get us talked about for the rest of the day. I didn't do much harm—a splashed wall, spilt apples, a broken window; but I saved the cross, as the cross will always be saved. It is at Westminster by now. I rather wonder you didn't stop it with the Donkey's Whistle."

"With the what?" asked Flambeau.

"I'm glad you've never heard of it," said the priest, making a face. "It's a foul thing. I'm sure you're too good a man for a Whistler. I couldn't have countered it even with the Spots myself; I'm not strong enough in the legs."

"What on earth are you talking about?" asked the other.

"Well, I did think you'd know the Spots," said Father Brown, agreeably surprised. "Oh, you can't have gone so very wrong yet!"

"How in blazes do you know all these horrors?" cried Flambeau.

The shadow of a smile crossed the round, simple face of his clerical opponent.

"Oh, by being a celibate simpleton, I suppose," he said. "Has it never struck you that a man who does next to nothing but hear men's real sins is not likely to be wholly unaware of human evil? But, as a matter of fact, another part of my trade, too, made me sure you weren't a priest."

"What?" asked the thief, almost gaping.

"You attacked reason," said Father Brown. "It's bad theology."

And even as he turned away to collect his property, the three policemen came out from under the twilight trees. Flambeau was an artist and a sportsman. He stepped back and swept Valentin a great bow.

"Do not bow to me, mon ami," said Valentin with silver clearness. "Let us both bow to our master."

And they both stood an instant uncovered while the little Essex priest blinked about for his umbrella.

FYODOR DOSTOEVSKY

THE SECOND SON OF A FORMER ARMY DOCTOR, DOSTOEVSKY was born in Moscow in 1821. He was educated at home and at a private school, but after the death of his mother in 1837 he was sent to St. Petersburg, entering the Army Engineering College, and in 1839 his father died. Though Dostoevsky graduated as a military engineer, he resigned in 1844 to devote himself to writing, publishing his first novel in 1846.

After being first sentenced to death in 1849 for supposed revolutionary activities, and then having that sentence reduced to imprisonment in Siberia, Dostoevsky spent four years in hard labor and five years as a soldier in Semipalatinsk.

He returned to St. Petersburg in 1854 as a writer dedicated to exploring the struggle between man and God, and began publishing books that have remained some of the greatest works of literature the world has known, among them *Notes from the Underground*, *Crime and Punishment*, *The Idiot*, and *The Possessed*; with the publication of *The Brothers Karamazov* in 1880, Dostoevsky was recognized in his own country as one of its great writers.

An epileptic all his life, Dostoevsky died in St. Petersburg on February 9, 1881, and was buried in St. Petersburg.

AN HONEST THIEF

BY FYODOR DOSTOEVSKY, TRANSLATED BY CONSTANCE GARNETT

One morning, just as I was about to set off to my office, Agrafena, my cook, washerwoman and housekeeper, came in to me and, to my surprise, entered into conversation.

She had always been such a silent, simple creature that, except her daily inquiry about dinner, she had not uttered a word for the last six years. I, at least, had heard nothing else from her.

"Here I have come in to have a word with you, sir," she began abruptly; "you really ought to let the little room."

"Which little room?"

"Why, the one next to the kitchen, to be sure."

"What for?"

"What for? Why, because folks do take in lodgers, to be sure."

"But who would take it?"

"Who would take it? Why, a lodger would take it, to be sure."

"But, my good woman, one could not put a bedstead in it; there wouldn't be room to move! Who could live in it?"

"Who wants to live there! As long as he has a place to sleep in. Why, he would live in the window."

"In what window?"

"In what window? As though you didn't know! The one in the passage, to be sure. He would sit there, sewing or doing anything else. Maybe he would sit on a chair, too. He's got a chair; and he has a table, too; he's got everything."

"Who is 'he' then?"

"Oh, a good man, a man of experience. I will cook for him. And I'll ask him three roubles a month for his board and lodging."

After prolonged efforts I succeeded at last in learning from Agrafena that an elderly man had somehow managed to persuade her to admit him into the kitchen as a lodger and boarder. Any notion Agrafena took into her head had to be carried out; if not, I knew she would give me no peace. When anything was not to her liking, she at once began to brood, and sank into a deep dejection that would last for a fortnight or three weeks. During that period my dinners were spoiled, my linen was mislaid, my floors were unscrubbed; in short, I had a great deal to put up with. I had observed long ago that this inarticulate woman was incapable of conceiving a project, of originating an idea of her own. But if anything like a notion or a project was by some means put into her feeble brain, to prevent its being carried out meant, for a time, her moral assassination. And so, as I cared more for my peace of mind than for anything else, I consented forthwith.

"Has he a passport anyway, or something of the sort?"

"To be sure, he has. He is a good man, a man of experience; three roubles he's promised to pay."

The very next day the new lodger made his appearance in my modest bachelor quarters; but I was not put out by this, indeed I was inwardly pleased. I lead as a rule a very lonely hermit's existence. I have scarcely any friends; I hardly ever go anywhere. As I had spent ten years never coming out of my shell, I had, of course, grown used to solitude. But another ten or fifteen years or more of the same solitary existence, with the same Agrafena, in the same bachelor quarters, was in truth a somewhat cheerless prospect. And therefore a new inmate, if well-behaved, was a heaven-sent blessing.

Agrafena had spoken truly; my lodger was certainly a man of experience. From his passport it appeared that he wan an old soldier, a fact which I should have known indeed from his face. An old soldier is easily recognised. Astafy Ivanovitch was a favourable specimen of his class. We got on very well together. What was best of all, Astafy Ivanovitch would sometimes tell a story, describing some incident in his own life. On the perpetual boredom of my existence such a story-teller was a veritable treasure. One day he told me one of these stories. It made an impression on me. The following event was what led to it.

I was left alone in the flat; both Astafy and Agrafena were out on business of their own. All of a sudden I heard from the inner room somebody—I fancied a stranger—come in; I went out; there actually was a stranger in the passage, a short fellow wearing no overcoat in spite of the cold autumn weather.

"What do you want?"

"Does a clerk called Alexandrov live here?"

"Nobody of that name here, brother. Good-bye."

"Why, the dvornik told me it was here," said my visitor, cautiously retiring towards the door.

"Be off, be off, brother, get along."

Next day after dinner, while Astafy Ivanovitch was fitting on a coat which he was altering for me, again someone came into the passage. I half opened the door.

Before my very eyes my yesterday's visitor, with perfect composure, took my wadded greatcoat from the peg and, stuffing it under his arm, darted out of the flat. Agrafena stood all the time staring at him, agape with astonishment and doing nothing for the protection of my property. Astafy Ivanovitch flew in pursuit of the thief and ten minutes later came back out of breath and empty-handed. He had vanished completely.

"Well, there's a piece of luck, Astafy Ivanovitch!"

"It's a good job your cloak is left! Or he would have put you in a plight, the thief!"

But the whole incident had so impressed Astafy Ivanovitch that I forgot the theft as I looked at him. He could not get over it. Every minute or two he would drop the work upon which he was engaged, and would describe over again how it had all happened, how he had been standing, how the greatcoat had been taken down before his very eyes, not a yard away, and how it had come to pass that he could not catch the thief. Then he would sit down to his work again, then leave it once more, and at last I saw him go down to the dvornik to tell him all about it, and to upbraid him for letting such a thing happen in this domain. Then he came back and began scolding Agrafena. Then he sat down to his work again, and long afterwards he was still muttering to himself how it had all happened, how he stood there and I was here, how before our eyes, not a yard away, the thief took the coat off the peg, and so on. In short, though Astafy Ivanovitch understood his business, he was a terrible slow-coach and busy-body.

"He's made fools of us, Astafy Ivanovitch," I said to him in the evening, as I gave him a glass of tea. I wanted to while away the time by recalling the story of the lost greatcoat, the frequent repetition of which, together with the great earnestness of the speaker, was beginning to become very amusing.

"Fools, indeed, sir! Even though it is no business of mine, I am put out. It makes me angry though it is not my coat that was lost. To my thinking there is no vermin in the world worse than a thief. Another takes what you can spare, but a thief steals the work of your hands, the sweat of your brow, your time . . . Ugh, it's nasty! One can't speak of it! It's too vexing. How is it you don't feel the loss of your property, sir?"

"Yes, you are right, Astafy Ivanovitch, better if the thing had been burnt; it's annoying to let the thief have it, it's disagreeable."

"Disagreeable! I should think so! Yet, to be sure, there are thieves and thieves. And I have happened, sir, to come across an honest thief."

"An honest thief? But how can a thief be honest, Astafy Ivanovitch?"

"There you are right indeed, sir. How can a thief be honest? There are none such. I only meant to say that he was an honest man, sure enough, and yet he stole. I was simply sorry for him."

"Why, how was that, Astafy Ivanovitch?"

"It was about two years ago, sir. I had been nearly a year out of a place, and just before I lost my place I made the acquaintance of a poor lost creature. We got acquainted in a public-house. He was a drunkard, a vagrant, a beggar, he had been in a situation of some sort, but from his drinking habits he had lost his work. Such a ne'er-do-well! God only knows what he had on! Often you wouldn't be sure if he's a shirt under his coat; everything he could lay his hands upon he would drink away. But he was not one to quarrel; he was a quiet fellow. A soft, good-natured chap. And he'd never ask, he was ashamed; but you could see for yourself the poor fellow wanted a drink, and you would stand it him. And so we got friendly, that's to say, he stuck to me . . . It was all one to me. And what a man he was, to be sure! Like a little dog he would follow me; wherever I went there he would be; and all that after our first meeting, and he as thin as a thread-paper! At first it was 'let me stay the night'; well, I let him stay.

"I looked at his passport, too; the man was all right.

"Well, the next day it was the same story, and then the third day he came again and sat all day in the window and stayed the night. Well, thinks I, he is sticking to me; give him food and drink and shelter at night, too—here am I, a poor man, and a hanger-on to keep as well! And before he came to me, he used to go in the same way to a government clerk's; he attached himself to him; they were always drinking together, but he, through trouble of some sort, drank himself into the grave. My man was called Emelyan Ilyitch. I pondered and pondered what I was to do with him. To drive him away I was ashamed. I was sorry for him; such a pitiful, godforsaken creature I never did set eyes on. And not a word said either; he does not ask, but just sits there and looks into your eyes like a dog. To think what drinking will bring a man down to!

"I keep asking myself how am I to say to him: 'You must be moving, Emelyanoushka, there's nothing for you here, you've come to the wrong place; I shall soon not have a bite for myself, how am I to keep you too?'

"I sat and wondered what he'd do when I said that to him. And I seemed to see how he'd stare at me, if he were to hear me say that, how long he would sit and not understand a word of it. And when it did get home to him at last, how he would get up from the window, would take up his bundle—I can see it now, the red-check handkerchief full of holes, with God knows what wrapped up in it, which he had always with him, and then how he would set his shabby old coat to rights, so that it would look decent and keep him warm, so that no holes would be seen—he was a man of delicate feelings! And how he'd open the door and go out with tears in his eyes. Well, there's no letting a man go to ruin like that . . . One's sorry for him.

"And then again, I think, how am I off myself? Wait a bit, Emelyanoushka, says I to myself, you've not long to feast with me: I shall soon be going away and then you will not find me.

"Well, sir, our family made a move; and Alexandr Filimonovitch, my master (now deceased, God rest his soul) said, 'I am thoroughly satisfied with you, Astafy Ivanovitch; when we come back from the country we will take you on again.' I had been butler with them; a nice gentleman he was, but he died that same year. Well, after seeing him off, I took my belongings, what little money I had, and I thought I'd have a rest for a time, so I went to an old woman I knew, and I took a corner in her room. There was only one corner free in it. She had been a nurse, so now she had a pension and a room of her own. Well, now, good-bye, Emelyanoushka, thinks I, you won't find me now, my boy.

"And what do you think, sir? I had gone out to see a man I knew, and when I came back in the evening, the first thing I saw was Emelyanoushka! There he was, sitting on my box and his check bundle beside him; he was sitting in his ragged old coat, waiting for me. And to while away the time he had borrowed a church book from the old lady, and was holding it wrong side upwards. He'd scented me out! My heart sank. Well, thinks I, there's no help for it—why didn't I turn him out. So I asked him straight off: 'Have you brought your passport, Emelyanoushka?'

"I sat down on the spot, sir, and began to ponder: will a vagabond like that be very much trouble to me? And on thinking it over it seemed he would not be much trouble. He must be fed, I thought. Well, a bit of bread in the morning, and to make it go down better I'll buy him an onion. At midday I should have to give him another bit of bread and an onion; and in the evening, onion again with kvass, with some more bread if he wanted it. And if some cabbage soup were to come our way, then we should both have had our fill. I am no great eater myself, and a drinking man, as we all know, never eats; all he wants is herb-brandy or green vodka. He'll ruin me with his drinking, I thought, but then another idea come into my head, sir, and took great hold on me. So much so that if Emelyanoushka had gone away I should have felt that I had nothing to live for, I do believe . . . I determined on the spot to be a father and guardian to him. I'll keep him from ruin, I thought, I'll wean him from the glass! You wait a bit, thought I; very well, Emelyanoushka, you may stay, only you must behave yourself; you must obey orders.

"Well, thinks I to myself, I'll begin by training him to work of some sort, but not all at once; let him enjoy himself a little first, and I'll look round and find something you are fit for, Emelyanoushka. For every sort of work a man needs a special ability, you know, sir. And I began to watch him on the quiet; I soon saw Emelyanoushka was a desperate character. I began, sir, with a word of advice: I said this and that to him. 'Emelyanoushka,' said I, 'you ought to take a thought and mend your ways. Have done with drinking! Just look what rags you go about in: that old coat of yours, if I may make bold to say so, is fit for nothing but a sieve. A pretty state of things! It's time to draw the line, sure enough.' Emelyanoushka sat and listened to me with his head hanging down. Would you believe it, sir? It had come to such a pass with him, he'd lost his tongue through drink and could not speak a word of sense. Talk to him of cucumbers and he's answer back about beans! He would listen and listen to me and then heave such a sigh. 'What are you sighing for, Emelyan Ilyitch?' I asked him.

"'Oh, nothing; don't you mind me, Astafy Ivanovitch. Do you know there were two women fighting in the street today, Astafy Ivanovitch? One upset the other woman's basket of cranberries by accident.'

"'Well, what of that?'

"'And the second one upset the other's cranberries on purpose and trampled them under foot, too.'

"'Well, and what of it, Emelyan Ilyitch?'

"'Why, nothing, Astafy Ivanovitch, I just mentioned it.'

"'Nothing, I just mentioned it!' Emelyanoushka, my boy, I thought, you've squandered and drunk away your brains!'

"'And do you know, a gentleman dropped a money-note on the pavement in Gorohovy Street, no, it was Sadovy Street. And a peasant saw it and said, "That's my luck"; and at the same time another man saw it and said, "No, it's my bit of luck. I saw it before you did."'

"'Well, Emelyan Ilyitch!'

"'And the fellows had a fight over it, Astafy Ivanovitch. But a policeman came up, took away the note, gave it back to the gentleman and threatened to take up both the men.'

"'Well, but what of that? What is there edifying about it, Emelyanoushka?'

"'Why, nothing to be sure. Folks laughed, Astafy Ivanovitch.'

"'Ach, Emelyanoushka! What do the folks matter? You've sold

your soul for a brass farthing! But do you know what I have to tell you, Emelyan Ilyitch?'

"'What, Astafy Ivanovitch?'

"'Take a job of some sort, that's what you must do. For the hundredth time I say to you, set to work, have some mercy on yourself!'

"'What could I set to, Astafy Ivanovitch? I don't know what job I could set to, and there is no one who will take me on, Astafy Ivanovitch.'

"'That's how you came to be turned off, Emelyanoushka, you drinking man!'

"'And do you know Vlass, the waiter, was sent for to the office today, Astafy Ivanovitch?'

"'Why did they send for him, Emelyanoushka?' I asked.

"'I could not say why, Astafy Ivanovitch. I suppose they wanted him there, and that's why they sent for him.'

"A-ach, thought I, we are in a bad way, poor Emelyanoushka! The Lord is chastising us for our sins. Well, sir, what is one to do with such a man?

"But a cunning fellow he was, and no mistake. He'd listen and listen to me, but at last I suppose he got sick of it. As soon as he sees I am beginning to get angry, he'd pick up his old coat and out he's slip and leave no trace. He'd wander about all day and come back at night drunk. Where he got the money from, the Lord only knows; I had no hand in that.

"'No,' said I, 'Emelyan Ilyitch, you'll come to a bad end. Give over drinking, mind what I say now, give it up! Next time you come home in liquor, you can spend the night on the stairs. I won't let you in!'

"After hearing that threat, Emelyanoushka sat at home that day and the next; but on the third he slipped off again. I waited and waited; he didn't come back. Well, at last I don't mind owning, I was in a fright, and I felt for the man too. What have I done to him? I thought. I've scared him away. Where's the poor fellow gone to now? He'll get lost maybe. Lord have mercy upon us!

"Night came on, he did not come. In the morning I went out into the porch; I looked, and if he hadn't gone to sleep in the porch! There he was with his head on the step, and chilled to the marrow of his bones.

"'What next, Emelyanoushka, God have mercy on you! Where will you go to next!'

"'Why, you were—sort of—angry with me, Astafy Ivanovitch, the other day, you were vexed and promised to put me to sleep in the porch, so I didn't—sort of—venture to come in, Astafy Ivanovitch, and so I lay down here ...'

"I did feel angry and sorry too.

"'Surely you might undertake some other duty, Emelyanoushka, instead of lying here guarding the steps,' I said.

"'Why, what other duty, Astafy Ivanovitch?'

"'You lost soul'—I was in such a rage, I called him that—'if you could but learn tailoring work! Look at your old rag of a coat! It's not enough to have it in tatters, here you are sweeping the steps with it! You might take a needle and boggle up your rags, as decency demands. Ah, you drunken man!'

"What do you think, sir? He actually did take a needle. Of course I said it in jest, but he was so scared he set to work. He took off his coat and began threading the needle. I watched him; as you may well guess, his eyes were all red and bleary, and his hands were all of a shake. He kept shoving and shoving the thread and could not get it through the eye of the needle; he kept screwing his eyes up and wetting the thread and twisting it in his fingers—it was no good! He gave it up and looked at me.

"'Well,' said I, 'this is a nice way to treat me! If there had been folks by to see, I don't know what I should have done! Why, you simple fellow, I said it you in joke, as a reproach. Give over your nonsense, God bless you! Sit quiet and don't put me to shame, don't sleep on my stairs and make a laughingstock of me.'

"'Why, what am I to do, Astafy Ivanovitch? I know very well I am a drunkard and good for nothing! I can do nothing but vex you, my bene—bene—factor . . .'

"And at that his blue lips began all of a sudden to quiver, and a tear ran down his white cheek and trembled on his stubbly chin, and then poor Emelyanoushka burst into a regular flood of tears. Mercy on us! I felt as though a knife were thrust into my heart! The sensitive creature! I'd never have expected it. Who could have guessed it? No, Emelyanoushka, thought I, I shall give you up altogether. You can go your way like the rubbish you are.

"Well, sir, why make a long story of it? And the whole affair is so trifling, it's not worth wasting words upon. Why, you, for instance, sir, would not have given a thought to it, but I would have given a great deal— if I had a great deal to give—that it never should have happened at all.

"I had a pair of riding breeches by me, sir, deuce take them, fine, first-rate riding breeches they were too, blue with a check on it. They'd been ordered by a gentleman from the country, but he would not have them after all; said they were not full enough, so they were left in my hands. It struck me they were worth something. At the second-hand dealer's I ought to get five silver roubles for them, or if not I could turn them into two pairs of trousers for Petersburg gentlemen and have a piece over for a waistcoat for myself. Of course for poor people like us everything comes in. And it happened just then that Emelyanoushka was having a sad time of it. There he sat day after day: he did not drink, not a drop passed his lips, but he sat and moped like an owl. It was sad to see him—he just sat and brooded. Well, thought I, either you've not a copper to spend, my lad, or else you're turning over a new leaf of yourself, you've given it up, you've listened to reason. Well, sir, that's how it was with us; and just then came a holiday. I went to vespers; when I came home I found Emelyanoushka sitting in the window, drunk and rocking to and fro.

"Ah! so that's what you've been up to, my lad! And I went to get something out of my chest. And when I looked in, the breeches were not there . . . I rummaged here and there; they'd vanished. When I'd ransacked everywhere and saw they were not there, something seemed to stab me to the heart. I ran first to the old dame and began accusing her; of Emelyanoushka I'd not the faintest suspicion, though there was cause for it in his sitting there drunk.

"'No,' said the old body, 'God be with you, my fine gentleman, what good are riding breeches to me? Am I going to wear such things? Why, a skirt I had I lost the other day through a fellow of your sort . . . I know nothing; I can tell you nothing about it,' she said.

"'Who has been here, who has been in?' I asked.

"'Why, nobody has been, my good sir,' says she; 'I've been here all the while; Emelyan Ilyitch went out and came back again; there he sits, ask him.'

"'Emelyanoushka,' said I, 'have you taken those new riding breeches for anything; you remember the pair I made for that gentleman from the country?'

"'No, Astafy Ivanovitch,' said he, 'I've not—sort of—touched them.'

"I was in a state! I hunted high and low for them—they were nowhere to be found. And Emelyanoushka sits there rocking himself to and fro. I was squatting on my heels and facing him and bending over the chest, and all at once I stole a glace at him . . . Alack, I thought; my heart suddenly grew hot within me and I felt myself flushing up too. And suddenly Emelyanoushka looked at me.

"'No, Astafy Ivanovitch,' said he, 'those riding breeches of yours, maybe, you are thinking, maybe, I took them, but I never touched them.'

"'But what can have become of them, Emelyan Ilyitch?'

"'No, Astafy Ivanovitch,' said he, 'I've never seen them.'

"'Why, Emelyan Ilyitch, I suppose, they've run off themselves, eh?'

"'Maybe they have, Astafy Ivanovitch.'

"When I heard him say that, I got up at once, went up to him, lighted the lamp and sat down to work to my sewing. I was altering a waistcoat for a clerk who lived below us. And wasn't there a burning pain and ache in my breast! I shouldn't have minded so much if I had put all the clothes I had in the fire. Emelyanoushka seemed to have an inkling of what a rage I was in. When a man is guilty, you know, sir, he scents trouble far off, like the birds of the air before a storm.

"'Do you know what, Astafy Ivanovitch,' Emelyanoushka began, and his poor old voice was shaking as he said the words, 'Antip Prohoritch, the apothecary, married the coachman's wife this morning, who died the other day—'

"I did give him a look, sir, a nasty look it was; Emelyanoushka understood it too. I saw him get up, go to the bed, and begin to rummage there for something. I waited—he was busy there a long time and kept muttering all the while, 'No, not there, where can the blessed things have got to!' I waited to see what he'd do; I saw him creep under the bed on all fours. I couldn't bear it any longer. 'What are you crawling about under the bed for, Emelyan Ilyitch?' said I.

"'Looking for the breeches, Astafy Ivanovitch. Maybe they've dropped down there somewhere.'

"'Why should you try to help a poor simple man like me,' said I, 'crawling on your knees for nothing, sir'—I called him that in my vexation.

"'Oh, never mind, Astafy Ivanovitch, I'll just look. They'll turn up, maybe, somewhere.'

"'H'm,' said I, 'look here, Emelyan Ilyitch!'

"'What is it, Astafy Ivanovitch?' said he.

"'Haven't you simply stolen them from me like a thief and a robber, in return for the bread and salt you've eaten here' said I.

"I felt so angry, sir, at seeing him fooling about on his knees before me.

"'No, Astafy Ivanovitch.'

"And he stayed lying as he was on his face under the bed. A long time he lay there and then at last crept out. I looked at him and the man was as white as a sheet. He stood up, and sat down near me in the window and sat so for some ten minutes.

"'No, Astafy Ivanovitch,' he said, and all at once he stood up and came towards me, and I can see him now; he looked dreadful. 'No, Astafy Ivanovitch,' said he, 'I never—sort of—touched your breeches.'

"He was all of a shake, poking himself in the chest with a trembling finger, and his poor old voice shook so that I was frightened, sir, and sat as though I was rooted to the window-seat.

"'Well, Emelyan Ilyitch,' said I, 'as you will, forgive me if I, in my foolishness, have accused you unjustly. As for the breeches, let them go hang; we can live without them. We've still our hands, thank God; we need not go thieving or begging from some other poor man; we'll earn our bread.'

"Emelyanoushka heard me out and went on standing there before me. I looked up, and he had sat down. And there he sat all the evening without a stirring. At last I lay down to sleep. Emelyanoushka went on sitting in the same place. When I looked out in the morning, he was lying curled up in his old coat on the bare floor; he felt too crushed even to come to bed. Well, sir, I felt no more liking for the fellow from that day, in fact for the first few days I hated him. I felt as one may say as though my own son had robbed me, and done me a deadly hurt. Ach, thought I, Emelyanoushka, Emelyanoushka! And Emelyanoushka, sir, went on drinking for a whole fortnight without stopping. He was drunk all the time, and regularly besotted. He went out in the morning and came back late at night, and for a whole fortnight I didn't get a word out of him. It was as though grief was gnawing at his heart, or as though he wanted to do for himself completely. At last he stopped: he must have come to the end of all he'd got, and then he sat in the window again. I remember he sat there without speaking for three days and three nights; all of a sudden I saw that he was crying. He was just sitting there, sir, and crying like anything; a perfect stream, as though he didn't know how his tears were flowing. And it's a sad thing, sir, to see a grown-up man and an old man, too, crying from woe and grief.

"'What's the matter, Emelyanoushka?' said I.

"He began to tremble so that he shook all over. I spoke to him for the first time since that evening.

"'Nothing, Astafy Ivanovitch.'

"'God be with you, Emelyanoushka, what's lost is lost. Why are you moping about like this?' I felt sorry for him.

"'Oh, nothing, Astafy Ivanovitch, it's no matter. I want to find some work to do, Astafy Ivanovitch.'

"'And what sort of work, pray, Emelyanoushka?'

"'Why, any sort; perhaps I could find a situation such as I used to have. I've been already to ask Fedosay Ivanitch. I don't like to be a burden to you, Astafy Ivanovitch. If I can find a situation, Astafy Ivanovitch, then I'll pay it you all back, and make you a return for all your hospitality.'

"'Enough, Emelyanoushka, enough; let bygones be bygones—and no more to be said about it. Let us go on as we used to do before.'

"'No, Astafy Ivanovitch, you, maybe, think—but I never touched your riding breeches.'

"'Well, have it your own way; God be with you, Emelyanoushka.'

"'No, Astafy Ivanovitch, I can't go on living with you, that's clear. You must excuse me, Astafy Ivanovitch.'

"'Why, God bless you, Emelyan Ilyitch, who's offending you and driving you out of the place—am I doing it?'

"'No, it's not the proper thing for me to live with you like this, Astafy Ivanovitch. I'd better be going.'

"He was so hurt, it seemed, he stuck to his point. I looked at him, and sure enough, up he got and pulled his old coat over his shoulders.

"'But where are you going, Emelyan Ilyitch? Listen to reason: what are you about? Where are you off to?'

"'No, good-bye, Astafy Ivanovitch, don't keep me now'—and he was blubbering again—'I'd better be going. You're not the same now.'

"'Not the same as what? I am the same. But you'll be lost by yourself like a poor helpless babe, Emelyan Ilyitch.'

"'No, Astafy Ivanovitch, when you go out now, you lock up your chest and it makes me cry to see it, Astafy Ivanovitch. You'd better let me go, Astafy Ivanovitch, and forgive me all the trouble I've given you while I've been living with you.'

"Well, sir, the man went away. I waited for a day; I expected he'd be back in the evening—no. Next day no sign of him, not the third day either. I couldn't eat, I couldn't sleep. The fellow had quite disarmed me. On the fourth day I went out to look for him; I peeped into all the taverns, to inquire for him—but no, Emelyanoushka was lost. 'Have you managed to keep yourself alive, Emelyanoushka?' I wondered. 'Perhaps he is lying dead under some hedge, poor drunkard, like a sodden long.' I went home more dead than alive. Next day I went out to look for him again. And I kept cursing myself that I'd been such a fool as to let the man go off by himself. On the fifth day it was a holiday—in the early morning I heard the door creak. I looked up and there was my Emelyanoushka coming in. His face was blue and his hair was covered with dirt as though he'd been sleeping in the street; he was as thin as a match. He took off his old coat, sat down on the chest and looked at me. I was delighted to see him, but I felt more upset about him than ever. For you see, sir, if I'd been overtaken in some sin, as true as I am here, sir, I'd have died like a dog before I'd have come back. But Emelyanoushka did come back. And a sad thing it was, sure enough, to see a man sunk so low. I began to look after him, to talk kindly to him, to comfort him.

"'Well, Emelyanoushka,' said I, 'I am glad you've come back. Had you been away much longer I should have gone to look for you in the taverns again today. Are you hungry?'

"'No, Astafy Ivanovitch.'

"'Come now, aren't you really? Here, brother, is some cabbage soup left over from yesterday; there was meat in it; it is good stuff. And here is some bread and onion. Come, eat it, it'll do you no harm.'

"I made him eat it, and I saw at once that the man had not tasted food for maybe three days—he was as hungry as a wolf. So it was hunger that had driven him to me. My heart was melted looking at the poor dear. 'Let me run to the tavern,' thought I, 'I'll get something to ease his heart, and then we'll make an end of it. I've no more anger in my heart against you, Emelyanoushka!' I brought him some vodka. 'Here, Emelyan Ilyitch, let us have a drink for the holiday. Like a drink? And it will do you good.' He then held out his hand, held it out greedily; he was just taking it and then he stopped himself. But a minute after I saw him take it, and lift it to his mouth, spilling it on his sleeve. But though he got it to his lips he set it down on the table again.

"'What is it, Emelyanoushka?'

"'Nothing, Astafy Ivanovitch, I—sort of—'

"'Won't you drink it?'

"'Well, Astafy Ivanovitch, I'm not—sort of—going to drink any more, Astafy Ivanovitch.'

"'Do you mean you've given it up altogether, Emelyanoushka, or are you only not going to drink today?'

"He did not answer. A minute later I saw him rest his head on his hand.

"'What's the matter, Emelyanoushka, are you ill?'

"'Why, yes, Astafy Ivanovitch, I don't feel well.'

"I took him and laid him down on the bed. I saw that he really was ill: his head was burning hot and he was shivering with fever. I sat by him all day; towards night he was worse. I mixed him some oil and onion and kvass and bread broken up.

"'Come, eat some of this,' said I, 'and perhaps you'll be better.' He shook his head. 'No,' said he, 'I won't have any dinner today, Astafy Ivanovitch.'

"I made some tea for him, I quite flustered our old woman—he was no better. Well, thinks I, it's a bad look-out! The third morning I went for a medical gentleman. There was one I knew living close by, Kostopravov by name. I'd made his acquaintance when I was in service with the Bosomyagins; he'd attended me. The doctor came and looked at him. 'He's in a bad way,' said he, 'it was no use sending for me. But if you like I can give him a powder.' Well, I didn't give him a powder, I thought that's just the doctor's little game; and then the fifth day came.

"He lay, sir, dying before my eyes. I sat in the window with my work in my hands. The old woman was heating the stove. We were all silent. My hear was simply breaking over him, the good-for-nothing fellow; I felt as if it were a son of my own I was losing. I knew that Emelyanoushka was looking at me. I'd seen the man all the day long making up his mind to say something and not daring to.

"At last I looked up at him; I saw such misery in the poor fellow's eyes. He had kept them fixed on me but, when he saw that I was looking at him, he looked down at once.

"'Astafy Ivanovitch.'

"'What is it, Emelyanoushka?'

"'If you were to take my old coat to a second-hand dealer's, how much do you think they'd give you for it, Astafy Ivanovitch?'

"'There's no knowing how much they'd give. Maybe they would give me a rouble for it, Emelyan Ilyitch.'

"But if I had taken it they wouldn't have given a farthing for it, but would have laughed in my face for bringing such a trumpery thing. I simply said that to comfort the poor fellow, knowing the simpleton he was.

"'But I was thinking, Astafy Ivanovitch, they might give you three roubles for it; it's made of cloth, Astafy Ivanovitch. How could they only give one rouble for a cloth coat?'

"'I don't know, Emelyan Ilyitch,' said I, 'if you are thinking of taking it you should certainly ask three roubles to begin with.'

"Emelyanoushka was silent for a time, and then he addressed me again—

"'Astafy Ivanovitch.'

"'What is it, Emelyanoushka?' I asked.

"'Sell my coat when I die, and don't bury me in it. I can lie as well without it; and it's a thing of some value—it might come in useful.'

"I can't tell you how it made my heart ache to hear him. I saw that the death agony was coming on him. We were silent again for a bit. So an hour passed by. I looked at him again: he was still staring at me, and when he met my eyes he looked down again.

"'Do you want some water to drink, Emelyan Ilyitch?' I asked.

"'Give me some, God bless you, Astafy Ivanovitch.'

"I gave him a drink.

"'Thank you, Astafy Ivanovitch,' said he.

"'Is there anything else you would like, Emelyanoushka?'

"'No, Astafy Ivanovitch, there's nothing I want, but I—sort of—'

"'What?'

"'I only—'

"'What is it, Emelyanoushka?'

"'Those riding breeches—it was—sort of—I who took them—Astafy Ivanovitch.'

"'Well, God forgive you, Emelyanoushka,' said I, 'you poor, sorrowful creature. Depart in peace.'

"And I was choking myself, sir, and the tears were in my eyes. I turned aside for a moment.

"'Astafy Ivanovitch—'

"I saw Emelyanoushka wanted to tell me something; he was trying to sit up, trying to speak, and mumbling something. He flushed red all over suddenly, looked at me . . . then I saw him turn white again, whiter and whiter, and he seemed to sink away all in a minute. His head fell back, he drew one breath and gave up his soul to God."

ANDRE DUBUS

ANDRE DUBUS WAS BORN IN 1936 IN LAKE CHARLES, Louisiana, and grew up in Lafayette, where he was educated by the Christian Brothers, a Catholic parochial school. He spent six years in the Marine Corps, becoming a captain; after leaving the Marines, he moved with his wife and four children to Iowa City, where he graduated from the University of Iowa Writers' Workshop with an MFA in creative writing.

Though he wrote one novel, *The Lieutenant,* Dubus is most famous for his many short story collections, among them *Separate Flights, Adultery and Other Choices, The Times Are Never So Bad, The Last Worthless Evening,* and his *Selected Stories.* His work garnered such important literary awards as the Rea Award for the Short Story for excellence in short fiction, and fellowships from the Guggenheim and MacArthur Foundations.

In July of 1986, he was seriously injured in a car accident. Driving from Boston to his home in Haverhill, Massachusetts, he stopped to aid two disabled motorists. As he helped one of them to the side of the highway, Dubus was struck by an oncoming car, critically injuring him and leaving him a paraplegic for the rest of his life. But the experience brought him a deeper relationship with God, renewing his Catholic faith. He died of a heart attack in 1999, and is buried in Elmwood Cemetery in Bradford, Massachusetts.

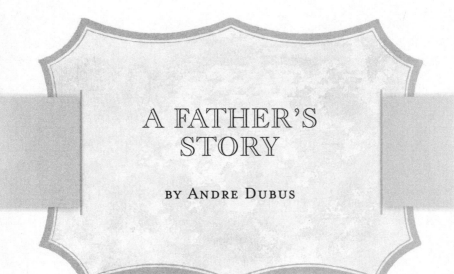

A FATHER'S STORY

BY ANDRE DUBUS

My name is Luke Ripley, and here is what I call my life: I own a stable of thirty horses, and I have young people who teach riding, and we board some horses, too. This is in northeastern Massachusetts. I have a barn with an indoor ring, and outside I've got two fenced-in rings and a pasture that ends at a woods with trails. I call it my life because it looks like it is, and people I know call it that, but it's a life I can get away from when I hunt and fish, and some nights after dinner when I sit in the dark in the front room and listen to opera. The room faces the lawn and the road, a two-lane country road. When cars come around the curve northwest of the house, they light up the lawn for an instant, the leaves of the maple out by the road and the hemlock closer to the window. Then I'm alone again, or I'd appear to be if someone crept up to the house and looked through a window: a big-gutted gray-haired guy, drinking tea and smoking cigarettes, staring out at the dark woods across the road, listening to a grieving soprano.

My real life is the one nobody talks about anymore, except Father Paul LeBoeuf, another old buck. He has a decade on me: he's sixty-four, a big man, bald on top with gray at the sides; when he had hair, it was black. His face is ruddy, and he jokes about being a whiskey priest, though he's not. He gets outdoors as much as he can, goes for a long walk every morning, and hunts and fishes with me. But I can't get him on a horse anymore. Ten years ago I could badger him into a trail ride; I had to give him a western saddle, and he'd hold the pommel and bounce through the woods with me, and be sore for days. He's looking at seventy with eyes that are younger than many I've seen in people in their twenties. I do not remember ever feeling the way they seem to; but I was lucky, because even as a child I knew that life would try me, and I must be strong to endure, though in those early days I expected to be tortured and killed for my faith, like the saints I learned about in school.

Father Paul's family came down from Canada, and he grew up speaking more French than English, so he is different from the Irish priests who abound up here. I do not like to make general statements, or even to hold general beliefs, about people's blood, but the Irish do seem happiest when they're dealing with misfortune or guilt, either their own or somebody else's, and if you think you're not a victim of either one, you can count on certain Irish priests to try to change your mind. On Wednesday nights Father Paul comes to dinner. Often he comes on other nights too, and once, in the old days when we couldn't eat meat on Fridays, we bagged our first ducks of the season on a Friday, and as we drove home from the marsh, he said: For the purposes of Holy Mother Church, I believe a duck is more a creature of water than land, and is not rightly meat. Sometimes he teases me about never putting anything in his Sunday collection, which he would not know about if I hadn't told him years ago. I would like to believe I told him so we could have philosophical talk at dinner, but probably the truth is I suspected he knew, and I did not want him to think I so loved money that I would not even give his church a coin on Sunday. Certainly the ushers who pass the baskets know me as a miser.

I don't feel right about giving money for buildings, places. This starts with the Pope, and I cannot respect one of them till he sells his house and everything in it, and that church too, and uses the money to feed the poor. I have rarely, and maybe never, come across saintliness, but I feel certain it cannot exist in such a place. But I admit, also, that

I know very little, and maybe the popes live on a different plane and are tried in ways I don't know about. Father Paul says his own church, St. John's, is hardly the Vatican. I like his church: it is made of wood, and has a simple altar and crucifix, and no padding on the kneelers. He does not have to lock its doors at night. Still it is a place. He could say Mass in my barn. I know this is stubborn, but I can find no mention by Christ of maintaining buildings, much less erecting them of stone or brick, and decorating them with pieces of metal and mineral and elements that people still fight over like barbarians. We had a Maltese woman taking riding lessons, she came over on the boat when she was ten, and once she told me how the nuns in Malta used to tell the little girls that if they wore jewelry, rings and bracelets and necklaces, in purgatory snakes would coil around their fingers and wrists and throats. I do not believe in frightening children or telling them lies, but if those nuns saved a few girls from devotion to things, maybe they were right. That Maltese woman laughed about it, but I noticed she wore only a watch, and that with a leather strap.

The money I give to the church goes in people's stomachs, and on their backs, down in New York City. I have no delusions about the worth of what I do, but I feel it's better to feed somebody than not. There's a priest in Times Square giving shelter to runaway kids, and some Franciscans who run a bread line; actually it's a morning line for coffee and a roll, and Father Paul calls it the continental breakfast for winos and bag ladies. He is curious about how much I am sending, and I know why: he guesses I send a lot, he has said probably more than tithing, and he is right; he wants to know how much because he believes I'm generous and good, and he is wrong about that; he has never had much money and does not know how easy it is to write a check when you have everything you will ever need, and the figures are mere numbers, and represent no sacrifice at all. Being a real Catholic is too hard; if I were one, I would do with my house and barn what I want the Pope to do with his. So I do not want to impress Father Paul, and when he asks me how much, I say I can't let my left hand know what my right is doing.

He came on Wednesday nights when Gloria and I were married, and the kids were young; Gloria was a very good cook (I assume she still is, but it is difficult to think of her in the present), and I liked sitting at the table with a friend who was also a priest. I was proud of my handsome and healthy children. This was long ago, and they were all very young and cheerful and often funny, and the three boys took care of their baby sister, and did not bully or tease her. Of course they did sometimes, with that excited cruelty children are prone to, but not enough so that it was part of her days. On the Wednesday after Gloria left with the kids and a U-Haul trailer, I was sitting on the front steps, it was summer, and I was watching cars go by on the road, when Father Paul drove around the curve and into the driveway. I was ashamed to see him because he is a priest and my family was gone, but I was relieved, too. I went to the car to greet him. He got out smiling, with a bottle of wine, and shook my hand, then pulled me to him, gave me a quick hug, and said: "It's Wednesday, isn't it? Let's open some cans."

With arms about each other we walked to the house, and it was good to know he was doing his work but coming as a friend, too, and I thought what good work he had. I have no calling. It is for me to keep horses.

In that other life, anyway. In my real one I go to bed early and sleep well and wake at four forty-five, for an hour of silence. I never want to get out of bed then, and every morning I know I can sleep for another four hours and still not fail at any of my duties. But I get up, so have come to believe my life can be seen in miniature in that struggle in the dark of morning. While making the bed and boiling water for coffee, I talk to God: I offer Him my day, every act of my body and spirit, my thoughts and moods, as a prayer of thanksgiving, and for Gloria and my children and my friends and two women I made love with after Gloria left. This morning offeratory is a habit from my boyhood in a Catholic school; or then it was a habit, but as I kept it and grew older it became a ritual. Then I say the Lord's Prayer, trying not to recite it, and one morning it occurred to me that a prayer, whether recited or said with concentration, is always an act of faith.

I sit in the kitchen at the rear of the house and drink coffee and smoke and watch the sky growing light before sunrise, the trees of the woods near the barn taking shape, becoming single pines and elms and oaks and maples. Sometimes a rabbit comes out of the treeline, or is already sitting there, invisible till the light finds him. The birds are awake in the trees and feeding on the ground, and the little ones, the purple finches and titmice and chickadees, are at the feeder I rigged outside the kitchen window; it is too small for pigeons to get a purchase. I sit and give myself to coffee and tobacco, that get me brisk again, and I watch and listen. In the first year or so after I lost my family, I played the radio in the mornings. But I overcame that, and now I rarely play it at all. Once in the mail I received a questionnaire asking me to write down everything I watched on television during the week they had chosen. At the end of those seven days I wrote in *The Wizard of Oz* and returned it. That was in winter and was actually a busy week for my television, which normally sits out the cold months without once warming up. Had they sent the questionnaire during baseball season, they would have found me at my set. People at the stables talk about shows and performers I have never heard of, but I cannot get interested; when I am in the mood to watch television, I go to a movie or read a detective novel. There are always good detective novels to be found, and I like remembering them next morning with my coffee.

I also think of baseball and hunting and fishing, and of my children. It is not painful to think about them anymore, because even if we had lived together, they would be gone now, grown into their own lives, except Jennifer. I think of death, too, not sadly, or with fear, though something like excitement does run through me, something more quickening than the coffee and tobacco. I suppose it is an intense interest, and an outright distrust: I never feel certain that I'll be here watching birds eating at tomorrow's daylight. Sometimes I try to think of other things, like the rabbit that is warm and breathing but not there till twilight. I feel on the brink of something about the life of the senses, but either am not equipped to go further or am not interested enough to concentrate. I have called all of this thinking, but it is not, because it is unintentional; what I'm really doing is feeling the day, in silence, and that is what Father Paul is doing too on his five-to-ten-mile walks.

When the hour ends I take an apple or carrot and I go to the stable and tack up a horse. We take good care of these horses, and no one rides them but students, instructors, and me, and nobody rides the horses we board unless an owner asks me to. The barn is dark and I turn on lights and take some deep breaths, smelling the hay and horses and their manure, both fresh and dried, a combined odor that you either like or you don't. I walk down the wide space of dirt between stalls, greeting the horses, joking with them about their quirks, and choose one for no reason at all other than the way it looks at me that morning. I get my old English saddle that has smoothed and darkened through the years, and go into the stall, talking to this beautiful creature who'll swerve out of a canter if a piece of paper blows in front of him, and if the barn catches fire and you manage to get him out he will, if he can get away from you, run back into the fire, to his stall. Like the smells that surround them, you either like them or you don't. I love them, so am spared having to try to explain why. I feed one the carrot or apple and tack up and lead him outside, where I mount, and we go down the driveway to the road and cross it and turn northwest and walk then trot then canter to St. John's.

A few cars are on the road, their drivers looking serious about going to work. It is always strange for me to see a woman dressed for work so early in the morning. You know how long it takes them, with the makeup and hair and clothes, and I think of them waking in the dark of winter or early light of other seasons, and dressing as they might for an evening's entertainment. Probably this strikes me because I grew up seeing my father put on those suits he never wore on weekends or his two weeks off, and so am accustomed to the men, but when I see these women I think something went wrong, to send all those dressed-up people out on the road when the dew hasn't dried yet. Maybe it's because I so dislike getting up early, but am also doing what I choose to do, while they have no choice. At heart I am lazy, yet I find such peace and delight in it that I believe it is a natural state, and in what looks like my laziest periods I am closest to my center. The ride to St. John's is fifteen minutes. The horses and I do it in all weather; the road is well plowed in winter, and there are only a few days a year when ice makes me drive the pickup. People always look at someone on horseback, and for a moment their faces change and many drivers and I wave to each other. Then at St. John's Father Paul and five or six regulars and I celebrate the Mass.

Do not think of me as a spiritual man whose every thought during those twenty-five minutes is at one with the words of the Mass. Each morning I try, each morning I fail, and know that always I will be a creature who, looking at Father Paul and the altar, and uttering prayers, will be distracted by scrambled eggs, horses, the weather, and memories and daydreams that have nothing to do with the sacrament I am about to receive. I can receive, though: the Eucharist, and also, at Mass and at other times, moments and even minutes of contemplation. But I cannot achieve contemplation, as some can; and so, having to face and forgive my own failures, I have learned from them both the necessity and wonder of ritual. For ritual allows those who cannot will themselves out of the secular to perform the spiritual, as dancing allows the tongue-tied man a ceremony of love. And, while my mind dwells on breakfast, or Major or Duchess tethered under the church eave, there is, as I take the Host from Father Paul and place it on my tongue and return to the pew, a feeling that I am thankful I have not lost in the forty-eight years since my first Communion. At its center is excitement; spreading out from it is the peace of certainty. Or the certainty of peace. One night Father Paul and I talked about faith. It was long ago, and all I remember is him saying: Belief is believing in God; faith is believing that God believes in you. That is the excitement, and the peace; then the Mass is over, and I go into the sacristy and we have a cigarette and chat, the mystery ends, we are two men talking like any two men on a morning in America, about baseball, plane crashes, presidents, governors, murders, the sun, the clouds. Then I go to the horse and ride back to the life people see, the one in which I move and talk, and most days I enjoy it.

IT IS LATE SUMMER NOW, THE TIME BETWEEN FISHING and hunting, but a good time for baseball. It has been two weeks since Jennifer left, to drive home to Gloria's after her summer visit. She is the only one who still visits; the boys are married and have children, and sometimes fly up for a holiday, or I fly down to visit one of them. Jennifer is twenty, and I worry about her the way fathers worry about daughters but not sons. I want to know what she's up to, and at the same time I don't. She looks athletic, and she is: she swims and runs and of course rides. All my children do. When she comes for six weeks in summer, the house is loud with girls, friends of hers since childhood, and new ones. I am glad she kept the girl friends. They have been young company for me and, being with them, I have been able to gauge her growth between summers. On their riding days, I'd take them back to the house when their lessons were over and they had walked the horses and put them back in the stalls, and we'd have lemonade or Coke, and cookies if I had some, and talk until their parents came to drive them home. One year their breasts grew, so I wasn't startled when I saw Jennifer in July. Then they were driving cars to the stable, and beginning to look like young women, and I was passing out beer and ashtrays and they were talking about college.

When Jennifer was here in summer, they were at the house most days. I would say generally that as they got older they became quieter, and though I enjoyed both, I sometimes missed the giggles and shouts. The quiet voices, just low enough for me not to hear from wherever I was, rising and falling in proportion to my distance from them, frightened me. Not that I believed they were planning or recounting anything really wicked, but there was a female seriousness about them, and it was secretive, and of course I thought: love, sex. But it was more than that: it was womanhood they were entering, the deep forest of it, and no matter how many women and men too are saying these days that there is little difference between us, the truth is that men find their way into that forest only on clearly marked trails, while women move about in it like birds. So hearing Jennifer and her friends talking so quietly, yet intensely, I wanted very much to have a wife.

But not as much as in the old days, when Gloria had left but her presence was still in the house as strongly as if she had only gone to visit her folks for a week. There were no clothes or cosmetics, but potted plants endured my neglectful care as long as they could, and slowly died; I did not kill them on purpose, to exorcise the house of her, but I could not remember to water them. For weeks, because I did not use it much, the house was as neat as she had kept it, though dust layered the order she had made. The kitchen went first: I got the dishes in and out of the dishwasher and wiped the top of the stove, but did not return cooking spoons and pot holders to their hooks on the wall, and soon the burners and oven were caked with spillings, the refrigerator had more space and was spotted with juices. The living room and my bedroom went next; I did not go into the children's rooms except on bad nights when I went from room to room and looked and touched and smelled, so they did not lose their order until a year later when the kids came for six weeks. It was three months before I ate the last of the food Gloria had cooked and frozen: I remember it was a beef stew, and very good. By then I had four cookbooks, and was boasting a bit, and talking about recipes with the women at the stables, and looking forward to cooking for Father Paul. But I never looked forward to cooking at night only for myself, though I made myself do it; on some nights I gave in to my daily temptation, and took a newspaper or detective novel to a restaurant. By the end of the second year, though, I had stopped turning on the radio as soon as I woke in the morning, and was able to be silent and alone in the evening too, and then I enjoyed my dinners.

It is not hard to live through a day, if you can live through a moment. What creates despair is the imagination, which pretends there is a future, and insists on predicting millions of moments, thousands of days, and so drains you that you cannot live the moment at hand. That is what Father Paul told me in those first two years, on some of the bad nights when I believed I could not bear what I had to: the most painful loss was my children, then the loss of Gloria, whom I still loved despite or maybe because of our long periods of sadness that rendered us helpless, so neither of us could break out of it to give a hand to the other. Twelve years later I believe ritual would have healed us more quickly than the repetitious talks we had, perhaps even kept us healed. Marriages have lost that, and I wish I had known then what I know now, and we had performed certain acts together every day, no matter how we felt, and perhaps then we could have subordinated feeling to action, for surely that is the essence of love. I know this from my distractions during Mass, and during everything else I do, so that my actions and feelings are seldom one. It does happen every day, but in proportion to everything else in a day, it is rare, like joy. The third most painful loss, which became second and sometimes first as months passed, was the knowledge that I could never marry again, and so dared not even keep company with a woman.

On some of the bad nights I was bitter about this with Father Paul, and I so pitied myself that I cried, or nearly did, speaking with damp eyes and breaking voice. I believe that celibacy is for him the same trial it is for me, not of the flesh, but the spirit: the heart longing to love. But the difference is he chose it, and did not wake one day to a life with thirty horses. In my anger I said I had done my service to love and chastity, and I told him of the actual physical and spiritual pain of practicing rhythm: nights of striking the mattress with a fist, two young animals lying side by side in heat, leaving the bed to pace, to smoke, to curse, and too passionate to question, for we were so angered and oppressed by our passion that we could see no further than our loins. So now I understand how people can be enslaved for generations before they throw down their tools or use them as weapons, the form of their slavery—the cotton fields, the shacks and puny cupboards and untended illnesses—absorbing their emotions and thoughts until finally they have little or none at all to direct with clarity and energy at the owners and legislators. And I told him of the trick of passion and its slaking: how during what we had to believe were safe periods, though all four children were conceived at those times, we were able with some coherence to question the tradition and reason and justice of the law against birth control, but not with enough conviction to soberly act against it, as though regular satisfaction in bed tempered our revolutionary as well as our erotic desires. Only when abstinence drove us hotly away from each other did we receive an urge so strong it lasted all the way to the drugstore and back; but always, after the release, we threw away the remaining condoms; and after going through this a few times, we knew what would happen, and from then on we submitted to the calendar she so precisely marked on the bedroom wall. I told him that living two lives each month, one as celibates, one as lovers, made us tense and short-tempered, so we snapped at each other like dogs.

To have endured that, to have reached a time when we burned slowly and could gain from bed the comfort of lying down at night with one who loves you and whom you love, could for weeks on end go to bed tired and peacefully sleep after a kiss, a touch of the hands, and then to be thrown out of the marriage like a bundle from a moving freight car, was unjust, was intolerable, and I could not or would not muster the strength to endure it. But I did, a moment at a time, a day, a night, except twice, each time with a different woman and more than a year apart, and this was so long ago that I clearly see their faces in my memory, can hear the pitch of their voices, and the way they pronounced words, one with a Massachusetts accent, one Midwestern, but I feel as though I only heard about them from someone else. Each rode at the stables and was with me for part of an evening; one was badly married, one divorced, so none of us was free. They did not understand this Catholic view, but they were understanding about my having it, and I remained friends with both of them until the married one left her husband and went to Boston, and the divorced one moved to Maine. After both those evenings, those good women, I went to Mass early while Father Paul was still in the confessional, and received his absolution. I did not tell him who I was, but of course he knew, though I never saw it in his eyes. Now my longing for a wife comes only once in a while, like a cold: on some late afternoons when I am alone in the barn, then I lock up and walk to the house, daydreaming, then suddenly look at it and see it empty, as though for the first time, and all at once I'm weary and feel I do not have the energy to broil meat, and I think of driving to a restaurant, then shake my head and go on to the house, the refrigerator, the oven; and some mornings when I wake in the dark and listen to the silence and run my hand over the cold sheet beside me; and some days in summer when Jennifer is here.

Gloria left first me, then the Church, and that was the end of religion for the children, though on visits they went to Sunday mass with me, and still do, out of a respect for my life that they manage to keep free of patronage. Jennifer is an agnostic, though I doubt she would call herself that, any more than she would call herself any other name that implied she had made a decision, a choice, about existence, death, and God. In truth she tends to pantheism, a good sign, I think; but not wanting to be a father who tells his children what they ought to believe, I do not say to her that Catholicism includes pantheism, like onions in a stew. Besides, I have no missionary instincts and do not believe everyone should or even could live with the Catholic faith. It is Jennifer's womanhood that renders me awkward. And womanhood now is frank, not like when Gloria was twenty and there were symbols:

high heels and cosmetics and dresses, a cigarette, a cocktail. I am glad that women are free now of false modesty and all its attention paid the flesh; but, still, it is difficult to see so much of your daughter, to hear her talk as only men and bawdy women used to, and most of all to see in her face the deep and unabashed sensuality of women, with no tricks of the eyes and mouth to hide the pleasure she feels at having a strong young body. I am certain, with the way things are now, that she has very happily not been a virgin for years. That does not bother me. What bothers me is my certainty about it, just from watching her walk across a room or light a cigarette or pour milk on cereal.

SHE TOLD ME ALL OF IT, WAKING ME THAT NIGHT WHEN I had gone to sleep listening to the wind in the trees and against the house, a wind so strong that I had to shut all but the lee windows, and still the house cooled; told it to me in such detail and so clearly that now, when she has driven the car to Florida, I remember it all as though I had been a passenger in the front seat, or even at the wheel. It started with a movie, then beer and driving to the sea to look at the waves in the night and the wind, Jennifer and Betsy and Liz. They drank a beer on the beach and wanted to go in naked but were afraid they would drown in the high surf. They bought another six-pack at a grocery store in New Hampshire, and drove home. I can see it now, feel it: the three girls and the beer and the ride on country roads where pines curved in the wind and the big deciduous trees swayed and shook as if they might leap from the earth. They would have some windows partly open so they could feel the wind; Jennifer would be playing a cassette, the music stirring them, as it does the young, to memories of another time, other people and places in what is for them the past.

She took Betsy home, then Liz, and sang with her cassette as she left the town west of us and started home, a twenty-minute drive on the road that passes my house. They had each had four beers, but now there were twelve empty bottles in the bag on the floor at the passenger seat, and I keep focusing on their sound against each other when the car shifted speeds or changed directions. For I want to understand that one moment out of all her heart's time on earth, and whether her history had any bearing on it, or whether her heart was then isolated from all it had known, and the sound of those bottles urged it. She was just leaving the town, accelerating past a night club on the right, gaining speed to climb a long, gradual hill, then she went up it, singing, patting the beat on the steering wheel, the wind loud through her few inches of open window, blowing her hair as it did the high branches alongside the road, and she looked up at them and watched the top of the hill for someone drunk or heedless coming over it in part of her lane. She crested to an open black road, and there he was: a bulk, a blur, a thing running across her head-lights, and she swerved left and her foot went for the brake and was stomping air above its pedal when she hit him, saw his legs and body in the air, flying out of her light, into the dark. Her brakes were screaming into the wind, bottles clinking in the fallen bag, and with the music and wind inside the car was his sound, already a memory but as real as an echo, that car-shuddering thump as though she had struck a tree. Her foot was back on the accelerator. Then she shifted gears and pushed it. She ejected the cassette and closed the window. She did not start to cry until she knocked on my bedroom door, then called: "Dad?"

Her voice, her tears, broke through my dream and the wind I heard in my sleep, and I stepped into jeans and hurried to the door, thinking harm, rape, death. All were in her face, and I hugged her and pressed her cheek to my chest and smoothed her blown hair, then led her, weeping, to the kitchen and sat her at the table where she could not speak, nor look at me; when she raised her face it fell forward again, as of its own weight, into her palms. I offered tea and she shook her head, and so I offered beer twice, then she shook her head, so I offered whiskey and she nodded. I had some rye that Father Paul and I had not finished last hunting season, and I poured some over ice and set it in front of her and was putting away the ice but stopped and got another glass and poured one for myself too, and brought the ice and bottle to the table where she was trying to get one of her long menthols out of the pack, but her fingers jerked like severed snakes, and I took the pack and lit one for her and took one for myself. I watched her shudder with her first swallow of rye, and push hair back from her face, it is auburn and gleamed in the overhead light, and I remembered how beautiful she looked riding a sorrel; she was smoking fast, then the sobs in her throat stopped, and she looked at me and said it, the words coming out with smoke: "I hit somebody. With the *car*."

Then she was crying and I was on my feet, moving back and forth, looking down at her, asking *Who? Where? Where?* She was pointing at the wall over the stove, jabbing her fingers and cigarette at it, her other hand at her eyes and twice in horror I actually looked at the wall. She finished the whiskey in a swallow and I stopped pacing and asking and poured another, and either the drink or the exhaustion of tears quieted her, even the dry sobs, and she told me; not as I tell it now, for that was later as again and again we relived it in the kitchen or living room, and, if in daylight, fled it on horseback out on the trails through the woods and, if at night, walked quietly around in the moonlit pasture, walked around and around it, sweating through our clothes. She told it in bursts, like she was a child again, running to me, injured from play. I put on boots and a shirt and left her with the bottle and her streaked face and a cigarette twitching between her fingers, pushed the door open against the wind, and eased it shut. The wind squinted and watered my eyes as I leaned into it and went to the pickup.

When I passed St. John's I looked at it, and Father Paul's little white rectory in the rear, and wanted to stop, wished I could as I could if he were simply a friend who sold hardware or something. I had forgotten my watch but I always know the time within minutes, even when a sound or dream or my bladder wakes me in the night. It was nearly two; we had been in the kitchen about twenty minutes; she had hit him around one-fifteen. Or her. The road was empty and I drove between blowing trees; caught for an instant in my lights, they seemed to be in panic. I smoked and let hope play its tricks on me: it was neither man nor woman but an animal, a goat or calf or deer on the road; it was a man who had jumped away in time, the collision of metal and body glancing not direct, and he had limped home to nurse bruises and cuts. Then I threw the cigarette and hope both out the window and prayed that he was alive, while beneath that prayer, a reserve deeper in my heart, another one stirred: that if he were dead, they would not get Jennifer.

From our direction, east and a bit south, the road to that hill and the night club beyond it and finally the town is, for its last four or five miles, straight through farming country. When I reached that stretch I slowed the truck and opened my window for the fierce air; on both sides were scattered farmhouses and barns and sometimes a silo, looking not like shelters but like unsheltered things the wind would flatten. Corn bent toward the road from a field on my right, and always something blew in front of me: paper, leaves, dried weeds, branches. I slowed approaching the hill, and went up it in second, staring through my open window at the ditch on the left side of the road, its weeds alive, whipping, a mad dance with the trees above them. I went over the hill and down and, opposite the club, turned right onto a side street of houses, and parked there, in the leaping shadows of trees. I walked back across the road to the club's parking lot, the wind behind me, lifting me as I strode, and I could not hear my boots on pavement. I walked up the hill, on the shoulder, watching the branches above me, hearing their leaves and the creaking trunks and the wind. Then I was at the top, looking down the road and at the farms and fields; the night was clear, and I could see a long way; clouds scudded past the half-moon and stars, blown out to sea.

I started down, watching the tall grass under the trees to my right, glancing into the dark of the ditch, listening for cars behind me; but as soon as I cleared one tree, its sound was gone, its flapping leaves and rattling branches far behind me, as though the greatest distance I had at my back was a matter of feet, while ahead of me I could see a barn two miles off. Then I saw her skid marks: short, and going left and downhill, into the other lane. I stood at the ditch, its weeds blowing; across it were trees and their moving shadows, like the clouds. I stepped onto its slope, and it took me sliding on my feet, then rump, to the bottom, where I sat still, my body gathered to itself, lest a part of me should touch him. But there was only tall grass, and I stood, my shoulders reaching the sides of the ditch, and I walked uphill, wishing for the flashlight in the pickup, walking slowly, and down in the ditch I could hear my feet in the grass and on the earth, and kicking cans and bottles. At the top of the hill I turned and went down, watching the ground above the ditch on my right, praying my prayer from the truck again, the first one, the one I would admit, that he was not dead, was in fact home, and began to hope again, memory telling me of lost pheasants and grouse I had shot, but they were small and the colors of their home, while a man was either there or not; and from that memory I left where I was and while walking in the ditch under the wind was in the deceit of imagination with Jennifer in the kitchen, telling her she had hit no one, or at least had not badly hurt anyone, when I realized he could be in the hospital now and I would have to think of a way to check there, something to say on the phone. I see now that, once hope returned, I should have been certain what it prepared for me: ahead of me, in high grass and the shadows of trees, I saw his shirt. Or that is all my mind would allow itself: a shirt, and I stood looking at it for the moments it took my mind to admit the arm and head and the dark length covered by pants. He lay face down, the arm I could see near his side, his head turned from me, on its cheek.

"Fella?" I said. I had meant to call, but it came out quiet and high, lost inches from my face in the wind. Then I said, "Oh, God," and felt Him in the wind and the sky moving past the stars and moon and the fields around me, but only watching me as He might have watched Cain or Job, I did not know which, and I said it again, and wanted to sink to the earth and weep till I slept there in the weeds. I climbed, scrambling up the side of the ditch, pulling at clutched grass, gained the top on hands and knees, and went to him like that, panting, moving through the grass as high and higher than my face, crawling under that sky, making sounds, too, like some animal, there being no words to let him know I was there with him now. He was long; that is the word that came to me, not tall. I kneeled beside him, my hands on my legs. His right arm was by his side, his left arm straight out from the shoulder, but turned, so his palm was open to the tree above us. His left cheek was clean-shaven, his eye closed, and there was no blood. I leaned forward to look at his open mouth and saw the blood on it, going down into the grass. I straightened and looked ahead at the wind blowing past me through grass and trees to a distant light, and I stared at the light, imagining someone awake out there, wanting someone to be, a gathering of old friends, or someone alone listening to music or painting a picture, then I figured it was a night light at a farmyard whose house I couldn't see. *Going*, I thought. *Still going*. I leaned over again and looked at dripping blood.

So I had to touch his wrist, a thick one with a watch and expansion band that I pushed up his arm, thinking *he's left-handed*, my three fingers pressing his wrist, and all I felt was my tough fingertips on that smooth underside flesh and small bones, then relief, then certainty. But against my will, or only because of it, I still don't know, I touched his neck, ran my fingers down as if petting, then pressed, and my hand sprang back as from fire. I lowered it again, held it there until it felt that faint beating that I could not believe. There was too much wind. Nothing could make a sound in it. A pulse could not be felt in it, nor could mere fingers in that wind feel the absolute silence of a dead man's artery. I was making sounds again; I grabbed his left arm and his waist, and pulled him toward me, and that side of him rose, turned and I lowered him to his back, his face tilted up toward the tree that was groaning, the tree and I the only sounds in the wind. Turning my face from his, looking down the length of him at his sneakers, I placed my ear on his heart, and heard not that but something else, and I clamped a hand over my exposed ear, heard something liquid and alive, like when you pump a well and after a few strokes you hear air and water moving in the pipe, and I knew I must raise his legs and cover him and run to a phone, while still I listened to his chest, thinking *raise with what? cover with what?* and amid the liquid sound I heard the heart, then lost it, and pressed my ear against bone, but his chest was quiet, and I did not know when the liquid had stopped, and do not know now when I heard air, a faint rush of it, and whether under my ear or at his mouth or whether I heard it at all. I straightened and looked at the light, dim and yellow. Then I touched his throat, looking him full in the face. He was blond and young. He could have been sleeping in the shade of a tree, but for the smear of blood from his mouth to his hair, and the night sky, and the weeds blowing against his head, and the leaves shaking in the dark above us.

I stood. Then I kneeled again and prayed for his soul to join in peace and joy all the dead and living; and, doing so, confronted my first sin against him, not stopping for Father Paul, who could have given him the last rites, and immediately then my second one, or, I saw then, my first, not calling an ambulance to meet me there, and I stood and turned into the wind, slid down the ditch and crawled out of it, and went up the hill and down it, across the road to the street of houses whose people I had left behind forever, so that I moved with stealth in the shadows to my truck.

When I came around the bend near my house, I saw the kitchen light at the rear. She sat as I had left her, the ashtray filled, and I looked at the bottle, felt her eyes on me, felt what she was seeing too: the dirt from my crawling. She had not drunk much of the rye. I poured some in my glass, with the water from melted ice, and sat down and swallowed some and looked at her and swallowed some more, and said: "He's dead."

She rubbed her eyes with the heels of her hands, rubbed the cheeks under them, but she was dry now.

"He was probably dead when he hit the ground. I mean, that's probably what killed—"

"Where was he?"

"Across the ditch, under a tree."

"Was he—did you see his face?"

"No. Not really. I just felt. For life, pulse. I'm going out to the car."

"What for? Oh."

I finished the rye, and pushed back the chair, then she was standing too.

"I'll go with you."

"There's no need."

"I'll go."

I took a flashlight from a drawer and pushed open the door and held it while she went out. We turned our faces from the wind. It was like on the hill, when I was walking, and the wind closed the distance behind me: after three or four steps I felt there was no house back there. She took my hand, as I was reaching for hers. In the garage we let go, and squeezed between the pickup and her little car, to the front of it, where we had more room, and we stepped back from the grill and I shone the light on the fender, the smashed headlight turned into it, the concave chrome staring to the right, at the garage wall.

"We ought to get the bottles," I said.

She moved between the garage and the car, on the passenger side, and had room to open the door and lift the bag. I reached out, and she gave me the bag and backed up and shut the door and came around the car. We sidled to the doorway, and she put her arm around my waist and I hugged her shoulders.

"I thought you'd call the police," she said.

We crossed the yard, faces bowed from the wind, her hair blowing away from her neck, and in the kitchen I put the bag of bottles in the garbage basket. She was working at the table: capping the rye and putting it away, filling the ice tray, washing the glasses, emptying the ashtray, sponging the table.

"Try to sleep now," I said.

She nodded at the sponge circling under her hand, gathering ashes. Then she dropped it in the sink and, looking me full in the face, as I had never seen her look, as perhaps she never had, being for so long a daughter on visits (or so it seemed to me and still does: that until then our eyes had never seriously met), she crossed to me from the sink and kissed my lips, then held me so tightly I lost balance, and would have stumbled forward had she not held me so hard.

I sat in the living room, the house darkened, and watched the maple and the hemlock. When I believed she was asleep I put on *La*

Bohème, and kept it at the same volume as the wind so it would not wake her. Then I listened to *Madame Butterfly*, and in the third act had to rise quickly to lower the sound: the wind was gone. I looked at the still maple near the window, and thought of the wind leaving farms and towns and the coast, going out over the sea to die on the waves. I smoked and gazed out the window. The sky was darker, and at daybreak the rain came. I listened to *Tosca*, and at six-fifteen went to the kitchen where Jennifer's purse lay on the table, a leather shoulder purse crammed with the things of an adult woman, things she had begun accumulating only a few years back, and I nearly wept, thinking of what sandy foundations they were: driver's license, credit card, disposable lighter, cigarettes, checkbook, ballpoint pen, cash, cosmetics, comb, brush, Kleenex, these the rite of passage from childhood, and I took one of them—her keys—and went out, remembering a jacket and hat when the rain struck me, but I kept going to the car, and squeezed and lowered myself into it, pulled the seat belt over my shoulder and fastened it and backed out, turning in the drive, going forward into the road, toward St. John's and Father Paul.

Cars were on the road, the workers, and I did not worry about any of them noticing the fender and light. Only a horse distracted them from what they drove to. In front of St. John's is a parking lot; at its far side, past the church and at the edge of the lawn, is an old pine, taller than the steeple now. I shifted to third, left the road, and, aiming the right headlight at the tree, accelerated past the white blur of church, into the black trunk growing bigger till it was all I could see, then I rocked in that resonant thump she had heard, had felt, and when I turned off the ignition it was still in my ears, my blood, and I saw the boy flying in the wind. I lowered my forehead to the wheel. Father Paul opened the door, his face white in the rain.

"I'm all right."

"What happened?"

"I don't know. I fainted."

I got out and went around to the front of the car, looked at the smashed light, the crumpled and torn fender.

"Come to the house and lie down."

"I'm all right."

"When was your last physical?"

"I'm due for one. Let's get out of this rain."

"You'd better lie down."

"No. I want to receive."

That was the time to say I want to confess, but I have not and will not. Though I could now, for Jennifer is in Florida, and weeks have passed, and perhaps now Father Paul would not feel that he must tell me to go to the police. And, for that very reason, to confess now would be unfair. It is a world of secrets, and now I have one from my best, in truth my only, friend.

Most of that day it rained, so it was only in the early evening, when the sky cleared, with a setting sun, that two little boys, leaving their confinement for some play before dinner, found him. Jennifer and I got that on the local news, which we listened to every hour, meeting at the radio, standing with cigarettes, until the one at eight o'clock; when she stopped crying, we went out and walked on the wet grass, around the pasture, the last of sunlight still in the air and trees. His name was Patrick Mitchell, he was nineteen years old, was employed by CETA, lived at home with his parents and brother and sister. The paper next day said he had been at a friend's house and was walking home, and I thought of that light I had seen, then knew it was not for him; he lived on one of the streets behind the club. The paper did not say then, or in the next few days, anything to make Jennifer think he was alive while she was with me in the kitchen. Nor do I know if we— I—could have saved him.

In keeping her secret from her friends, Jennifer had to perform so often, as I did with Father Paul and at the stables, that I believe the acting, which took more of her than our daylight trail rides and our night walks in the pasture, was her healing. Her friends teased me about wrecking the car. When I carried her luggage out to the car on that last morning, we spoke only of the weather for her trip—the day was clear, with a dry cool breeze—and hugged and kissed, and I stood watching as she started the car and turned it around. But then she shifted to neutral and put on the parking brake and unclasped the belt, looking at me all the while, then she was coming to me, as she had that night in the kitchen, and I opened my arms.

I have said I talk with God in the mornings, as I start my day, and sometimes as I sit with coffee, looking at the birds, and the woods. Of course He has never spoken to me, but that is not something I require. Nor does He need to. I know Him, as I know the part of myself that knows Him, that felt Him watching from the wind and the night as I kneeled over the dying boy. Lately I have taken to arguing with Him, as I can't with Father Paul, who, when he hears my monthly confession, has not heard and will not hear anything of failure to do all that one can to save an anonymous life, of injustice to a family in their grief, of deepening their pain at the chance and mystery of death by giving them nothing—no one—to hate. With Father Paul I feel lonely about this, but not with God. When I received the Eucharist while Jennifer's car sat twice-damaged, so redeemed, in the rain, I felt neither loneliness nor shame, but as though He were watching me, even from my tongue, intestines, blood, as I have watched my sons at times in their young lives when I was able to judge but without anger, and so keep silent while they, in the agony of their youth, decided how they must act; or found reasons, after their actions, for what they had done. Their reasons were never as good or as bad as their actions, but they needed to find them, to believe they were living by them, instead of the awful solitude of the heart.

I do not feel the peace I once did: not with God, nor the earth, or anyone on it. I have begun to prefer this state, to remember with fondness the other one as a period of peace I neither earned nor deserved. Now in the mornings while I watch purple finches driving larger titmice from the feeder, I say to Him: I would do it again. For when she knocked on my door, then called me, she woke what had flowed dormant in my blood since her birth, so that what rose from the bed was not a stable owner or a Catholic or any other Luke Ripley I had lived with for a long time, but the father of a girl.

And He says: I am a Father too.

Yes, I say, as You are a Son Whom this morning I will receive; unless You kill me on the way to church, then I trust You will receive me. And as a Son You made Your plea.

Yes, He says, but I would not lift the cup.

True, and I don't want You to lift it from me either. And if one of my sons had come to me that night, I would have phoned the police and told them to meet us with an ambulance at the top of the hill.

Why? Do you love them less?

I tell Him no, it is not that I love them less, but that I could bear the pain of watching and knowing my sons' pain, could bear it with pride as they took the whip and nails. But You never had a daughter and, if You had, You could not have borne her passion.

So, He says, you love her more than you love Me.

I love her more than I love truth.

Then you love in weakness, He says.

As You love me, I say, and I go with an apple or carrot out to the barn.

SHUSAKU ENDO

SHUSAKU ENDO, THE INTERNATIONALLY RENOWNED JAPANESE novelist, playwright, essayist, screenwriter, and short story author, was born in 1923 in Tokyo, and lived with his parents in Manchuria until their divorce in 1933. He was then raised by his mother's family, and was baptized a Catholic in 1935. Persecuted and humiliated for his belief during his childhood, and further oppressed in his young adulthood, his faith in God and Christ only deepened.

He studied French literature at the University of Lyon from 1950 to 1953, and began publishing upon his return to Japan; his writing continually explored the issues of faith and doubt, East versus West, and a deeper understanding of how Christ could be comprehended within the context of the Eastern culture. His most important books are the novels *Silence*, *The Samurai*, and *Deep River*, as well as the study *A Life of Jesus*.

Endo died in 1996 of complications due to renal disease. A museum dedicated to his life and his literary career can be found in Sotome, Japan.

THE FINAL MARTYRS

BY SHUSAKU ENDO,
TRANSLATED BY VAN C. GESSEL

In the Uragami district not far from Nagasaki is a village called Nakano. Today it's a part of Hashiguchi-chō, but once it was a tiny community known simply as Nakano Village.

Early in the Meiji period, a man named Kisuke lived in this village. Physically he was as huge as an elephant, but his cowardice belied his size, and he was ineffectual no matter what task he was set to do. He tried with all his might to succeed, but whether he was planting rice paddies, or harvesting the plants, or helping out with roof-thatching in early spring at the orders of the village co-operative union, in the end his youthful co-workers, unable to watch his clumsiness any longer, would always end up lending him a hand.

"I hate working with you, Kisuke. We always have to fix things up after you've finished." When his compatriots Kanzaburō and Zenno-suke complained to him in this manner, Kisuke contracted his huge body as much as possible, and all he could do was bow his head deeply and say: "Forgive me. Kanzaburō, please forgive me!"

Another problem was that, despite his youth, Kisuke was a hopeless sissy. He should have had no cause for fear, since his size and strength exceeded that of most young men his age. But let a single snake cross the road in front of him, and he would freeze in terror. Had some pranksters from the village draped a snake's corpse over the end of a pole and brought it to Kisuke, saying, "Kisuke, this is for you!" his face would have paled like that of a little girl.

Once Kisuke, on his way home from working in the fields, was challenged to a fight by two drunken young men from a neighboring village. The two trouble-makers had, of course, thrown down the gauntlet knowing full well that Kisuke was the infamous coward of Nakano village.

Kisuke retreated to the edge of the road and covered his trembling face with one hand. "Please pardon me. Please forgive me."

The two men, understandably disgusted with Kisuke for quivering like a baby when he was twice the size of a normal man, retorted: "Hey, you call yourself a man? If you're a man, up with your fists. C'mon, your fists!"

Then they taunted him, coaxing him to prove he was a man by stripping down and showing them the evidence. Kisuke pleaded with them not to make him do that, but his cowering posture had the adverse effect of filling his opponents with a sadistic pleasure. "Come on, strip down! So you won't, eh?"

For the sheer fun of it, they rubbed Kisuke's face into the ground as they might have tormented a puppy-dog.

The villagers of Nakano were legitimately irate when they learned how Kisuke had come stealing back into the village that night, stripped even of his loincloth and concealing his private parts. In Nakano village the proscribed Christian faith had been practiced in secret over the years, unbeknown to the officials, and precisely because there was so much solidarity among the villagers, they could not forgive the fact that Kisuke had been taken for a fool by young men from another community. The youths of the village vowed they would never again speak to such a weakling, and the children, in their own callow way, began throwing horse dung and stones at the tumbledown shack where Kisuke and his mother lived.

Still, it made the villagers sad to see Kisuke set out for the fields each day with his hoe on his shoulder and his eyes lowered in misery. The elders from the co-operative began quoting Jesus' words to the young people: "Whosoever shall smite thee on thy right cheek, turn to him the other also." The residents of Nakano half grudgingly forgave Kisuke, who had become a laughing-stock in another village.

Because the villagers in Nakano in the Uragami district had sustained their belief in Christianity, in violation of the prohibition against the faith that the new Meiji government had inherited from the Tokugawa shogunate, their village organization was slightly different from those in other hamlets populated by Buddhist adherents. The Christian villages of Kyushu established various organizations based on age which in today's terms would be described as a "youth group," an "adult group," a "children's association" and a "women's organization." These groups together formed the religious league known as the "cooperative union." Names such as the "Santa Maria Union" or the "Jesus Union" were attached to each organization, and the union heads were elected to perform various duties. To assist the union heads, one, and sometimes several, service volunteers were put into place. Based on an entry in the Christian historical documents that reads, "The number of union heads and service volunteers should be determined on the basis of location and circumstances," it appears that the number of these officials varied from village to village.

Kisuke belonged to the young people's organization in his village, but the level of his faith can be determined from the following anecdote.

In the spring of one year a beggar came to live on the outskirts of the village. But he was no ordinary beggar. He was a leper, and his fingers and toes were gnarled, all the hair had fallen from his head, and his eyes were half blinded. He had been driven from one village to the next before he finally arrived in Nakano, where he was fortunate enough to be able to lay himself down in an abandoned hut beside the banks of the river that flowed near the village.

Because the leaders of the co-operative were responsible not only for governing the village but for playing the role of priests who strengthened the faith of the villagers, they taught their followers how they should treat this beggar. They related how in olden days Jesus had stretched forth His hand to the lepers, and they ordered the union members to take turns caring for the supplicant. The villagers thereupon set up a schedule by which each would deliver rice balls and medicine every day to the riverside hut.

It was in early summer some two months later that Kisuke's turn came. This was an act of mercy that even a child could perform, and Kanzaburō and Zennosuke from his youth group merely told him: "Kisuke, just like the chief said, he's a poor, unfortunate invalid, so be sure you take him some warm rice balls during the day and again at night."

On his assigned day, as he set out to work in the fields, Kisuke had his mother prepare the medications and the rice balls as everyone had instructed him. That afternoon, he headed for the deserted riverbed. It was an early summer's day, warm enough to squeeze out a little perspiration, and when he stepped down into the riverbed, the stench of reeds rotted to their roots attacked his nose. The roof of the decaying hut peeked almost blackly from between the reeds. He could hear not a single sound; he wondered what the beggar was doing. It was so quiet all around him, he felt ill at ease.

When he arrived at the doorway, nervously clutching the bag containing the rice and medicines, the splintered door made an eerie sound as it creaked open. When fearfully he peered inside, the face of the beggar, with eye-sockets gaping like caverns and bereft of a nose, appeared before Kisuke.

"Uwaaah!"

Hurling the bag down, Kisuke fled from the hut, nearly stumbling as he made for the riverbed. The beggar had just grabbed on to the pillar and pulled himself to his feet, intending to go out and drink some stagnant water in the riverbed.

After he raced back to the village, Kisuke refused to return to the hut ever again, no matter how much his fellow-villagers entreated him. As always, in his childlike way he simply pleaded: "Please forgive me. Please forgive me!"

The union heads and elder rulers of the village harshly chastened Kisuke for his lack of charity, citing the example of St. Sebastian, who had held lepers in his arms to keep them warm. Absorbing the rebuke, Kisuke made one more attempt to deliver a package of rice balls in the evening, but no sooner had he left the village than he came running back. He clutched his hands together in entreaty: "I'll do anything else you ask. But please don't make me do this!"

At that time one of the village rulers, a man named Taira no Kunitarō, who would later be martyred at the Sakura-chō prison in Nagasaki, remarked with a gloomy expression: "One day Kisuke's cowardice may cause him to become like Judas, who betrayed our Savior."

IN THE FIFTH YEAR OF THE ANSEI ERA (1858), THE Tokugawa shogunate abandoned its long tradition of isolationism and signed a trade agreement with the United States. The eighth article of that treaty stipulated that "American citizens residing in Japan shall be allowed free exercise of their own religion, and will be allowed to erect places of worship near their dwellings." This effectively did away with the use of *fumie*. Similar treaties were signed with Britain, France, Russia, and Holland the following year.

In 1859 the Parisian missionary, Father Girard,[1] who had been waiting for some time at Naha in Okinawa, entered Edo as a priest for the French Embassy in the capital. He was followed the next year by Revd Bernard Petitjean,[2] who landed at Nagasaki and erected a church in the Ōura hills to the south of Nagasaki with the help of Japanese carpenters. This was the original structure of the Ōura Church that was demolished by the atomic bomb.

The Japanese of the day, who called this church the "French Temple," flocked curiously around to observe the construction of the chapel, but before long they stopped coming, owing perhaps to harassment from the government. Even though the treaty had permitted the practice of the Christian faith by foreigners, the ban on the religion among the Japanese continued. Both Father Petitjean and Father Laucaigne,[3] who reached Japan a year later, had heard while still in their native lands that some believers still secretly continued to follow the faith they had been taught when St. Francis Xavier came to this island nation in the Far East. Once the chapel was built, the first mission they had to carry out was to locate these "hidden" Christians.

But a month passed, then another month, and the chapel still had no visitors. The two priests frequently set out for Nagasaki and the environs of Uragami. Sometimes they would give sweets to children, at other times they would pretend to have fallen from a horse. But not a single Japanese came forward to confess in secret that he was a Christian.

The situation changed on the afternoon of 17 March 1865. That afternoon, Father Petitjean was kneeling at the altar in prayer. It was quiet that afternoon in the chapel. The door creaked faintly but, certain that this must be a police patrolman peeking in half in jest, he continued praying. Someone quietly approached him. When he turned round, a peasant woman dressed in a worker's smock stood stiff as a rod.

"The statue . . . ?" She spoke softly. "Where is the statue of Santa Maria?"

At her words Father Petitjean rose from the prayer altar. He spoke not a word, but his trembling finger indicated a two-foot statue of the Holy Mother positioned to the right of the altar.

"Ah, Santa Maria!" the woman cried. "Oh my, how sweet the Holy Child is!"

This was the initial exchange between the first priest who had come to Japan after over two hundred years of exclusionary policies and the *kakure* Christians of Japan. The hidden Christians, while pretending on the surface to be followers of Buddhism, had secretly continued to intone their ancient Latin prayers and to live the teachings of the Church preached to them by their parents in Nagasaki and Uragami, as well as in out-of-the-way villages facing the sea, and on islands in the harbor such as Gotÿ and Hirado.

In this way contact was established with the faithful, but the government had still not granted freedom of worship. To ward off persecution, Fathers Petitjean and Laucaigne decided to visit the villages and islands where the believers were hidden. They shaved off their curly locks and whiskers, donned wigs made of black-dyed fur from the hemp palm tree and put on peasant clothing. Under cover of darkness they climbed into a boat and traveled from village to village, guided by believers who led them along valley footpaths.

The government officials naturally were aware of the priests' movements. One of the magistrates of Nagasaki at the time, Governor Tokunaga of Iwami, had been tracking down Christians in the Uragami district, and in the summer of 1867 he gave orders to 170 constables to arrest any believers who had violated the prohibition on Christianity. On 15 July, just past midnight, Nakano village was raided. This was the beginning of the great suppression that came to be known as the "fourth persecution at Uragami."[4]

July is the month when typhoons hammer Kyushu. Heavy rains had fallen from morning on the fifteenth. By night the rains had been joined by wind.

Amidst the raging storm the village slept like the dead, but at that late hour constables carrying paper lanterns had already begun to surround the village of Nakano.

In a thatched-roof shed at the crossroads by the village shrine, three young men kept night watch, listening to the sound of the rain and the howling of the wind as they sipped their tea, unaware of what was happening outside. The faithful in Nakano called this shed the "Francis Xavier Chapel." It was a secret place where the villagers could hold their private meetings and offer up their prayers.

The three young night guards were Kanzaburō, Zennosuke, and Kisuke, who dozed in a corner of the room clutching the knees of his work clothes.

Casting an occasional glance towards Kisuke, Kanzaburō and Zennosuke were discussing whether they were prepared to die for their faith if, by chance, they should be subjected to the tortures of persecution.

"Well, I might be afraid. I might be afraid, but in that moment I know that the Lord Jesus would help me," Kanzaburō declared defiantly. "I'm determined to endure torture to the very end."

"What about Kisuke?" Looking a bit uneasy, Zennosuke deflected the focus of the conversation. They glanced at their huge friend, who was sawing logs beneath the flickering light of the candle.

"He has a weakness for pain, after all, so I imagine he'd whimper in agony. Why, maybe he might even abandon the Lord Jesus and 'topple.'"

"Topple," of course, meant to forsake one's faith. They had known Kisuke since childhood, but as they thought of his usual cowardice and awkwardness, they had the distinct impression that he would be the first among the young people of the village to howl in torment. They remembered the words that the village elder, Kunitarō, had muttered with a dark expression: "One day Kisuke's cowardice may cause him to become like Judas, who betrayed our Savior." He had uttered the warning as though he were a prophet.

"What time is it?" Kanzaburō asked.

"Must be about 2 a.m."

Just then, mingling with the sounds of the wind and rain, they heard the piercing tone of a whistle. At that signal the constables who had been waiting on the outskirts of the city with lassos and clubs in hand stormed along the levee and into Nakano village. What followed were the sounds of doors being broken in, and the shouts of the constables. In later years Kanzaburō, who survived the whole ordeal, described the situation that night in the following words:

"Zennosuke escaped out the lattice door. Kisuke was caught with one of the ropes. I put my hands behind my back, and told them to go ahead and tie me up. 'Don't try to bewitch us!' they shouted, and they seemed very afraid of me and wouldn't come near. They threw a lasso round me and three of them tied me up tight. I couldn't breathe, and I passed out. They revived me by giving me water and smelling-salts. Then they dragged me off and stuck me in the village headman's rice granary.

"Some people had their heads cracked open and were covered with blood. Others were tightly bound up. By the time the sun had started to shine in the east, nearly a hundred had been arrested. Then they beat us on our backsides with whips and drove us out of the rice granary. The officers wore headbands tied behind their heads, and they waved their naked swords. We had to run lickety-split down to Nagasaki, where they put us in the prison at Sakura-chō."

His manner of expression was crude, but it painted a vivid picture of the events of that night.

And so the fourth persecution at Uragami began. Once the inconsequential invalids and women and children were released from the Sakura-chō prison, thirty-eight men, including young men and their aged leaders, were stuffed into a narrow, stifling cell. Included in this group were Kanzaburō, Zennosuke, and the face and large body of Kisuke, who, needless to say, was panic-stricken.

The next day several of the men were hauled before the court. Those who refused to "topple" were submitted to a torture known as *dodoi.* Their arms and legs, throat and chest were bound with ropes, which were knotted together in one spot behind their backs. Then they were hoisted up on to a cross, while officers who stood below struck them fiercely with poles and whips. They were lowered to the ground and water was poured over them. The ropes would absorb the water and constrict tightly, gnawing into the flesh of the captives. Those who remained in the cell heard cries like the dark yowls of wild creatures coming from the court, punctuated by taunts from the officers.

"Kisuke, be brave!"

Withstanding the cries of torment, Kanzaburō at once commanded and encouraged Kisuke, who sat to his side pale and clutching the bars of the cell.

"Pray to Santa Maria. To Santa Maria . . ."

The others in the cell joined in a chorus of prayers for protection to the Holy Mother Mary, as though the idea had occurred to them only after Kanzaburō's remark. Amid the muffled, praying voices, Kisuke alone clung desperately to the bars, his pale lips quivering.

"Be brave, Kisuke!"

But suddenly, as if he had gone mad, Kisuke cried out in a loud voice. He was yelling to a warder standing outside the cell. "Please forgive me! Please forgive me!"

The other Christians scrambled to put their hands over Kisuke's mouth and silence his cries. But in his lunatic state Kisuke had more than sufficient strength to brush off three or four men.

"Hey! I can't take it anymore. I'll topple! Officer! I'll topple!"

The officer opened the thick cell door and lugged Kisuke out. The view they had of Kisuke from behind—being kicked and falling to the ground, falling and rising again and again as he was led away to the court—was hideous. He was taken before the officials to provide them with a fingerprint that would serve as proof that he had "toppled."

With a cold shudder Kanzaburō watched the retreating figure of his childhood friend as he was transformed into Judas, just as Kunitarō had prophesied. Once he had provided the officers with his thumbprint, Kisuke, no doubt ashamed, fled across the courtyard without even a glance toward the cell.

After Kisuke's apostasy, three other believers, unable to endure the *dodoi* torture, swore oaths to renounce their faith. It was painful to watch as trusted comrades one after another committed the act of betrayal. Perhaps even amidst their pain, the remaining thirty-four men had sealed a silent promise amongst themselves that they would never apostatize. They did not bend to any subsequent torture. The officers finally seemed to have given up, and for the time being ceased their physical abuse, and the men were moved to a tiny barracks in the Nagasaki hills, at a place called Kojima.

Three months passed. In October of that year, unbeknown to any of the prisoners, the Tokugawa shogunate collapsed.

INEVITABLY, FOREIGN DIPLOMATS WERE DISTRESSED ABOUT the persecution of Kyushu Christians. They put considerable pressure on the new Meiji government to stop these incidents, but because the new rulers themselves had not yet decided on a policy toward religion, all they could do was give the same vague sort of reply that the shogunate had given in regard to Christianity. In reality, notice-boards were erected in Nagasaki neighborhoods reading: "Prohibition on Practice of Christianity Continues as Before. Practice of Heretical Beliefs Strictly Prohibited." As a desperate measure the Meiji government broke with the defunct shogunate's practice of lumping Christianity together with "heretical beliefs," and listed them separately.

But protests from various consular bodies rejected this wily tactic. Kido Takayoshi,[5] one of the Meiji oligarchs, took the matter seriously and changed the initial policy of punishing all the Christian faithful, deciding instead to exile only the prominent members of the flock to various provinces, then observing the attitudes of the remaining captives before deciding upon follow-up measures.

With these orders, twenty-eight of the thirty-eight prisoners from Nakano village were banished to Tsuwano in Iwami province. This took place in July, precisely one year after they were originally apprehended.

On the morning of 20 July, beneath a whitely shrouding morning mist, a small freighter awaited the criminals at the port of Nagasaki. Out in the offing a 1500-ton steamship stood ready. They were put on this vessel and transported as far as Onomichi. From there they proceeded to Hiroshima, then set out along the San'in highway over the mountains to Tsuwano.

Just outside the castle town of Tsuwano is a hill known as Maiden hill. The Kōrinji Temple erected on this hill became the prison where they were to live out the rest of their lives.

At first their lives at Kōrinji were relaxed. The officials, in their customary fashion, believed that because they were dealing with dirt-farmers it would be a simple matter to change the hearts of these men in short order merely by lecturing them thoroughly on religion. Their daily ration included five cups of rice, 73 mon worth of vegetables, and one square of paper, which for men who were no better than lowly peasants made for a tolerably comfortable life. Day after day, Buddhist clerics from the temple and Shintÿ priests came to sermonize to them. The Christians listened in silence to these lectures. When pressure was placed on them to apostalize, however, not one of them would nod his head in the affirmative. Finally the authorities had to subject them once again to torture.

The comparatively abundant ration of food they had been receiving was reduced to a single pinch of salt and a watery porridge. Their bedding was taken away and replaced with thin straw mats. Their clothing was restricted to the unlined summer kimonos they had been wearing when they were arrested.

Winter in San'in turned bitter cold in October. The tortures were carried out next to the 65-square-meter pond in the garden of the Kōrinji. Stripped of their clothing, the Christians were stood one at a time beside the pond. Seventy-liter barrels filled with water were set beside them, and an officer with a long-handled dipper stood in wait.

"Then you will not apostatize?"

"I will not." At that answer, each Christian was shoved into the pond, which was topped with a thin layer of ice. The water splashed as they struck it. When they floated to the surface, the officer jabbed at them with his dipper. Later on, Kanzaburō described the sufferings of that day as follows:

"My body turned cold and froze, and I began to shake and my teeth chattered, and I couldn't see any more. The world started spinning. Just when I felt I had breathed my last, the officer said: "Come out now." They had put a hook on the end of a meter-long bamboo shaft, and they coiled my hair round the end of the hook and pulled me in with all their might. Once they'd hauled me out of the water, they raked away the snow, and they built a log fire using two bundles of brushwood as kindling. They dried and warmed me there by the fire, then gave me some smelling-salts until I came to. I can't begin to describe the pain I felt that day."

Once the water torture was completed, the prisoners were taken to the 1-meter cell. This was a one square-meter box, with bars of 6-centimeter-square poles placed at 3-centimeter intervals; the only opening was a hole at about eye-level for the providing of food. It was, of course, so cramped that the prisoners had to bend over before they could even crawl into the cell.

As a result of the tortures and the savage cold of the Tsuwano winter, the Christians began dying one after another. The first to die was a twenty-seven-year-old man named Wasaburō. He survived for twenty days in the 1-meter cell, but his strength finally failed and he died.

The next to die from the tortures was a thirty-two-year-old man named Yasutarō. To all appearances Yasutarō was a feeble fellow, but he went out of his way to offer the meager food given him to others, and he willingly took on unpleasant chores such as cleaning their toilet. He was forced to sit out in the snow for three days and three nights, after which he was placed in the 1-meter cell, where he died with his body bent over.

Kanzaburō was able to speak with Yasutarō three days before his death. In one of his letters, Kanzaburō writes: "I told him I thought he must be feeling very alone there in the tiny cell. But he answered:

'No, I'm not at all lonely. Ever since I was nine years old, a person who looks just like Santa Maria, dressed in a blue kimono and veil, has told me stories, so I haven't been the least bit lonely. But please don't tell this to anyone while I'm still alive.' And just three days after he said that to me, he died a truly noble death."

With their comrades dying one after another, some of the surviving Christians began to lose heart. Finally, one particularly bitter winter night, sixteen men declared that they would forsake their faith. They were immediately released from the cell and given warm food and *sake*, and several days later they descended from the mountain.

Ten men remained. Included in their number were Kanzaburō and Zennosuke. There in the 1-meter cell they had to fight against their memories of the mountains, the houses and their families at home. More than anything else, these memories weakened their resolve.

"I wonder what's happened to Kisuke?" Sometimes Kanzaburō would think of the face and massive form of the friend he had not seen since they were together in the prison at Sakura-chō. It was almost as if Kanzaburō could still see engraved on the back of his eyelids the retreating figure of Kisuke as the officers shoved him towards the court to offer his thumbprint. "He's so cowardly . . . If he weren't so spineless, Kisuke would have been able to hold on to his faith . . ."

Around this time the officials came up with a new means to increase the torment of the ten Christians who had endured the water torture and the 1-meter cell. Their new strategy was to bring relatives of the believers to Tsuwano and to abuse them before the eyes of the men. The officials conjectured that it would be meaningless to torture the hearty brothers of their captives; it would be far more effective, they reasoned, to afflict their aged mothers and younger brothers and sisters.

In February twenty-six women and children were packed on to a ship and transported to Tsuwano. A new cell was assembled in the garden of the Kōrinji Temple, and the newly arrived captives were placed in it.

Kanzaburō's younger sister, Matsu, and his younger brother, Yūjirō, were among the new prisoners. Matsu was fifteen and Yūjirō was twelve.

The children were tortured without mercy. A boy of ten called Suekichi refused to apostatize even though oil was poured on both his hands and they were set alight. A five-year-old child was fed nothing for two days, then taunted with sweets by officers, but he merely shook his head firmly. His answer to the officer was: "My mother told me that if I didn't give up Christianity I could go to Paradise, and that when I got to Paradise, they'd have things even more delicious than those sweets."

Yūjirō was stripped naked and exposed to the frigid wind, where he was lashed to a cross made of logs and left to hang. At night an officer would throw water on him. He was beaten with whips. The whip handles were jabbed into his ears and nose. Being a child of twelve, he wailed in a loud voice that was clearly audible to Kanzaburō in his 1-meter cell. As elder brother he could offer no help other than his own prayers.

After a week Yūjirō's body began to turn pale and puffy. His heart had weakened. The alarmed officers ceased their tortures and turned him over to his sister Matsu. Gasping for breath with his head cradled in Matsu's lap, Yūjirō wept: "Matsu, please forgive me. I tried not to cry like that. I thought about the Lord Jesus' torture and tried not to shout out. But it hurt so much, I ended up screaming. My faith is so weak, please forgive me, Matsu."

Near dawn, clutching Matsu's hand, the young boy died. That morning the officers brought in a coffin, quickly placed the corpse inside it, and took it away without a word.

After his younger brother's murder, even Kanzaburō felt his heart was being ripped open. He didn't want to contemplate apostatizing, but it was unbearable to think that the same kind of torture might be applied to his sister Matsu.

"Why won't the Lord Jesus help us? Why does the Lord Jesus watch in silence while these children endure such horrible torture?" Doubts began to seep into his mind because the Lord gave them no answer in their extremity. He grew frightened of God's icy silence. It was at this time that Kanzaburō's faith began to waver.

"Why do we put up with this? What kind of religion makes you sacrifice your brothers and sisters?" Kanzaburō beat his head against the wooden poles of his 1-meter cell in order to drive away these haunting thoughts. The skin on his head split open and he began to bleed, but still he continued to strike his head on the pillar. Battering his head like this was the only means he had to overcome these frightening ideas. "Zennosuke! Zennosuke!" he yelled to his friend. "Pray for me!"

But no answer came, and he could not tell whether Zunnosuke was alive or dead.

Four days after Yūjirō died, Kanzaburō decided that his heart could bear no more of this misery. Vacantly he stared through the hole in the cell door at the garden of the Kōrinji temple. An officer was talking with a man who appeared to be a beggar. The pauper's body was wrapped in a straw mat, and he leaned on a tall cane as he bowed his head over and over to the officer.

Kanzaburō felt as though he had seen that posture and that manner of bowing before. But he couldn't remember where.

Suddenly the officer raised his hand and beat the beggar roughly. The frightened beggar looked as though he were going to run away, but he staggered back two or three steps and halted.

Can that be Kisuke? Kanzaburō was astounded. Why in the world would Kisuke . . . ?

But it was in fact Kisuke who came walking towards the cell after the officer sent him tottering. It was the same Kisuke who had staggered away from prison at Sakura-chō in Nagasaki two years before.

Why has that coward Kisuke come here?

When the beggar passed in front of his cell, he appeared to have journeyed far before coming here to Tsuwano, and his face was pitch-black with whiskers and mud, but Kanzaburō could distinguish traces of the unforgettable bulk of his childhood friend.

With a dull clatter the officer jerked the door of the cell open and shoved the beggar inside. After the officer left, there was silence for a long while. Eventually Kanzaburō shouted: "Is that you, Kisuke? Is the man who just came into this cell by chance Kisuke of Nakano village?"

"Yes . . ." A thin voice like the buzz of a mosquito responded. "Yes . . . Who are you?"

"It's me." Rubbing his face against the opening in the cell, Kanzaburō called out his name. "Why did you come here? What in hell are you doing here?" His voice was flooded with all the spite and anger he had felt these several years towards his childhood friend. "You gave them your fingerprint at the jail in Sakura-chō, so why have you come here?" No answer came for a time. Then at last a dull-witted answer reached his ears. It was Kisuke's voice, pleading as if through tears.

"Please forgive me. Please forgive me."

Then falteringly Kisuke began to explain to Kanzaburō. Everyone in the cell listened quietly to his words. From time to time as Kisuke spoke they heard the footsteps of the guards, and in fear Kisuke would stop speaking. At nightfall the cold became even more bitter, and a powdery snow began to fall.

After Kisuke, unable to bear the cries of his comrades as they suffered the *dodoi* torture at Sakura-chō, had offered his fingerprint to the officials, he could no longer return to Nakano village. He wanted to see his parents and sisters, but the shame of having betrayed his faith and the pain of having abandoned his friends forced him to take refuge in Nagasaki. There he had worked as a stevedore in the great harbor.

"I reckoned I'd been forsaken by the Lord and by Santa Maria, so I abandoned myself to *sake* and evil activities to try to forget about all of you."

As a tearful Kisuke made his confession, the men in the cell sighed and nodded their heads.

Though he drank *sake* and paid for women, Kisuke was unable to forget the agony in his heart. But at this point he could no longer go to the authorities and retract his declaration of apostasy, thereby declaring himself a Christian once again. His cowardice prevented him from making such a declaration and having to listen again to the screams of those undergoing the *dodoi* torture. Those dark, bestial cries still echoed hauntingly at the core of his ears. To block out those voices, Kisuke fled from Nagasaki to the fishing village of Shirogoe. There he took on work with a fisherman's family. He felt the physical exhaustion that came from rowing a boat and hauling in ropes would be a better means than *sake* and women to quell the pain in his heart.

But one day when Kisuke and his employer brought a catch of fish to Nagasaki for the first time in several months, he had to witness an unexpected scene. Officers at the dock were shoving prisoners on to two freighters. Pelted with jeers from the assembled crowd and poked with poles by the officers, the prisoners were driven like animals on to the boats. Kisuke stood on his toes and peered over the shoulders of the crowd, and there he saw that the prisoners were women and children he knew from Nakano village. The familiar faces of Matsu and Yūjirō were among the captives. Their eyes were lowered in grief, and with drooping heads they sat down without a word in the water-soaked ship.

"Those are Christian prisoners." Kisuke's employer poked his shoulder. "They're fools, aren't they?"

Kisuke averted his eyes and nodded to his employer, who was staring into his face.

That night he went out on to the sea-shore and sat alone staring at the dark ocean.

What can a coward like me do? A coward like me?

Listening to the sound of the dark waves that pushed in and broke, broke and then retreated, Kisuke felt a bitterness towards God surging up from the depths of his heart. There are two types of people—those born with strong hearts and courage, and those who are craven and clumsy. From their childhood Kanzaburō and Zennosuke had been strong of will. So even when they were subjected to persecution, they had been able to maintain their faith. But me—I'm spineless by nature, and my knees buckle and I turn pale if someone just lifts a hand against me. Because I was born like that, even though I want to believe in the Lord Jesus' teachings, in no way can I put up with torture.

If only I hadn't been born in these times . . .

If Kisuke had lived in the distant past when freedom of religion was accessible, even if he had not been one of the valiant souls, he wouldn't have ended up in this predicament of betraying the Lord Jesus and Santa Maria.

Why was I born to such a fate?

That thought made Kisuke resent God's lack of compassion.

It happened just as Kisuke stood and was about to leave the beach. He heard a voice calling to him from behind. He turned round, but no one was there. It was neither the voice of a man nor a woman. But he had heard the voice echoing clearly amidst the sound of the black ocean waves.

"All you have to do is go and be with the others. If you're tortured again and you become afraid, it's all right to run away. It's all right to betray me, but go follow the others."

Kisuke stopped in his tracks and looked out at the sea in a daze. He pressed his fists against his face and wept aloud. When Kisuke had finished his story, the Christians in the cell were silent, emitting not even a cough. As they sat in confinement they knew from the sharp stab at their skin that the snow was gradually piling up outside. Kanzaburō felt that the tortures he had endured these two years, and the fact that his brother had died without abandoning the faith, had not been in vain.

The next morning the officers unlocked the door to the 1-meter cell to interrogate Kisuke. If Kisuke would not agree to apostatize, he would be thrown into the icy lake in the garden of the temple. As he listened to the rasp of the lock and to Kisuke's faltering footsteps, Kanzaburō whispered: "Kisuke. If it hurts you, it's all right to apostatize. It's all right. The Lord Jesus is pleased just because you came here. He is pleased."

---

1. Prudence Séraphin Barthélemy Girard, a French missionary born in 1821, went to work in Japan in 1858. He died in 1867 in a fire that destroyed the church he built in Yokohama.
2. Father Petitjean (1829–84) reached Nagasaki in 1863, where he helped build the Ōura chapel. He died in Nagasaki and was buried in the chapel.
3. Joseph Marie Laucaigne (1838–85) came to Japan in 1863 and assisted Petitjean in his missionary work. He also worked in Nagasaki and Osaka. He took care of Petitjean during his final illness, then became fatally ill himself.
4. Uragami was first raided by authorities searching for *kakure* Christians in 1790, in 1842, and again in 1859. During this fourth raid, which lasted from 1867 to 1873, over a hundred were jailed, sixty of whom died from torture and exposure.
5. Kido (1833–77) was instrumental in putting together a coalition of domains that toppled the Tokugawa shogunate and ushered in the Meiji restoration of 1867.

HELEN NORRIS

BORN IN MIAMI, FLORIDA, IN 1916, HELEN NORRIS GREW up in Montgomery, Alabama, on her family's farm, where she began writing stories as a child. She attended the University of Alabama, where in 1938 she received her AB; she then stayed on to receive her Master of Arts in 1940. Her first novel, *Something More Than Earth*, was written for her thesis, and published the same year.

While raising her children—she married after graduation and moved to Birmingham—Norris stopped writing, but picked it up again in the late 1950s, writing the novels *For the Glory of God* and *More Than Seven Watchmen*. Only after her retirement from Huntingdon College in Montgomery in 1979 did Norris begin writing and publishing short stories, and it is this form that has brought her the most accolades: five of her stories have appeared in the *O. Henry Prize Story* collections, and two of her stories have been made into television films: *The Christmas Wife* and *The Cracker Man*. Her collections include *The Christmas Wife: Stories, Water Into Wine*, and *The Burning Glass: Stories*.

The recipient of the Harper Lee Award for Alabama's Distinguished Writer, Norris has also served as Poet Laureate for the State of Alabama. She now resides in Black Rock, North Carolina.

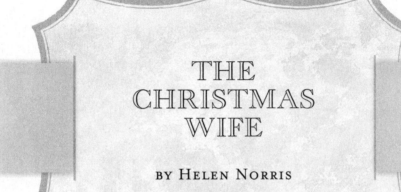

THE
CHRISTMAS
WIFE

by Helen Norris

His name was Tanner, a reasonable man in his early sixties, desiring peace, a measure of joy, and reassurance. All that was submerged. The tip of the iceberg was a seasoned smile that discouraged excesses and a way of looking, "That's fine but not today." His marriage had fitted him like a glove, but now his wife Florence was dead for three years. And so it came to pass that Christmas was a problem.

Not a large problem, but one that niggled when the weather turned and got a little worse with blackbirds swarming in the elm trees, on the move. And here he was looking out at the falling leaves, chewing his November turkey in a restaurant down the block, and going nowhere. Except to his son's in California (Christmas with palm trees!), to his daughter-in-law with the fugitive eyes and his grandsons bent on concussions, riding their wagons down the stairs at dawn, whaling the daylights out of their toys. During the long, safe years of his marriage his hand had been firmly, as they say, on the helm. He had been in control. It alarmed him that now he was not in control, even of his holidays, especially of Christmas. A courtly man with a sense of tradition, he liked his Christmases cast in the mold, which is to say he liked them the way they had always been.

Now, the best thing about Thanksgiving was its not being Christmas. It held Christmas at bay. But then the days shortened and the wind swept them into the gutter along with the leaves. And it rained December . . .

He had seen the advertisement several times that fall, a modest thing near the real-estate ads in the Sunday paper, the boxed-in words: "Social Arrangements," and underneath in a smaller type: "Of All Kinds." He had thought it amusing. At the bottom a phone number and then an address.

Actually the address was a little elusive. He passed it twice without seeing the sign. It would have been better perhaps to have phoned, but he wanted to maintain a prudent flexibility. Inside, the lighting was dim and decidedly pink. It proceeded, he saw, from a large hanging lamp that swung from the ceiling, an opulent relic with a porcelain globe painted over with roses. The wind of his entrance had set it in motion and he stood in the rosy bloom of its shadows. He was conscious of pictures in massive frames—one directly before him, a half-draped woman with one raised foot stepping out of something, perhaps a pool—a carpet eroded slightly with wear, a faint sweetish smell of baking food. To his left a man was bent over a desk. Incredibly he seemed to be mending his shoe. Filing cabinets flanked him on either side. For a silent moment they studied each other. What Tanner observed was a dark, smallish face of uncertain age, possibly foreign, with a dusting of beard, a receding hairline, and rimless glasses with one frosted lens. He managed some irony: "Are you the social arranger?"

"I am at your service." The man swept the shoe neatly into his lap, and then he repeated, "I am at your service."

"Yes," Tanner said. "Your ad is tantalizing but a little unclear. The scope of your service . . ."

The man interrupted. "It is very clear. We make social arrangements of all kinds."

"Splendid! Then perhaps I can rely on you."

"We are discreet."

"Oh, I assure you, no call for discretion." Then he laid it before them both, making it seem a spontaneous thing, almost as if the occasion inspired it. The arranger clearly was not deceived. With his unfrosted lens he seemed to perceive how long it had lain on the floor of the mind, how a little each day it had taken its shape and resisted being swept with the leaves to the gutter.

"I am by nature a sociable man." The arranger inclined his head with enthusiasm. "I live alone. My wife is dead. Christmas has become . . . what I require is a Christmas companion. A lady of my age or a little younger. Not handsome or charming. But simply . . . agreeable. Reasonable health. A good digestion, since I shall look forward to cooking for the occasion."

The other was making notes on the back of an envelope. "My secretary," he said, "is out with the flu. An inconvenience." Then he looked up and past Tanner's head. "Overnight, I presume?"

Tanner said lightly, "I've consulted the calendar. Christmas arrives this year on a Saturday. Actually I should prefer the lady for the weekend. But I wish it to be most clearly understood: the bedrooms are separate."

The arranger put down his pencil and adjusted the frosted, then the unfrosted lens. He propelled his chair backward ever so slightly into the burning heart of his files.

"There is a difficulty?" Tanner asked, concealing his unease. "Christmas, I'm sure, is a difficult time. But there must be a few in your files who live alone and would welcome a pleasant holiday with no strings attached." He stared with some irony at the array of cabinets.

"My secretary at the moment . . . Your request is reasonable. We shall consult our files. There is the matter of the fee."

Tanner was ready. "I am prepared to pay a fee of five hundred dollars for a suitable person. And, I may add, a bonus of one hundred to be paid in advance to the lady herself in case she wishes to make some holiday preparation." He had made an impression. He saw it at once. And then, without really intending it, he explained, "I arrived at these figures by checking the cost of a trip to my son's and concluding that this would serve almost as well and be on the whole a great deal more convenient." He turned to go. "In the meantime I shall check on your agency."

"Of course. It is welcomed. Your name and number? A few facts for the files."

"I shall drop by again."

"But your telephone number?"

"I shall be in touch." He left at once. He was again in control of his life, his seasons. The knowledge exhilarated him. He took a deep breath of the chilly air. Halfway down the block he stopped before a store window and studied the objects on display with care. Some plumbing equipment, secondhand it seemed. He was not after all in the best part of town. The bowl of a lavatory brimmed with live holly. In the mirror above it his own face was smiling.

As he moved away he played with the idea of stopping it there, of letting the plan of it be the whole. He sniffed at the edges. The scent of it, crisp, indefinable, a little exotic, was in the wind as he turned the corner.

Before a profitable sale of his business had left him retired and now, as he told himself, dangerously free, he had been an architect. A few years ago he had built for a friend a small vacation house back in the mountains, a comfortable distance away from the city. It was quite the nicest thing of its kind he had done. "Do me something you'd like for yourself." With such an order how could he resist giving all of its contours his gravest attention? He recalled it now with a growing pleasure, how it made its alliance with rock and sky. It was in the year after Florence died, and perhaps it was some of his lost communion that he poured without knowing it into the house.

When he returned to the tiny apartment, haunted with furniture, where he had lived since the death of his wife, he looked at it with a critical eye and found it hostile to holiday cheer. He rang up his friend, who was now in Chicago. What about the house? Using it for the holiday? Well, would you mind . . . ? Well, of course he wouldn't mind.

When the key arrived in the mail he put it into his pocket and went for a walk. He watched the gray squirrels loitering in the park and the leaves crusting the benches and the sun going down through a network of fog. He reminded himself that what he wanted was the mountain air like a ripening plum and the smell of burning wood in the morning. He wanted the cooking. He wanted the house he had made and loved and the presence of a woman, simply her presence, to give it the seal of a Christmas past. There was no woman of his acquaintance whom he could ask to cancel her plans and give him a Christmas out of her life. In return for what? With a woman he knew, there would be the question, the expectation, the where-are-we-going? to spoil the fine bouquet of the season. In the morning he drove to the arranger.

Actually he had meant to check on the agency, but then it had come to seem that part of the adventure, perhaps the whole of the adventure, was not to do so. So that now the unlikely aspect of the office, with its lamp and the rocking circles of light and its unpleasant piney odor of cleanser, and of the arranger, today without tie and faintly disheveled, did not disturb but even elated him. He was startled and then amused to observe that one of the pictures on the wall had been changed. The one he had particularly noted before of the woman emerging half-draped from a pool had now been replaced by a pasture with cows.

"It occurs to me," said Tanner, "that I don't know your name."

"I have a card somewhere." The arranger rummaged, overturning a vase full of pencils. He was looking flushed, even feverish, but perhaps it was only the rosy light. "My secretary is out . . ." He abandoned the search. "But your name . . . we don't have it. Do we have your name? We require references for the protection of all."

"You have found someone for me?"

The arranger fixed him with the unfrosted eye and gave his desk chair a provocative swivel and coughed for a while. "I believe," he said, "we have just the party." After a pause he propelled himself backward into his files. He caressed the drawers lightly with delicate fingers and opened one with an air of cunning. And swiftly removing a card, he called out: "I think, I do think, this is what you require. I shall read you details, and then of course you can judge for yourself."

Tanner said firmly, "I don't at all wish to know the details. I rely on your judgment." It seemed to him suddenly to spoil the occasion to have the woman read out like a bill of fare.

The arranger was visibly disappointed, as if he had suffered a rejection of sorts. But presently he shrugged and closed the drawer carefully. Still holding the card, he propelled himself forward and into his desk.

Tanner said, "I have here a list of my own: pertinent facts, a reference or two."

The arranger took it and scanned it slowly. Then very quickly the matter was concluded. Tanner was handed a map of the city marked with an X where he was to wait for the lady in question to step from the 2:20 bus on the afternoon of the day before Christmas.

"But I should be happy . . ."

"She wishes it so," said the arranger reverently. And as Tanner was leaving, he called out gravely, "She is one who has recently entered my files. A rare acquisition."

Tanner bowed. "I shall treat her accordingly."

It had occurred to him of course—how could it not have?—that the whole thing could well be a jolly rip-off. While he waited with his car packed with holiday treats, no woman would emerge from that bus or the next or the next. The phone would ring on in an empty office. I'm sorry, the number is no longer in use. But because he so richly deserved this Christmas he could not believe it would really be so. And if it were . . . then he would drive slowly and quietly home and slowly and quietly get Christmas drunk. Part of the reward of growing older was precisely this trick one seemed to acquire of holding two possible futures in mind, of preferring one while allowing the other.

He found, on the whole, in the days that followed that it was best to assume that the lady would appear and to give his attention to preparation: a miniature tree, a wreath for the mantel, the mincemeat pies on which he prided himself, the small turkey stuffed with his own invention, the imported Chablis. He had always done most of the holiday meal when Florence was alive. He spent a great deal of time on the gifts, one nice one for her and several smaller things (he wished now that he had permitted himself a few details such as height and weight), a gift for himself in case she failed him in that department.

And of course the day came and the hour struck. With the trunk of his car neatly loaded, he was waiting by the curb. When he saw the bus coming he got out of the car. And there she was, the last to descend, as if she had lingered to look him over. Clutching a small bag, she stood alone looking down at the pavement and then up at him, the winter sun in her narrowed eyes. And she was so unmistakably what she was, a bit of merchandise sent out on approval, that he knew her at once with a catch in his throat and a small despair.

"I'm John Tanner," he offered and gave her his arm, and then as he assisted her into the car, "I've been looking forward to this for days." She wanly smiled.

After that as he drove and kept up a patter of talk to put them both at ease, he remembered how she looked, without looking at her: sand-colored hair (he guessed it was dyed), colorless eyes, a small thin face. He thought she could be in her middle fifties. She rarely spoke, and when she did her voice had a breathless hesitation—very soft, so low that he scarcely heard her.

So he said to her: "Don't be uneasy. I'm really a very comfortable person. This is new to me too. But I said to myself, why not, why not."

She coughed a little.

Then they were climbing into the mountains and the air became damp with fallen leaves and notably colder. When they reached the road that led to the house, already the dark was lapping at the trees in the valley below. And around the curve was the house before him exactly as he had made it to be—clean-lined, beached on the rock with pines leaning into it, breasting the wave of sweet gums and oaks that foamed at its base.

He thought how much he had always liked it. "I built it," he said to her. "Not with my hands. Perhaps you were told I'm an architect by trade." He wondered suddenly what she had been told and if it had made her decide to come, or if after all the money was the whole of it.

"I'll go first," he said. "The steps are narrow." With a shyness he had not expected to feel, he climbed through a thicket of wild young shrubs that had marched through the summer to take the stairs. Her plaintive cough like the cry of a bird pursued him into the dusk that gathered about the door. It summoned the longing out of his soul. At that moment he wished that this Christmas were past, over and done with along with the rest. His hands were trembling when he turned the key.

Inside it was dark, with a faint little warmth from the windows that lately had drunk up the sun. He switched on the light and paused to see the great curving room spring to greet and enfold him, exactly as he had created it to do, all the sweeping half-circle of wood and stone, brown, rose, and gray. It calmed and restored him as it always had. He noted the lovely stone curve of the mantel and below it the faggots laid ready to light. Beneath his match they sprang into bloom. And when he turned round the fireshine was kindling the great tile stove, the hub of the wheel, the heart of the house, with its own special curve like a hive of bees. How he loved that stove! He had found it in an old hunting lodge near Vienna where he went for a week after Florence had died. He had bought it and had it dismantled with care and shipped to this place, then reassembled, while he ordered and

implored, agonized and exulted, till again every tile was exactly in place—
only one of them cracked, and that still mourned and unspoken like a
guilty secret.

He turned to share it all with the woman behind him, but she was
warming her hands in the blaze of the fire. So now he would fill the
hive with good oak and a little pine for the seethe and flair. Till the
translucent bricks that encircled its base would be gemmed and ringed
into amber and garnet. The hunting scenes on the creamy tiles would
shimmer and glow and appear to change from moment to moment—
the deer and the boar, the flowers, the trees, all richly orange and yellow and brown, as if honey had seeped through the hive to stain them.
And the circle of the house would draw close and warm. Guests had
always exclaimed: but where, but how? The children accepted without
a word. They ran to embrace it and warm their faces. When something
is right the children will know it.

He drew the curtains against the night. Then he showed her her
room done neatly in white, and assured her the chill would be gone in
an hour. While the daylight held he loaded the stove with wood from
the generous pile banked against the rock outside. He unloaded food
from the trunk of his car and all the rest. He busied himself and
refused to think beyond the task at hand. He could hear her coughing
in a stifled way.

While he was checking the fire in the stove he recalled with a start
and a sense of shame that he had not asked or been told her name.
Again she was warming her hands by the hearth. He stood behind her
with an armful of wood. "What shall I call you? You must tell me your
name." He made it sound as gracious and easy as possible.

She turned to him then. "My name is Cherry."

He found it a fatuous, unlikely name for the woman before him. He wondered if it had been invented for him. He would not trust himself to repeat it. He said instead, "Please call me John."

Her eyes were colorless, he observed again, and reflected the fire, the room, himself. He could find in them nothing of the woman behind them. They seemed in a strange way not to see him. The flesh beneath them looked faintly bruised. The cheekbones were firm and slightly rouged. There were small, parenthetical lines at the corners of a thin and somber mouth, which he noted with relief was free of rouge. He said to her kindly, "You seem to be coughing. Perhaps we have something here that would help."

She withdrew from him then. Her eyes shut him out. "Oh, no, I'm fine. It's just . . . well, I had the flu but I'm over it now. But when night comes on . . . I cough just a little."

He reassured her. "The flu is everywhere. I've really remarkable resistance to it."

"I'm really quite well."

"Of course," he said and winced to recall that clearly he had specified reasonable health. He could explain now her stifled voice in the car. "I've made a little light chowder for supper. Something very light. It will warm you up and be just the thing. I've always made it for Christmas Eve."

"That would be nice. I can help you with it."

But he would not have it. He placed her in a chair before the fire with a throw from the sofa around her shoulders and told her to rest her voice and be still. Then to get her into the spirit of things he found the wreath made of ribbon and holly and balanced it on the mantel before her. And he added a length of pine to the stove. He opened the vents to make it hum for her like a hiveful of bees in the manner its maker had meant it to do—a trick of construction he had never fathomed. The tiles had taken on a splendid sheen. He wanted to tell her to turn and watch.

While he was warming their supper in the kitchen, she came and stood in the archway, her eyes pale as glass, her hands, transparent with blue veins, clutching the sill like roots. He had put on his dark-rimmed glasses for the work. She looked at him with a kind of alarm as if he became even more the stranger, almost as if she surprised an intruder. But he led her back to the chair by the fire. He scolded her heartily, "I want you well by Christmas." The words and gestures sprang naturally out of the last years with Florence.

He served them both from trays by the fire, making it all seem easy and festive. She ate very little. He poured her a glass of Tokay, and while she sipped it, her face not pink from the fire, he got out the tree and began to trim it with the tiny carved figures he and Florence had found in a shop in Munich before their son was born. He told her about them. She put down her glass and began to help. One of the small figures slipped from her fingers. When he bent to retrieve it he saw that her eyes were swimming in tears. "Don't worry," he said. "They're quite indestructible."

She fought for control. "It's my glasses," she said. "I don't see without them."

"Of course. Where are they? I'll get them for you." He rose at once. She drew in her breath. "I forgot to bring them."

Or had she thought he would find them unpleasing? He was really impatient. Should he have specified in the beginning that he wanted a woman who could manage to see?

Finally he asked, "Shall I put on some music? Or would you just rather call it a day?" He did not like to say "go to bed," an innocent phrase that had been corrupted.

"It's what you want."

"It's what you want too."

But she shook her head. She was paid to pleasure him, to enjoy what he offered. He was suddenly struck with how easily the shape of a thing could change and take on the color of prostitution. A practiced woman would take care to conceal it, but in her innocence she underlined it. He rose and removed the throw he had placed on her shoulders. His voice was grave. "If I'm to have my way . . . I want you to have a good night's sleep."

The evening was gone. He could not retrieve it, nor would he have done so. His heart was heavy. He lowered the lights. Her face was uncertain but she moved away past the stove that sang softly like a bird in the dusk, throwing its shadows on floor and wall. She looked at it briefly and passed without comment. Perhaps she could scarcely see it at all. Her gesture summed up for him the failure of the day.

HE TRIED TO SLEEP. THE WIND HAD RISEN. THE PINES above his bedroom were stroking the roof. In the room beyond he could hear her coughing. Wasn't she after all what he had ordered—a nothing who would not intrude or assert or assess or be?

He tossed in despair. Christmas is dangerous, it's too hot to handle, it's a handful of roots breeding—what did the poem say?—memory and desire. Get another day. Fourth of July, Labor Day. Don't pit yourself against Christmas. You lose. You can't contain it. It runs backward into a shop in Munich. It echoes . . . It's calling your own name down a well.

He slept a little. And in his dream the social arranger took off his glasses and lo, behind them his eyes were laughing. The eye once hidden by the frosted lens was crinkled with laughter. Why are you laughing? Tanner approached him and saw, peering, that the eye was a stone and cracked into pieces.

He awoke, dispossessed. The dark ran liquid through his veins. The wind whipped him into some distant gutter.

When daylight came he lay grimly rehearsing his script for the day. If order prevails all things are possible and even tolerable. The key of course is to be in control. His shoulder was stiff from hauling the wood. He had raised his window to sleep in the cold, and now he heard the sound of a distant axe breaking, breaking the early day.

He had the turkey in the oven, the pilaf thawing, and the salad prepared before she appeared for her morning coffee. The patches of dark were still under her eyes, but her face was rested. She seemed to have taken great care with her dress. Her sand-colored hair was combed back from her face, and now he decided the color was hers. He could see the gray. She was wearing a wine-colored jumper with a gray-green, high-necked blouse beneath. They might be a nod at the Christmas colors. There was something childlike about her dress and her slender figure, and touching about her desire to please.

He drank a third cup of coffee with her, and some of the grayness drained out of his soul. She pronounced the smell of his cooking agreeable. In the glance of her eyes around the room there was something of readiness, almost he might say of anticipation. And suddenly the day began to be possible.

"Were you warm enough in the night?" he asked.

"Oh, yes. Oh, yes."

"You're not coughing today."

"Oh, no. I'm well."

After he had coaxed the stove into shimmer and the comfortable song it could sing in the morning after a night of lying fallow, he drew the curtains away from the windows, a tender curve of them like a sickle moon, the way he had planned them in the beginning. The mist was milky in the pines and the hollows.

Before she arose he had laid his gifts for her around the tree. She looked at them with a troubled face. "I didn't know."

"How could you know? It would spoil the surprise."

But she left him quickly and returned with an unwrapped heavy tin. "I was saving it for dinner." She handed it to him, then took it away and put it with the other things beside the tree. His heart misgave him. It was fruitcake of course. He had never liked it. But what else came in round tins painted with holly and weighed enough to crush the bones of your foot?

He put on some music. He made her sit in state on the sofa. Then he found his glasses on the sink in the kitchen and put them on her. "I want you to see. Can you see?" he asked.

She looked around her and down at her hands. "Oh, yes, I can."

"Are you sure you can?"

"Oh, yes. Oh, yes."

"Well, at least you will see things the way I do." He had to laugh. She looked like a small, obedient child who was given permission to try her father's glasses. They diminished her face and gave her an owlish air of wisdom. Then he handed her the packages one by one—first, the teakwood tray, then a fragile porcelain cup and saucer with a Christmas scene. For Christmases to come. And to remind her, he said, of this very day. Then a small, lacquered music box that played a carol. While it finished its song he opened the tie he had bought for himself and exclaimed at the colors. He declared that a friend had secretly left it on the seat of his car. She held her things on the tray in her lap and watched him with pale and troubled eyes, their trouble magnified by his glasses. "Do you like them?" he asked.

"Oh, yes. They're lovely."

Then he watched while she opened the tall ribboned box with the figurine, a bit of Lladro that came from Spain. She drew out the blue-and-gray girl with the pure, grave face and the goose in her arms. She held it silently. Then she touched the smooth, child's head with her hand. "Do you like it?" he asked.

"Oh, yes. I do."

"I knew you would like it." She looked at him, puzzled. "Oh, yes, I knew it . . . It reminds me," he said, "a little of you."

What he meant, he realized, was that Florence would like it . . . and that it also reminded him a little of her. But there was one box more, the largest of all. "But you've given too much." She was reluctant to open it, almost distracted. He could tell she was thinking of the whole of her cost, the somber transaction with the seedy purveyor.

"What is too much? This Christmas has never happened before."
And he added gaily, "Whatever you don't like will have been too much.
We can toss it into the stove and burn it."

She smiled at that and opened the box. She lifted the dark green,
floor-length woolen robe, severe, elegant, very formal. "Try it on," he
commanded. She did so obediently. He crossed the room to appraise
it from a distance and pronounced it too long. He saw with dismay he
had bought it for Florence, her height, her coloring. But it seemed to
do now surprisingly well. It coaxed her colorless eyes into green. "I like
it on you. You must leave it on till the room is warm."

But she took it off at once. "It's much too fine." She folded it carefully and put it back in its box.

THE DINNER WENT WELL, AND SHE SEEMED TO ENJOY
it. He insisted she wear his glasses while eating. It was prudent, he
said, to consume nothing on faith. At his urging she took a second
helping of pie. He allowed himself a generous slice of her cake and
declared it superior. He toasted her fruitcake, herself, and the day. Her
face was flushed to a pink with the wine. Her hair fell softly against her
cheek. She brushed it away with the back of her hand, which was worn
and expressive, with a tracery of veins. He had seen such a hand on a
painting in Prague.

He allowed her to rest for a while after eating. Then he told her
about the lake below the house, hidden from view because of the trees.
"Would you like to walk down?"

"Oh, yes," she said.

At his bidding she put on a sweater he had packed for himself and then her coat. She drew a flimsy scarf over her head. He looked with doubt at her fragile shoes. But she said they were all she had brought along. "No matter," he said. "I'll keep you from falling."

Outside it was sunless and clear and cold. The mist had vanished. The path was hardly a path at all. He had to steady her over the rocks. She was light and insubstantial against him. In the trees around them festive with moss the squirrels were stammering, cracking their nuts and pitting the shells. Under their feet the acorns of water oaks crackled like flames. And then the lake was down below like a rent in the fabric of moss and leaves. Strange birds were skimming it looking for fish, with haunting cries that poured through the trees and summoned them to the water's edge.

He guided her down. Once she slipped but he caught her and held her safe. She was shivering a little. "Are you cold?"

"Oh, no."

He held her arm tightly to reassure her. The lake was polished and gray as steel. Across it a line of young bamboo was green, as if it were spring on the other side.

"It's very deep. And somewhere in the middle is a splendid boat that sank beneath me without any warning."

He watched her eyes look up and smile. "Were you fishing?" she asked.

"Yes, that I was. And the fish I had caught went down with the boat. When I came up for air they were swimming around me laughing like crazy."

He had made her laugh, in a way he could always make Florence laugh when he sounded foolish. Her laughter warmed him in some deep place that had long been sunless. Not the laughter itself, but the way he could pluck it out of her throat, summon it out of whatever she was.

He ventured, regretting the small deception: "You remind me of someone I used to know whose name was Beth. Do you think you would mind if I called you that?"

"Oh, no."

He was more than relieved to be rid of the name which he could not bring himself to repeat. He was holding her firmly. The edge of her scarf fell against his face as if she had touched him. It released him into the cold, still air. The birds were circling, ringing them with their plangent calls, weaving them into the water and trees. She coughed a little and the shudder of her body against his own was mirrored down in the polished lake. Her image in water joined to his was clearer to him than the woman he held.

As if it had lain in wait for him there, he remembered a time before the boat had vanished. It was in the summer they were building the house, the only one then for miles around. The workmen had all gone home for the day. He rowed himself to the middle of the lake and waited. He never knew why it was he had waited. And suddenly along the line of the shore a woman was walking who seemed to be Florence: the shape of her body, the way she moved, as she was in the years before her illness. Her head was bent. She was looking for something at the water's edge. He could see her reflection just below moving with her like a walking companion. Abruptly she knelt and, leaning over the slight embankment, she plunged one arm deep into the water. In the waning light he could see the gleam of her bare white arm as it disappeared. For a terrible moment he was sure she would fall and join the woman in the water below. The whole of the lake was moving in ripples, around him, past him to where she knelt. He could not call. He simply willed her, willed her to rise. And she rose and looked at him across the water. And then she turned and walked into the trees. He had never known who the woman was . . . or if she was.

The woman beside him coughed. "Do you swim?" he asked.

"Oh, no," she said.

He waited a little. "Would you like to go back?"

"Whatever you say."

They climbed the hill slowly, clinging together, pausing at intervals to catch their breath and release it in mingling clouds to the air. A rising wind sprayed their faces with leaves. He felt they were plunging deep into winter. The rock supporting the house above them loomed pearl gray in the evening light. Below them the lake had been sucked into shadow.

IN THE NIGHT HE AWOKE WITH A COLD, CLEAR SENSE that Florence had called him. He lay still listening. But of course not Florence. Then he heard the sharp cough, but it did not come from the room next to his. It came from another part of his world, and it seemed on the move like the call of a bird, caged in the circle he had made of a house. It shattered his dark. Finally he put on a robe and found her in the living room with her hands and her body pressed to the stove. She stood in darkness. But she had pulled the drapery back from the window, and in the moonlight he could see her clearly, motionless as if she were carved in marble.

He switched on a lamp. She turned to him quickly a face that was stricken with grief and shame. "I'm sorry, I'm sorry."

"Were you cold?" he asked.

"A little cold. But the cough is worse when I'm lying down. I was afraid of waking you."

He saw that she had thrown over her own dressing gown the robe he had given. "You're not to worry. I'm here to help." He noted her trembling and built up the fire.

"I'm sorry," she repeated. "I've spoiled it all."

"You haven't spoiled a thing." He fetched her a chair.

He found a jar of honey in the kitchen and a lemon he had packed; and he fed her spoonfuls of the mixture as if she were a child . . . as if he were giving Florence her medicine when she woke in the night.

"Thank you," she said. "I'm so sorry."

"You mustn't talk."

She sat by the stove, her body subdued, in an attitude of profound despair. He pulled the robe close about her shoulders and waited silently beside her chair. He felt he was on the edge of something, a depth, a life he did not want to explore. A lonely woman who had waited for years for a door to open and now was in terror of seeing it close? He drew away. Nothing is simple, he said to himself. Nothing is ever, ever simple. Though what he meant by it he could not say. He saw his own life as an endless struggle to make the complex simple.

Commanding her silence, he turned out the lamp. He drew up a chair for himself and sat near her, and waited as he had waited in the night with Florence after the stroke had forbidden her speech. The moonlight was cold on her trembling form. The circle of light at the base of the stove drew him down and ringed him with glimmering warmth. He sat half dozing in a strange sort of peace, because it was good to be with a woman on a Christmas night. And because he had bound her voice and its power to give him more.

After a time, when her trembling had stopped, he gave her another spoonful of syrup and sent her to bed with the rest of it.

In the night through the wall he could hear her weeping. He lay with some reservoir within him filling with tears. The walk through the wood had brought a memory of Florence, the sharpest one. She had been moving ahead through the trees of another wood. He had heard the rustle of her shoes in the leaves, and then nothing. He thought she had stopped to peel moss from the bark of a fallen trunk for her garden at home. And so he had come on her fallen body. Then the long limbo of her stroke and death, when slowly, slowly she had withdrawn. As he thought of it now, and had scarcely let himself think it before, there had been a period before that day when she had withdrawn herself ever so lightly. In fact for some years: "Whatever you think . . . whatever you like . . . if it's what you want." His will was hers, his desires her own. It was almost as if her helpless years were a further step in a long dependence. He had liked the deference of her will to his. He liked to arrange the life for them both. Perhaps it was true— he saw now it was—he had struck her down in her vital self and summoned compliance out of her soul. And in compliance was bred withdrawal. Yet surely, surely it was what he wanted. Making a house or making a marriage, always he had to be in control. Her death had ended his long dominion. He must admit he had reigned with spirit . . . and a certain flair.

Genial husband, genial host. And now in the dark he knew himself as the social arranger. That seedy figure in the heart of his files he had conjured out of his own deep need. The woman weeping behind the wall—weeping for a reason he could not explain—was made to his order. He remembered with shame how he had denied her a past or a name. As if he would grant her permission to be . . . what he wished, when he wished.

HE AWOKE WITH A START. THE WINDOWS WERE OPALES-cent with ice. The needles of the pines where threads of crystal. Their boughs lay heavy along the roof. He rose to shake up the fire in the stove with a thunderous clamor, for the final time. He built the flame on the hearth again. And when she emerged, her eyes faintly rimmed, the lines gone deep at the corners of her mouth, he stood before her in new humility. Today he allowed her to help him with breakfast, a good one to last them for the drive into town. Then while the kitchen was alive and steaming with the cleaning up, he asked: "If you hadn't come . . ." He began again. "If you had spent Christmas in the usual way, where would it be?"

She was washing dishes and did not answer. He heard her silence, again with relief. He said with good humor, "But the rule is you have to take half the leftovers back to wherever it is you would be if you weren't here now." He was restored as the genial host.

After a little he went into the living room and stood at the crescent line of the windows. He could see the frozen forest below, shimmering with amber light in the sun. Beside him the warmth of flame on the hearth. It seemed to him that his was enough forever—the ice-filled trees, the flame-filled room in the midst of ice, all this ice with a heart of fire. He was conscious that she had entered the room. For a moment he asked for the trees along the mountain road to break beneath their burden of ice and cut them off for another day.

He turned to see her. She was pressing her hands to the tiles of the stove—worn hands the color of the ancient tiles. "I'll show you a secret," he said to ease her. "There's a tile that was cracked, and no one knows where it is but me. And I've never told."

She seemed not to hear. It was almost time to put her back in the box, like the blue-and-gray girl with the goose in her arms. And so he told her, "I shall always remember this time . . . these days."

She sucked in her breath and turned away. He stopped and waited. She began to cry. "What is it?" he asked.

But she turned again and walked to the fire. "You're so good," she said in a stifled voice. "You're so kind."

He was moved. "But that shouldn't . . ."

"Oh, yes. Oh, yes."

He said something he had not intended to say then, perhaps never to say: "But it doesn't really have to end with this . . . But I can't go on picking you up at a bus stop."

She faced him, weeping, shaking her head.

"You've not enjoyed it?"

"Oh, yes. Oh, yes. It's the loveliest time I've ever had."

"Then why . . . ? I assumed . . . Why would you be in his files . . .

why would you be willing to come at all unless . . ." Then a kind of light seemed to dawn in his mind, as if he had known it all along. "You work for him," he said. "You're the secretary who was out with the flu."

She did not deny it. She wept on into her handkerchief, coughing as if he had called up her illness. "Are you?" he asked. She nodded her head. She could not speak. "But it's all right . . . it's all right. Why should I care? I really don't care if you work for the charlatan. He made this weekend possible, didn't he?"

She gave him a final, stricken look. "I'm his wife too."

"His wife!"

She wept.

He was stunned. "But why?"

Through her tears she told him. "There was no one else. And we needed the money. You don't know. The bills."

"But his files . . . the files."

"They're full of other things, not names: cleaning aids . . . other things. We have nothing at all. I bought these clothes with the money you gave." Her voice sank to a hopeless whisper. "He said I should do it. It would be all right. He said you were safe."

"Safe!"

"He said you were . . ."

"Safe?"

She did not answer.

"No one is safe! How could he send you out like this? How could he know I was safe, walking in out of the street like that?" His anger released him from hurt and chagrin. He paced the length of the curving room. He said to himself: I've been taken . . . had.

He turned to her from the end of the room. The stove beyond him was deep in whispers. The ice outside slipped and fell from the trees. "Can you approve of this . . . man? Can you love this man?"

"He's my husband," she wept.

He was forced to see with what grace she suffered them both.

AND SO HE DID INDEED PUT HER BACK IN THE BOX. He drove her to the bus stop and waited in the car, talking lightly of the winter ahead and the spring when perhaps he would take a trip to the West. When the bus arrived he helped her on with her packages. The music box gave a stifled cry. He saw her safely seated at the rear. Then he watched while her bus moved off and away, picking up speed with a grinding of gears, moving faster and farther away past the winter and into spring and on through a shower of summer leaves, and never reaching her destination.

FLANNERY O'CONNOR

THE ONLY CHILD OF A MIDDLE-CLASS CATHOLIC FAMILY, Flannery O'Connor was born in Savannah, Georgia, in 1925. At age six she was already interested in drawing and writing, and her literary endeavors were encouraged by her father early on. In 1938 the family moved to O'Connor's mother's hometown of Milledgeville, Georgia, as her father's lupus no longer allowed him to work; he died in 1940. At age 16, she enrolled at Georgia State College for Women there in Milledgeville, studying sociology, and after graduating in 1945 after only three years, she attended the University of Iowa's Writers Workshop. There she began what became a literary career that saw the awarding of three O. Henry awards, grants from *The Kenyon Review*, the National Institute of Arts and Letters, and the Ford Foundation, and residencies at Yaddo, an important artists' colony in New York.

But in 1950 she began to develop the first signs of lupus, and she was forced to move home to Milledgeville, where her mother took care of her for the rest of her life. It was here she wrote her most important stories, and here that her Catholic worldview played its greatest role in honing her tough and funny and fiercely Christian fiction. Her books include the novels *Wise Blood* and *The Violent Bear It Away*, though she is best known for her two story collections, *A Good Man Is Hard to Find* and the posthumously published

Everything That Rises Must Converge. Her collection of essays on faith, art, and writing, *Mystery and Manners*, remains a classic meditation on what it means to be a Christian and to practice the habit of art. She died August 3, 1964, at home in Milledgeville.

A GOOD MAN IS
HARD TO FIND

by Flannery O'Connor

The grandmother didn't want to go to Florida. She wanted to visit some of her connections in east Tennessee and she was seizing at every chance to change Bailey's mind. Bailey was the son she lived with, her only boy. He was sitting on the edge of his chair at the table, bent over the orange sports section of the *Journal*. "Now look here, Bailey," she said, "see here, read this," and she stood with one hand on her thin hip and the other rattling the newspaper at his bald head. "Here this fellow that calls himself The Misfit is aloose from the Federal Pen and headed toward Florida and you read here what it says he did to these people. Just you read it. I wouldn't take my children in any direction with a criminal like that aloose in it. I couldn't answer to my conscience if I did."

Bailey didn't look up from his reading so she wheeled around then and faced the children's mother, a young woman in slacks, whose face was as broad and innocent as a cabbage and was tied around with a green head-kerchief that had two points on the top like a rabbit's ears. She was sitting on the sofa, feeding the baby his apricots out of a jar. "The children have been to Florida before," the old lady said. "You all ought to take them somewhere else for a change so they would see different parts of the world and be broad. They never have been to east Tennessee."

The children's mother didn't seem to hear her but the eight-year-old boy, John Wesley, a stocky child with glasses, said, "If you don't want to go to Florida, why dontcha stay at home?" He and the little girl, June Star, were reading the funny papers on the floor.

"She wouldn't stay at home to be queen for a day," June Star said without raising her yellow head.

"Yes and what would you do if this fellow, The Misfit, caught you?" the grandmother asked.

"I'd smack his face," John Wesley said.

"She wouldn't stay at home for a million bucks," June Star said. "Afraid she'd miss something. She has to go everywhere we go."

"All right, Miss," the grandmother said. "Just remember that the next time you want me to curl your hair."

June Star said her hair was naturally curly.

The next morning the grandmother was the first one in the car, ready to go. She had her big black valise that looked like the head of a hippopotamus in one corner, and underneath it she was hiding a basket with Pitty Sing, the cat, in it. She didn't intend for the cat to be left alone in the house for three days because he would miss her too much and she was afraid he might brush against one of the gas burners and accidentally asphyxiate himself. Her son, Bailey, didn't like to arrive at a motel with a cat.

She sat in the middle of the back seat with John Wesley and June Star on either side of her. Bailey and the children's mother and the baby sat in front and they left Atlanta at eight forty-five with the mileage on the car at 55890. The grandmother wrote this down because she thought it would be interesting to say how many miles they had been when they got back. It took them twenty minutes to reach the outskirts of the city.

The old lady settled herself comfortably, removing her white cotton gloves and putting them up with her purse on the shelf in front of the back window. The children's mother still had on slacks and still had her head tied up in a green kerchief, but the grandmother had on a navy blue straw sailor hat with a bunch of white violets on the brim and a navy blue dress with a small white dot in the print. Her collars and cuffs were white organdy trimmed with lace and at her neckline she had pinned a purple spray of cloth violets containing a sachet. In case of an accident, anyone seeing her dead on the highway would know at once that she was a lady.

She said she thought it was going to be a good day for driving, neither too hot nor too cold, and she cautioned Bailey that the speed limit was fifty-five miles an hour and that the patrolmen hid themselves behind billboards and small clumps of trees and sped out after you before you had a chance to slow down. She pointed out interesting details of the scenery: Stone Mountain; the blue granite that in some places came up to both sides of the highway; the brilliant red clay banks slightly streaked with purple; and the various crops that made rows of green lace-work on the ground. The trees were full of silver-white sunlight and the meanest of them sparkled. The children were reading comic magazines and their mother had gone back to sleep.

"Let's go through Georgia fast so we won't have to look at it much," John Wesley said.

"If I were a little boy," said the grandmother, "I wouldn't talk about my native state that way. Tennessee has the mountains and Georgia has the hills."

"Tennessee is just a hillbilly dumping ground," John Wesley said, "and Georgia is a lousy state too."

"You said it," June Star said.

"In my time," said the grandmother, folding her thin veined fingers, "children were more respectful of their native states and their parents and everything else. People did right then. Oh look at the cute little pickaninny!" she said and pointed to a Negro child standing in the door of a shack. "Wouldn't that make a picture, now?" she asked and they all turned and looked at the little Negro out of the back window. He waved.

"He didn't have any britches on," June Star said.

"He probably didn't have any," the grandmother explained. "Little niggers in the country don't have things like we do. If I could paint, I'd paint that picture," she said.

The children exchanged comic books.

The grandmother offered to hold the baby and the children's mother passed him over the front seat to her. She set him on her knee and bounced him and told him about the things they were passing. She rolled her eyes and screwed up her mouth and stuck her leathery thin face into his smooth bland one. Occasionally he gave her a far-away smile. They passed a large cotton field with five or six graves fenced in the middle of it, like a small island. "Look at the graveyard!" the grandmother said, pointing it out. "That was the old family burying ground. That belonged to the plantation."

"Where's the plantation?" John Wesley asked.

"Gone with the Wind," said the grandmother. "Ha. Ha."

When the children finished all the comic books they had brought, they opened the lunch and ate it. The grandmother ate a peanut butter sandwich and an olive and would not let the children throw the box and the paper napkins out the window. When there was nothing else to do they played a game by choosing a cloud and making the other two guess what shape it suggested. John Wesley took one the shape of a cow and June Star guessed a cow and John Wesley said, no, an automobile, and June Star said he didn't play fair, and they began to slap each other over the grandmother.

The grandmother said she would tell them a story if they would keep quiet. When she told a story, she rolled her eyes and waved her head and was very dramatic. She said once when she was a maiden lady she had been courted by a Mr. Edgar Atkins Teagarden from Jasper, Georgia. She said he was a very good-looking man and a gentleman and that he brought her a watermelon every Saturday afternoon with his initials cut in it, E. A. T. Well, one Saturday, she said, Mr. Teagarden brought the watermelon and there was nobody at home and he left it on the front porch and returned in his buggy to Jasper, but she never got the watermelon, she said, because a nigger boy ate it when he saw the initials, E. A. T.! This story tickled John Wesley's funny bone and he giggled and giggled but June Star didn't think it was any good. She said she wouldn't marry a man that just brought her a watermelon on Saturday. The grandmother said she would have done well to marry Mr. Teagarden because he was a gentleman and had bought Coca-Cola stock when it first came out and that he had died only a few years ago, a very wealthy man.

They stopped at The Tower for barbecued sandwiches. The Tower was a part stucco and part wood filling station and dance hall set in a clearing outside of Timothy. A fat man named Red Sammy Butts ran it and there were signs stuck here and there on the building and for miles up and down the highway saying, TRY RED SAMMY'S FAMOUS BARBECUE. NONE LIKE FAMOUS RED SAMMY'S! RED SAM! THE FAT BOY WITH THE HAPPY LAUGH! A VETERAN! RED SAMMY'S YOUR MAN!

Red Sammy was lying on the bare ground outside The Tower with his head under a truck while a gray monkey about a foot high, chained to a small chinaberry tree, chattered nearby. The monkey sprang back into the tree and got on the highest limb as soon as he saw the children jump out of the car and run toward him.

Inside, The Tower was a long dark room with a counter at one end and tables at the other and dancing space in the middle. They all sat down at a board table next to the nickelodeon and Red Sam's wife, a tall burnt-brown woman with hair and eyes lighter than her skin, came and took their order. The children's mother put a dime in the machine and played "The Tennessee Waltz," and the grandmother said that tune always made her want to dance. She asked Bailey if he would like to dance but he only glared at her. He didn't have a naturally sunny disposition like she did and trips made him nervous. The grandmother's brown eyes were very bright. She swayed her head from side to side and pretended she was dancing in her chair. June Star said play something she could tap to so the children's mother put in another dime and played a fast number and June Star stepped out onto the dance floor and did her tap routine.

"Ain't she cute?" Red Sam's wife said, leaning over the counter. "Would you like to come be my little girl?"

"No I certainly wouldn't," June Star said. "I wouldn't live in a broken-down place like this for a million bucks!" and she ran back to the table.

"Ain't she cute?" the woman repeated, stretching her mouth politely.

"Aren't you ashamed?" hissed the grandmother.

Red Sam came in and told his wife to quit lounging on the counter and hurry up with these people's order. His khaki trousers reached just to his hip bones and his stomach hung over them like a sack of meal swaying under his shirt. He came over and sat down at a table nearby and let out a combination sigh and yodel. "You can't win," he said. "You can't win," and he wiped his sweating red face off with a gray handkerchief. "These days you don't know who to trust," he said. "Ain't that the truth?"

"People are certainly not nice like they used to be," said the grandmother.

"Two fellers come in here last week," Red Sammy said, "driving a Chrysler. It was a old beat-up car but it was a good one and these boys looked all right to me. Said they worked at the mill and you know I let them fellers charge the gas they bought? Now why did I do that?"

"Because you're a good man!" the grandmother said at once.

"Yes'm, I suppose so," Red Sam said as if he were struck with this answer.

His wife brought the orders, carrying the five plates all at once without a tray, two in each hand and one balanced on her arm. "It isn't a soul in this green world of God's that you can trust," she said. "And I don't count nobody out of that, not nobody," she repeated, looking at Red Sammy.

"Did you read about that criminal, The Misfit, that's escaped?" asked the grandmother.

"I wouldn't be a bit surprised if he didn't attack this place right here," said the woman. "If he hears about it being here, I wouldn't be none surprised to see him. If he hears it's two cent in the cash register, I wouldn't be a tall surprised if he . . ."

"That'll do," Red Sam said. "Go bring these people their Co'-Colas," and the woman went off to get the rest of the order.

"A good man is hard to find," Red Sammy said. "Everything is getting terrible. I remember the day you could go off and leave your screen door unlatched. Not no more."

He and the grandmother discussed better times. The old lady said that in her opinion Europe was entirely to blame for the way things were now. She said the way Europe acted you would think we were made of money and Red Sam said there was no use talking about it, she was exactly right. The children ran outside into the white sunlight and looked at the monkey in the lacy chinaberry tree. He was busy catching fleas on himself and biting each one carefully between his teeth as if it were a delicacy.

They drove off again into the hot afternoon. The grandmother took cat naps and woke up every few minutes with her own snoring. Outside of Toombsboro she woke up and recalled an old plantation that she had visited in this neighborhood once when she was a young lady. She said the house had six white columns across the front and that there was an avenue of oaks leading up to it and two little wooden trellis arbors on either side in front where you sat down with your suitor after a stroll in the garden. She recalled exactly which road to turn off to get to it. She knew that Bailey would not be willing to lose any time looking at an old house, but the more she talked about it, the more she wanted to see it once again and find out if the little twin arbors were still standing. "There was a secret panel in this house," she said craftily, not telling the truth but wishing that she were, "and the story went that all the family silver was hidden in it when Sherman came though but it was never found . . ."

"Hey!" John Wesley said. "Let's go see it! We'll find it! We'll poke all the woodwork and find it! Who lives there? Where do you turn off at? Hey Pop, can't we turn off there?"

"We never have seen a house with a secret panel!" June Star shrieked. "Let's go to the house with the secret panel! Hey Pop, can't we go see the house with the secret panel!"

"It's not far from here, I know," the grandmother said. "It wouldn't take over twenty minutes."

Bailey was looking straight ahead. His jaw was as rigid as a horseshoe. "No," he said.

The children began to yell and scream that they wanted to see the house with the secret panel. John Wesley kicked the back of the front seat and June Star hung over her mother's shoulder and whined desperately into her ear that they never had any fun even on their vacation, that they could never do what THEY wanted to do. The baby began to scream and John Wesley kicked the back of the seat so hard that his father could feel the blows in his kidney.

"All right!" he shouted and drew the car to a stop at the side of the road. "Will you all shut up? Will you all just shut up for one second? If you don't shut up, we won't go anywhere."

"It would be very educational for them," the grandmother murmured.

"All right," Bailey said, "but get this: this is the only time we're going to stop for anything like this. This is the one and only time."

"The dirt road that you have to turn down is about a mile back," the grandmother directed. "I marked it when we passed."

"A dirt road," Bailey groaned.

After they had turned around and were headed toward the dirt road, the grandmother recalled other points about the house, the beautiful glass over the front doorway and the candle-lamp in the hall. John Wesley said that the secret panel was probably in the fireplace.

"You can't go inside this house," Bailey said. "You don't know who lives there."

"While you all talk to the people in front, I'll run around behind and get in a window," John Wesley suggested.

"We'll all stay in the car," his mother said.

They turned onto the dirt road and the car raced roughly along in a swirl of pink dust. The grandmother recalled the times when there were no paved roads and thirty miles was a day's journey. The dirt road was hilly and there were sudden washes in it and sharp curves on dangerous embankments. All at once they would be on a hill, looking down over the blue tops of trees for miles around, then the next minute, they would be in a red depression with the dust-coated trees looking down on them.

"This place had better turn up in a minute," Bailey said, "or I'm going to turn around."

The road looked as if no one had traveled on it in months.

"It's not much farther," the grandmother said and just as she said it, a horrible thought came to her. The thought was so embarrassing that she turned red in the face and her eyes dilated and her feet jumped up, upsetting her valise in the corner. The instant the valise moved, the newspaper top she had over the basket under it rose with a snarl and Pitty Sing, the cat, sprang onto Bailey's shoulder.

The children were thrown to the floor and their mother, clutching the baby, was thrown out the door onto the ground; the old lady was thrown into the front seat. The car turned over once and landed right-side-up in a gulch off the side of the road. Bailey remained in the driver's seat with the cat—gray-striped with a broad white face and an orange nose—clinging to his neck like a caterpillar.

As soon as the children saw they could move their arms and legs, they scrambled out of the car, shouting, "We've had an ACCIDENT!" The grandmother was curled up under the dashboard, hoping she was injured so that Bailey's wrath would not come down on her all at once. The horrible thought she had had before the accident was that the house she had remembered so vividly was not in Georgia but in Tennessee.

Bailey removed the cat from his neck with both hands and flung it out the window against the side of a pine tree. Then he got out of the car and started looking for the children's mother. She was sitting against the side of the red gutted ditch, holding the screaming baby, but she only had a cut down her face and a broken shoulder. "We've had an ACCIDENT!" the children screamed in a frenzy of delight.

"But nobody's killed," June Star said with disappointment as the grandmother limped out of the car, her hat still pinned to her head but the broken front brim standing up at a jaunty angle and the violet spray hanging off the side. They all sat down in the ditch, except the children, to recover from the shock. They were all shaking.

"Maybe a car will come along," said the children's mother hoarsely.

"I believe I have injured an organ," said the grandmother, pressing her side, but no one answered her. Bailey's teeth were clattering. He had on a yellow sport shirt with bright blue parrots designed in it and his face was as yellow as the shirt. The grandmother decided that she would not mention that the house was in Tennessee.

The road was about ten feet above and they could see only the tops of the trees on the other side of it. Behind the ditch they were sitting in there were more woods, tall and dark and deep. In a few minutes they saw a car some distance away on top of a hill, coming slowly as if the occupants were watching them. The grandmother stood up and waved both arms dramatically to attract their attention. The car continued to come on slowly, disappeared around a bend and appeared again, moving even slower, on top of the hill they had gone over. It was a big black battered hearse-like automobile. There were three men in it.

It came to a stop just over them and for some minutes, the driver looked down with a steady expressionless gaze to where they were sitting, and didn't speak. Then he turned his head and muttered something to the other two and they got out. One was a fat boy in black trousers and a red sweat shirt with a silver stallion embossed on the front of it. He moved around on the right side of them and stood staring, his mouth partly open in a kind of loose grin. The other had on khaki pants and a blue striped coat and a gray hat pulled down very low, hiding most of his face. He came around slowly on the left side. Neither spoke.

The driver got out of the car and stood by the side of it, looking down at them. He was an older man than the other two. His hair was just beginning to gray and he wore silver-rimmed spectacles that gave him a scholarly look. He had a long creased face and didn't have on any shirt or undershirt. He had on blue jeans that were too tight for him and was holding a black hat and a gun. The two boys also had guns.

"We've had an ACCIDENT!" the children screamed.

The grandmother had the peculiar feeling that the bespectacled man was someone she knew. His face was as familiar to her as if she had known him all her life but she could not recall who he was. He moved away from the car and began to come down the embankment, placing his feet carefully so that he wouldn't slip. He had on tan and white shoes and no socks, and his ankles were red and thin. "Good afternoon," he said. "I see you all had you a little spill."

"We turned over twice!" said the grandmother.

"Oncet," he corrected. "We seen it happen. Try their car and see will it run, Hiram," he said quietly to the boy with the gray hat.

"What you got that gun for?" John Wesley asked. "Whatcha gonna do with that gun?"

"Lady," the man said to the children's mother, "would you mind calling them children to sit down by you? Children make me nervous. I want all you all to sit down right together there where you're at."

"What are you telling US what to do for?" June Star asked.

Behind them the line of woods gaped like a dark open mouth. "Come here," said their mother.

"Look here now," Bailey began suddenly, "we're in a predicament! We're in . . ."

The grandmother shrieked. She scrambled to her feet and stood staring. "You're The Misfit!" she said. "I recognized you at once!"

"Yes'm," the man said, smiling slightly as if he were pleased in spite of himself to be known, "but it would have been better for all of you, lady, if you hadn't of reckernized me."

Bailey turned his head sharply and said something to his mother that shocked even the children. The old lady began to cry and The Misfit reddened.

"Lady," he said, "don't you get upset. Sometimes a man says things he don't mean. I don't reckon he meant to talk to you thataway."

"You wouldn't shoot a lady, would you?" the grandmother said and removed a clean handkerchief from her cuff and began to slap at her eyes with it.

The Misfit pointed the toe of his shoe into the ground and made a little hole and then covered it up again. "I would hate to have to," he said.

"Listen," the grandmother almost screamed, "I know you're a good man. You don't look a bit like you have common blood. I know you must come from nice people!"

"Yes mam," he said, "finest people in the world." When he smiled he showed a row of strong white teeth. "God never made a finer woman than my mother and my daddy's heart was pure gold," he said. The boy with the red sweat shirt had come around behind them and was standing with his gun at his hip. The Misfit squatted down on the ground. "Watch them children, Bobby Lee," he said. "You know they make me nervous." He looked at the six of them huddled together in front of him and he seemed to be embarrassed as if he couldn't think of anything to say. "Ain't a cloud in the sky," he remarked, looking up at it. "Don't see no sun but don't see no cloud neither."

"Yes, it's a beautiful day," said the grandmother. "Listen," she said, "you shouldn't call yourself The Misfit because I know you're a good man at heart. I can just look at you and tell."

"Hush!" Bailey yelled. "Hush! Everybody shut up and let me handle this!" He was squatting in the position of a runner about to sprint forward but he didn't move.

"I pre-chate that, lady," The Misfit said and drew a little circle in the ground with the butt of his gun.

"It'll take a half a hour to fix this here car," Hiram called, looking over the raised hood of it.

"Well, first you and Bobby Lee get him and that little boy to step over yonder with you," The Misfit said, pointing to Bailey and John Wesley. "The boys want to ast you something," he said to Bailey. "Would you mind stepping back in them woods there with them?"

"Listen," Bailey began, "we're in a terrible predicament! Nobody realizes what this is," and his voice cracked. His eyes were as blue and intense as the parrots in his shirt and he remained perfectly still.

The grandmother reached up to adjust her hat brim as if she were going to the woods with him but it came off in her hand. She stood staring at it and after a second she let it fall on the ground. Hiram pulled Bailey up by the arm as if he were assisting an old man. John Wesley caught hold of his father's hand and Bobby Lee followed. They went off toward the woods and just as they reached the dark edge, Bailey turned and supporting himself against a gray naked pine trunk, he shouted, "I'll be back in a minute, Mamma, wait on me!"

"Come back this instant!" his mother shrilled but they all disappeared into the woods.

"Bailey Boy!" the grandmother called in a tragic voice but she found she was looking at The Misfit squatting on the ground in front of her. "I just know you're a good man," she said desperately. "You're not a bit common!"

"Nome, I ain't a good man," The Misfit said after a second as if he had considered her statement carefully, "but I ain't the worst in the world neither. My daddy said I was a different breed of dog from my brothers and sisters. 'You know,' Daddy said, 'it's some that can live their whole life out without asking about it and it's others has to know why it is, and this boy is one of the latters. He's going to be into everything!'" He put on his black hat and looked up suddenly and then away deep into the woods as if he were embarrassed again. "I'm sorry I don't have on a shirt before you ladies," he said, hunching his shoulders slightly. "We buried our clothes that we had on when we escaped and we're just making do until we can get better. We borrowed these from some folks we met," he explained.

"That's perfectly all right," the grandmother said. "Maybe Bailey has an extra shirt in his suitcase."

"I'll look and see terrectly," The Misfit said.

"Where are they taking him?" the children's mother screamed.

"Daddy was a card himself," The Misfit said. "You couldn't put anything over on him. He never got in trouble with the Authorities though. Just had the knack of handling them."

"You could be honest too if you'd only try," said the grandmother. "Think how wonderful it would be to settle down and live a comfortable life and not have to think about somebody chasing you all the time."

The Misfit kept scratching in the ground with the butt of his gun as if he were thinking about it. "Yes'm, somebody is always after you," he murmured.

The grandmother noticed how thin his shoulder blades were just behind his hat because she was standing up looking down on him. "Do you ever pray?" she asked.

He shook his head. All she saw was the black hat wiggle between his shoulder blades. "Nome," he said.

There was a pistol shot from the woods, followed closely by another.

Then silence. The old lady's head jerked around. She could hear the wind move through the tree tops like a long satisfied insuck of breath. "Bailey Boy!" she called.

"I was a gospel singer for a while," The Misfit said. "I been most everything. Been in the arm service, both land and sea, at home and abroad, been twict married, been an undertaker, been with the railroads, plowed Mother Earth, been in a tornado, seen a man burnt alive oncet," and he looked up at the children's mother and the little girl who were sitting close together, their faces white and their eyes glassy. "I even seen a woman flogged," he said.

"Pray, pray," the grandmother began, "pray, pray . . ."

"I never was a bad boy that I remember of," The Misfit said in an almost dreamy voice, "but somewheres along the line I done something wrong and got sent to the penitentiary. I was buried alive," and he looked up and held her attention to him by a steady stare.

"That's when you should have started to pray," she said. "What did you do to get sent to the penitentiary that first time?"

"Turn to the right, it was a wall," The Misfit said, looking up again at the cloudless sky. "Turn to the left, it was a wall. Look up it was a ceiling, look down it was a floor. I forget what I done, lady. I set there and set there, trying to remember what it was I done and I ain't recalled it to this day. Oncet in a while, I would think it was coming to me, but it never come."

"Maybe they put you in by mistake," the old lady said vaguely.

"Nome," he said. "It wasn't no mistake. They had the papers on me."

"You must have stolen something," she said.

The Misfit sneered slightly. "Nobody had nothing I wanted," he said. "It was a head-doctor at the penitentiary said what I had done was kill my daddy but I known that for a lie. My daddy died in nineteen ought nineteen of the epidemic flu and I never had a thing to do with it. He was buried in the Mount Hopewell Baptist churchyard and you can go there and see for yourself."

"If you would pray," the old lady said, "Jesus would help you."

"That's right," The Misfit said.

"Well then, why don't you pray?" she asked trembling with delight suddenly.

"I don't want no hep," he said. "I'm doing all right by myself."

Bobby Lee and Hiram came ambling back from the woods. Bobby Lee was dragging a yellow shirt with bright blue parrots in it.

"Thow me that shirt, Bobby Lee," The Misfit said. The shirt came flying at him and landed on his shoulder and he put it on. The grandmother couldn't name what the shirt reminded her of. "No, lady," The Misfit said while he was buttoning it up, "I found out the crime don't matter. You can do one thing or you can do another, kill a man or take a tire off his car, because sooner or later you're going to forget what it was you done and just be punished for it."

The children's mother had begun to make heaving noises as if she couldn't get her breath. "Lady," he asked, "would you and that little girl like to step off yonder with Bobby Lee and Hiram and join your husband?"

"Yes, thank you," the mother said faintly. Her left arm dangled helplessly and she was holding the baby, who had gone to sleep, in the other. "Hep that lady up, Hiram," The Misfit said as she struggled to climb out of the ditch, "and Bobby Lee, you hold onto that little girl's hand."

"I don't want to hold hands with him," June Star said. "He reminds me of a pig." The fat boy blushed and laughed and caught her by the arm and pulled her off into the woods after Hiram and her mother.

Alone with The Misfit, the grandmother found that she had lost her voice. There was not a cloud in the sky nor any sun. There was nothing around her but woods. She wanted to tell him that he must pray. She opened and closed her mouth several times before anything came out. Finally she found herself saying, "Jesus. Jesus," meaning, Jesus will help you, but the way she was saying it, it sounded as if she might be cursing.

"Yes'm," The Misfit said as if he agreed. "Jesus thown everything off balance. It was the same case with Him as with me except He hadn't committed any crime and they could prove I had committed one because they had the papers on me. Of course," he said, "they never shown me my papers. That's why I sign myself now. I said long ago, you get you a signature and sign everything you do and keep a copy of it. Then you'll know what you done and you can hold up the crime to the punishment and see do they match and in the end you'll have something to prove you ain't been treated right. I call myself The Misfit," he said, "because I can't make what all I done wrong fit what all I gone through in punishment."

There was a piercing scream from the woods, followed closely by a pistol report. "Does it seem right to you, lady, that one is punished a heap and another ain't punished at all?"

"Jesus!" the old lady cried. "You've got good blood! I know you wouldn't shoot a lady! I know you come from nice people! Pray! Jesus, you ought not to shoot a lady. I'll give you all the money I've got!"

"Lady," The Misfit said, looking beyond her far into the woods, "there never was a body that give the undertaker a tip."

There were two more pistol reports and the grandmother raised her head like a parched old turkey hen crying for water and called, "Bailey Boy, Bailey Boy!" as if her heart would break.

"Jesus was the only One that ever raised the dead," The Misfit continued, "and He shouldn't have done it. He thown everything off balance. If He did what He said, then it's nothing for you to do but thow away everything and follow Him, and if He didn't, then it's nothing for you to do but enjoy the few minutes you got left the best way you can by killing somebody or burning down his house or doing some other meanness to him. No pleasure but meanness," he said and his voice had become almost a snarl.

"Maybe He didn't raise the dead," the old lady mumbled, not knowing what she was saying and feeling so dizzy that she sank down in the ditch with her legs twisted under her.

"I wasn't there so I can't say He didn't," The Misfit said. "I wisht I had of been there," he said, hitting the ground with his fist. "It ain't right I wasn't there because if I had of been there I would of known. Listen lady," he said in a high voice, "if I had of been there I would of known and I wouldn't be like I am now." His voice seemed about to crack and the grandmother's head cleared for an instant. She saw the man's face twisted close to her own as if he were going to cry and she murmured, "Why you're one of my babies. You're one of my own children!" She reached out and touched him on the shoulder. The Misfit sprang back as if a snake had bitten him and shot her three times through the chest. Then he put his gun down on the ground and took off his glasses and began to clean them.

Hiram and Bobby Lee returned from the woods and stood over the ditch, looking down at the grandmother who half sat and half lay in a puddle of blood with her legs crossed under her like a child's and her face smiling up at the cloudless sky.

Without his glasses, The Misfit's eyes were red-rimmed and pale and defenseless-looking. "Take her off and thow her where you thown the others," he said, picking up the cat that was rubbing itself against his leg.

"She was a talker, wasn't she?" Bobby Lee said, sliding down the ditch with a yodel.

"She would of been a good woman," The Misfit said, "if it had been somebody there to shoot her every minute of her life."

"Some fun!" Bobby Lee said.

"Shut up, Bobby Lee," The Misfit said. "It's no real pleasure in life."

LEO TOLSTOY

LEO TOLSTOY WAS BORN IN 1828 IN TULA PROVINCE, RUSSIA.
His parents died when he was a child, and he was brought up by relatives, later
studying law and oriental languages at Kazan University. He grew disappointed
with the quality of the education he was receiving there, and returned to his
hometown of Yasnaya Polyana, spending much of his time there and in Moscow
and St. Petersburg. In 1851 he and his older brother left for the Caucasus, where
they enlisted with an artillery regiment. This was when he began his writing
career, publishing the autobiographical trilogy *Childhood*, *Boyhood*, and *Youth*.

In 1857 he visited France, Switzerland, and Germany, and it was during
these trips that he came to a spiritual crisis that turned him from authoring
books on privileged society to a deeply held belief in the teaching of Christ.
His epic novel *War and Peace* appeared between 1865 and 1869, and his other
masterpiece, *Anna Karenina*, was published from 1873 to 1877. Later, his book
on the Christian life, *A Confession* and *What I Believe* (which was banned in
1884), resulted in his being excommunicated from the Russian Orthodox
Church in 1901 for his writing's radical stance on the importance of a personal
relationship with Christ, and the perceived anarchist stance "turning the other
cheek" was believed to embrace. He died of pneumonia on November 7, 1910,
at a railway station far from home after choosing to live his life as an ascetic.

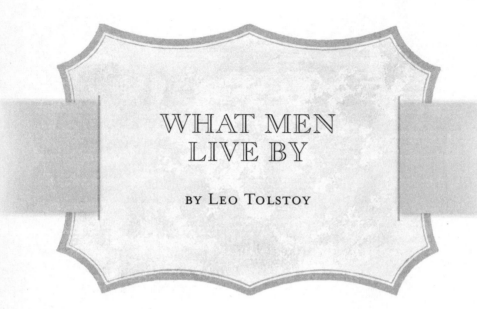

WHAT MEN LIVE BY

BY LEO TOLSTOY

"We know that we have passed out of death into life, because we love the brethren. He that loveth not abideth in death." —1 "Epistle St. John" iii. 14.

"Whoso hath the world's goods, and beholdeth his brother in need, and shutteth up his compassion from him, how doth the love of God abide in him? My little children, let us not love in word, neither with the tongue; but in deed and truth." —iii. 17–18.

"Love is of God; and every one that loveth is begotten of God, and knoweth God. He that loveth not knoweth not God; for God is love." —iv. 7–8.

"No man hath beheld God at any time; if we love one another, God abideth in us." —iv. 12.

"God is love; and he that abideth in love abideth in God, and God abideth in him." —iv. 16.

"If a man say, I love God, and hateth his brother, he is a liar; for he that loveth not his brother whom he hath seen, how can he love God whom he hath not seen?" —iv. 20.

I

A shoemaker named Simon, who had neither house nor land of his own, lived with his wife and children in a peasant's hut and earned his living by his work. Work was cheap but bread was dear, and what he earned he spent for food. The man and his wife had but one sheep-skin coat between them for winter wear, and even that was worn to tatters, and this was the second year he had been wanting to buy sheep-skins for a new coat. Before winter Simon saved up a little money: a three-rouble note lay hidden in his wife's box, and five roubles and twenty kopeks were owed him by customers in the village.

So one morning he prepared to go to the village to buy the sheep-skins. He put on over his shirt his wife's wadded nankeen jacket, and over that he put his own cloth coat. He took the three-rouble note in his pocket, cut himself a stick to serve as a staff, and started off after breakfast. "I'll collect the five roubles that are due to me," thought he, "add the three I have got, and that will be enough to buy sheep-skins for the winter coat."

He came to the village and called at a peasant's hut, but the man was not at home. The peasant's wife promised that the money should be paid next week, but she would not pay it herself. Then Simon called on another peasant, but this one swore he had no money, and would only pay twenty kopeks which he owed for a pair of boots Simon had mended. Simon then tried to buy the sheep-skins on credit, but the dealer would not trust him.

"Bring your money," said he, "then you may have your pick of the skins. We know what debt-collecting is like." So all the business the shoemaker did was to get the twenty kopeks for boots he had mended, and to take a pair of felt boots a peasant gave him to sole with leather.

Simon felt downhearted. He spent the twenty kopeks on vodka and started homewards without having bought any skins. In the morning he had felt the frost; but now, after drinking the vodka, he felt warm, even without a sheep-skin coat. He trudged along, striking his stick on the frozen earth with one hand, swinging the felt boots with the other, and talking to himself.

"I'm quite warm," said he, "though I have no sheep-skin coat. I've had a drop and it runs through all my veins. I need no sheep-skins. I go along and don't worry about anything. That's the sort of man I am! What do I care? I can live without sheep-skins. I don't need them. My wife will fret, to be sure. And, true enough, it is a shame; one works all day long, and then does not get paid. Stop a bit! If you don't bring that money along, sure enough I'll skin you, blessed if I don't. How's that? He pays twenty kopeks at a time! What can I do with twenty kopeks? Drink it—that's all one can do! Hard up, he says he is! So he may be—but what about me? You have a house, and cattle, and everything; I've only what I stand up in! You have corn of your own growing; I have to buy every grain. Do what I will, I must spend three roubles every week for bread alone. I come home and find the bread all used up, and I have to fork out another rouble and a half. So just pay up what you owe, and no nonsense about it!"

By this time he had nearly reached the shrine at the bend of the road. Looking up, he saw something whitish behind the shrine. The daylight was fading, and the shoemaker peered at the thing without being able to make out what it was. "There was no white stone here before. Can it be an ox? It's not like an ox. It has a head like a man, but it's too white; and what could a man be doing there?"

He came closer, so that it was clearly visible. To his surprise it really was a man, alive or dead, sitting naked, leaning motionless against the shrine. Terror seized the shoemaker, and he thought, "Some one has killed him, stripped him, and left him there. If I meddle I shall surely get into trouble."

So the shoemaker went on. He passed in front of the shrine so that he could not see the man. When he had gone some way, he looked back, and saw that the man was no longer leaning against the shrine, but was moving as if looking towards him. The shoemaker felt more frightened than before, and thought, "Shall I go back to him, or shall I go on? If I go near him something dreadful may happen. Who knows who the fellow is? He has not come here for any good. If I go near him he may jump up and throttle me, and there will be no getting away. Or if not, he'd still be a burden on one's hands. What could I do with a naked man? I couldn't give him my last clothes. Heaven only help me to get away!"

So the shoemaker hurried on, leaving the shrine behind him— when suddenly his conscience smote him, and he stopped in the road.

"What are you doing, Simon?" said he to himself. "The man may be dying of want, and you slip past afraid. Have you grown so rich as to be afraid of robbers? Ah, Simon, shame on you!"

So he turned back and went up to the man.

II

Simon approached the stranger, looked at him and saw that he was a young man, fit, with no bruises on his body, but evidently freezing and frightened, and he sat there leaning back without looking up at Simon, as if too faint to lift his eyes. Simon went close to him, and then the man seemed to wake up. Turning his head, he opened his eyes and looked into Simon's face. That one look was enough to make Simon fond of the man. He threw the felt boots on the ground, undid his sash, laid it on the boots, and took off his cloth coat.

"It's not a time for talking," said he. "Come, put this coat on at once!" And Simon took the man by the elbows and helped him to rise. As he stood there, Simon saw that his body was clean and in good condition, his hands and feet shapely, and his face good and kind. He threw his coat over the man's shoulders, but the latter could not find the sleeves. Simon guided his arms into them, and drawing the coat well on, wrapped it closely about him, tying the sash round the man's waist.

Simon even took off his torn cap to put it on the man's head, but then his own head felt cold, and he thought: "I'm quite bald, while he has long curly hair." So he put his cap on his own head again. "It will be better to give him something for his feet," thought he; and he made the man sit down, and helped him to put on the felt boots, saying, "There, friend, now move about and warm yourself. Other matters can be settled later on. Can you walk?"

The man stood up and looked kindly at Simon, but could not say a word.

"Why don't you speak?" said Simon. "It's too cold to stay here, we must be getting home. There now, take my stick, and if you're feeling weak, lean on that. Now step out!"

The man started walking and moved easily, not lagging behind.

As they went along, Simon asked him, "And where do you belong to?"

"I'm not from these parts."

"I thought as much. I know the folks hereabouts. But how did you come to be there by the shrine?"

"I cannot tell."

"Has some one been ill-treating you?"

"No one has ill-treated me. God has punished me."

"Of course God rules all. Still, you'll have to find food and shelter somewhere. Where do you want to go to?"

"It is all the same to me."

Simon was amazed. The man did not look like a rogue, and he spoke gently, but yet he gave no account of himself. Still Simon thought, "Who knows what may have happened?" And he said to the stranger: "Well then, come home with me, and at least warm yourself awhile."

So Simon walked towards his home, and the stranger kept up with him, walking at his side. The wind had risen and Simon felt it cold under his shirt. He was getting over his tipsiness by now, and began to feel the frost. He went along sniffling and wrapping his wife's coat round him, and he thought to himself: "There now—talk about sheep-skins! I went out for sheep-skins and come home without even a coat to my back, and what is more, I'm bringing a naked man along with me. Matryona won't be pleased!" And when he thought of his wife he felt sad; but when he looked at the stranger and remembered how he had looked up at him at the shrine, his heart was glad.

III

Simon's wife had everything ready early that day. She had cut wood, brought water, fed the children, eaten her own meal, and now she sat thinking. She wondered when she ought to make bread: now or tomorrow? There was still a large piece left.

"If Simon has had some dinner in town," thought she, "and does not eat much for supper, the bread will last out another day."

She weighed the piece of bread in her hand again and again, and thought: "I won't make any more today. We have only enough flour left to bake one batch; We can manage to make this last out till Friday."

So Matryona put away the bread and sat down at the table to patch her husband's shirt. While she worked she thought how her husband was buying skins for a winter coat.

"If only the dealer does not cheat him. My good man is much too simple; he cheats nobody, but any child can take him in. Eight roubles is a lot of money—he should get a good coat at that price. Not tanned skins, but still a proper winter coat. How difficult it was last winter to get on without a warm coat. I could neither get down to the river, nor go out anywhere. When he went out he put on all we had, and there was nothing left for me. He did not start very early today, but still it's time he was back. I only hope he has not gone on the spree!"

Hardly had Matryona thought this, when steps were heard on the threshold, and some one entered. Matryona stuck her needle into her work and went out into the passage. There she saw two men: Simon, and with him a man without a hat, and wearing felt boots.

Matryona noticed at once that her husband smelt of spirits. "There now, he has been drinking," thought she. And when she saw that he was coatless, had only her jacket on, brought no parcel, stood there silent, and seemed ashamed, her heart was ready to break with disappointment. "He has drunk the money," thought she, "and has been on the spree with some good-for-nothing fellow whom he has brought home with him."

Matryona let them pass into the hut, followed them in, and saw that the stranger was a young, slight man, wearing her husband's coat. There was no shirt to be seen under it, and he had no hat. Having entered, he stood, neither moving, nor raising his eyes, and Matryona thought: "He must be a bad man—he's afraid."

Matryona frowned, and stood beside the oven looking to see what they would do.

Simon took off his cap and sat down on the bench as if things were all right.

"Come, Matryona; if supper is ready, let us have some."

Matryona muttered something to herself and did not move, but stayed where she was, by the oven. She looked first at the one and then at the other of them, and only shook her head. Simon saw that his wife was annoyed, but tried to pass it off. Pretending not to notice anything, he took the stranger by the arm.

"Sit down, friend," said he, "and let us have some supper."

The stranger sat down on the bench.

"Haven't you cooked anything for us?" said Simon.

Matryona's anger boiled over. "I've cooked, but not for you. It seems to me you have drunk your wits away. You went to buy a sheepskin coat, but come home without so much as the coat you had on, and bring a naked vagabond home with you. I have no supper for drunkards like you."

"That's enough, Matryona. Don't wag your tongue without reason. You had better ask what sort of man—"

"And you tell me what you've done with the money?"

Simon found the pocket of the jacket, drew out the three-rouble note, and unfolded it.

"Here is the money. Trifonof did not pay, but promises to pay soon."

Matryona got still more angry; he had bought no sheep-skins, but had put his only coat on some naked fellow and had even brought him to their house.

She snatched up the note from the table, took it to put away in safety, and said: "I have no supper for you. We can't feed all the naked drunkards in the world."

"There now, Matryona, hold your tongue a bit. First hear what a man has to say."

"Much wisdom I shall hear from a drunken fool. I was right in not wanting to marry you—a drunkard. The linen my mother gave me you drank; and now you've been to buy a coat—and have drunk it too!"

Simon tried to explain to his wife that he had only spent twenty kopeks; tried to tell how he had found the man—but Matryona would not let him get a word in. She talked nineteen to the dozen, and dragged in things that had happened ten years before.

Matryona talked and talked, and at last she flew at Simon and seized him by the sleeve.

"Give me my jacket. It is the only one I have, and you must needs take it from me and wear it yourself. Give it here, you mangy dog, and may the devil take you."

Simon began to pull off the jacket, and turned a sleeve of it inside out; Matryona seized the jacket and it burst its seams. She snatched it up, threw it over her head and went to the door. She meant to go out, but stopped undecided—she wanted to work off her anger, but she also wanted to learn what sort of a man the stranger was.

IV

Matryona stopped and said: "If he were a good man he would not be naked. Why, he hasn't even a shirt on him. If he were all right, you would say where you came across the fellow."

"That's just what I am trying to tell you," said Simon. "As I came to the shrine I saw him sitting all naked and frozen. It isn't quite the weather to sit about naked! God sent me to him, or he would have perished. What was I to do? How do we know what may have happened to him? So I took him, clothed him, and brought him along. Don't be so angry, Matryona. It is a sin. Remember, we all must die one day."

Angry words rose to Matryona's lips, but she looked at the stranger and was silent. He sat on the edge of the bench, motionless, his hands folded on his knees, his head drooping on his breast, his eyes closed, and his brows knit as if in pain. Matryona was silent, and Simon said: "Matryona, have you no love of God?"

Matryona heard these words, and as she looked at the stranger, suddenly her heart softened towards him. She came back from the door, and going to the stove she got out the supper. Setting a cup on the table, she poured out some kvas. Then she brought out the last piece of bread, and set out a knife and spoons.

"Eat, if you want to," said she.

Simon drew the stranger to the table.

"Take your place, young man," said he.

Simon cut the bread, crumbled it into the broth, and they began to eat. Matryona sat at the corner of the table resting her head on her hand and looking at the stranger.

And Matryona was touched with pity for the stranger, and began to feel fond of him. And at once the stranger's face lit up; his brows were no longer bent, he raised his eyes and smiled at Matryona.

When they had finished supper, the woman cleared away the things and began questioning the stranger. "Where are you from?" said she.

"I am not from these parts."

"But how did you come to be on the road?"

"I may not tell."

"Did some one rob you?"

"God punished me."

"And you were lying there naked?"

"Yes, naked and freezing. Simon saw me and had pity on me. He took off his coat, put it on me and brought me here. And you have fed me, given me drink, and shown pity on me. God will reward you!"

Matryona rose, took from the window Simon's old shirt she had been patching, and gave it to the stranger. She also brought out a pair of trousers for him.

"There," said she, "I see you have no shirt. Put this on, and lie down where you please, in the loft or on the oven."

The stranger took off the coat, put on the shirt, and lay down in the loft. Matryona put out the candle, took the coat, and climbed to where her husband lay.

Matryona drew the skirts of the coat over her and lay down, but could not sleep; she could not get the stranger out of her mind.

When she remembered that he had eaten their last piece of bread and that there was none for tomorrow, and thought of the shirt and trousers she had given away, she felt grieved; but when she remembered how he had smiled, her heart was glad.

Long did Matryona lie awake, and she noticed that Simon also was awake—he drew the coat towards him.

"Simon!"

"Well?"

"You have had the last of the bread, and I have not put any to rise. I don't know what we shall do tomorrow. Perhaps I can borrow some of neighbor Martha."

"If we're alive we shall find something to eat."

The woman lay still awhile, and then said, "He seems a good man, but why does he not tell us who he is?"

"I suppose he has his reasons."

"Simon!"

"Well?"

"We give; but why does nobody give us anything?"

Simon did not know what to say; so he only said, "Let us stop talking," and turned over and went to sleep.

V

In the morning Simon awoke. The children were still asleep; his wife had gone to the neighbor's to borrow some bread. The stranger alone was sitting on the bench, dressed in the old shirt and trousers, and looking upwards. His face was brighter than it had been the day before.

Simon said to him, "Well, friend; the belly wants bread, and the naked body clothes. One has to work for a living. What work do you know?"

"I do not know any."

This surprised Simon, but he said, "Men who want to learn can learn anything."

"Men work and I will work also."

"What is your name?"

"Michael."

"Well, Michael, if you don't wish to talk about yourself, that is your own affair; but you'll have to earn a living for yourself. If you will work as I tell you, I will give you food and shelter."

"May God reward you! I will learn. Show me what to do."

Simon took yarn, put it round his thumb and began to twist it.

"It is easy enough—see!"

Michael watched him, put some yarn round his own thumb in the same way, caught the knack, and twisted the yarn also.

Then Simon showed him how to wax the thread. This also Michael mastered. Next Simon showed him how to twist the bristle in, and how to sew, and this, too, Michael learned at once.

Whatever Simon showed him he understood at once, and after three days he worked as if he had sewn boots all his life. He worked without stopping, and ate little. When work was over he sat silently, looking upwards. He hardly went into the street, spoke only when necessary, and neither joked nor laughed. They never saw him smile, except that first evening when Matryona gave them supper.

VI

Day by day and week by week the year went round. Michael lived and worked with Simon. His fame spread till people said that no one sewed boots so neatly and strongly as Simon's workman, Michael; and from all the district round people came to Simon for their boots, and he began to be well off.

One winter day, as Simon and Michael sat working, a carriage on sledge-runners, with three horses and with bells, drove up to the hut. They looked out of the window; the carriage stopped at their door, a fine servant jumped down from the box and opened the door. A gentleman in a fur coat got out and walked up to Simon's hut. Up jumped Matryona and opened the door wide. The gentleman stooped to enter the hut, and when he drew himself up again his head nearly reached the ceiling, and he seemed quite to fill his end of the room.

Simon rose, bowed, and looked at the gentleman with astonishment. He had never seen any one like him. Simon himself was lean, Michael was thin, and Matryona was dry as a bone, but this man was like some one from another world: red-faced, burly, with a neck like a bull's, and looking altogether as if he were cast in iron.

The gentleman puffed, threw off his fur coat, sat down on the bench, and said, "Which of you is the master bootmaker?"

"I am, your Excellency," said Simon, coming forward.

Then the gentleman shouted to his lad, "Hey, Fedka, bring the leather!"

The servant ran in, bringing a parcel. The gentleman took the parcel and put it on the table.

"Untie it," said he. The lad untied it.

The gentleman pointed to the leather.

"Look here, shoemaker," said he, "do you see this leather?"

"Yes, your honor."

"But do you know what sort of leather it is?"

Simon felt the leather and said, "It is good leather."

"Good, indeed! Why, you fool, you never saw such leather before in your life. It's German, and cost twenty roubles."

Simon was frightened, and said, "Where should I ever see leather like that?"

"Just so! Now, can you make it into boots for me?"

"Yes, your Excellency, I can."

Then the gentleman shouted at him: "You can, can you? Well, remember whom you are to make them for, and what the leather is. You must make me boots that will wear for a year, neither losing shape nor coming unsewn. If you can do it, take the leather and cut it up; but if you can't, say so. I warn you now, if your boots come unsewn or lose shape within a year, I will have you put in prison. If they don't burst or lose shape for a year, I will pay you ten roubles for your work."

Simon was frightened, and did not know what to say. He glanced at Michael and nudging him with his elbow, whispered: "Shall I take the work?"

Michael nodded his head as if to say, "Yes, take it."

Simon did as Michael advised, and undertook to make boots that would not lose shape or split for a whole year.

Calling his servant, the gentleman told him to pull the boot off his left leg, which he stretched out.

"Take my measure!" said he.

Simon stitched a paper measure seventeen inches long, smoothed it out, knelt down, wiped his hand well on his apron so as not to soil the gentleman's sock, and began to measure. He measured the sole, and round the instep, and began to measure the calf of the leg, but the paper was too short. The calf of the leg was as thick as a beam.

"Mind you don't make it too tight in the leg."

Simon stitched on another strip of paper. The gentleman twitched his toes about in his sock, looking round at those in the hut, and as he did so he noticed Michael.

"Whom have you there?" asked he.

"That is my workman. He will sew the boots."

"Mind," said the gentleman to Michael, "remember to make them so that they will last me a year."

Simon also looked at Michael and saw that Michael was not looking at the gentleman, but was gazing into the corner behind the gentleman, as if he saw some one there. Michael looked and looked, and suddenly he smiled, and his face became brighter.

"What are you grinning at, you fool?" thundered the gentleman. "You had better look to it that the boots are ready in time."

"They shall be ready in good time," said Michael.

"Mind it is so," said the gentleman, and he put on his boots and his fur coat, wrapped the latter round him, and went to the door. But he forgot to stoop, and struck his head against the lintel.

He swore and rubbed his head. Then he took his seat in the carriage and drove away.

When he had gone, Simon said: "There's a figure of a man for you! You could not kill him with a mallet. He almost knocked out the lintel, but little harm it did him."

And Matryona said: "Living as he does, how should he not grow strong? Death itself can't touch such a rock as that."

VII

Then Simon said to Michael: "Well, we have taken the work, but we must see we don't get into trouble over it. The leather is dear, and the gentleman hot-tempered. We must make no mistakes. Come, your eye is truer and your hands have become nimbler than mine, so you take this measure and cut out the boots. I will finish off the sewing of the vamps."

Michael did as he was told. He took the leather, spread it out on the table, folded it in two, took a knife and began to cut out.

Matryona came and watched him cutting, and was surprised to see how he was doing it. Matryona was accustomed to seeing boots made, and she looked and saw that Michael was not cutting the leather for boots, but was cutting it round.

She wished to say something, but she thought to herself: "Perhaps I do not understand how gentleman's boots should be made. I suppose Michael knows more about it—and I won't interfere."

When Michael had cut up the leather, he took a thread and began to sew not with two ends, as boots are sewn, but with a single end, as for soft slippers.

Again Matryona wondered, but again she did not interfere. Michael sewed on steadily till noon. Then Simon rose for dinner, looked around, and saw that Michael had made slippers out of the gentleman's leather.

"Ah," groaned Simon, and he thought, "How is it that Michael, who has been with me a whole year and never made a mistake before, should do such a dreadful thing? The gentleman ordered high boots, welted, with whole fronts, and Michael has made soft slippers with single soles, and has wasted the leather. What am I to say to the gentleman? I can never replace leather such as this."

And he said to Michael, "What are you doing, friend? You have ruined me! You know the gentleman ordered high boots, but see what you have made!"

Hardly had he begun to rebuke Michael, when "rat-tat" went the iron ring that hung at the door. Some one was knocking. They looked out of the window; a man had come on horseback, and was fastening his horse. They opened the door, and the servant who had been with the gentleman came in.

"Good day," said he.

"Good day," replied Simon. "What can we do for you?"

"My mistress has sent me about the boots."

"What about the boots?"

"Why, my master no longer needs them. He is dead."

"Is it possible?"

"He did not live to get home after leaving you, but died in the carriage. When we reached home and the servants came to help him alight, he rolled over like a sack. He was dead already, and so stiff that he could hardly be got out of the carriage. My mistress sent me here, saying: 'Tell the bootmaker that the gentleman who ordered boots of him and left the leather for them no longer needs the boots, but that he must quickly make soft slippers for the corpse. Wait till they are ready, and bring them back with you.' That is why I have come."

Michael gathered up the remnants of the leather; rolled them up, took the soft slippers he had made, slapped them together, wiped them down with his apron, and handed them and the roll of leather to the servant, who took them and said: "Good-bye, masters, and good day to you!"

VIII

Another year passed, and another, and Michael was now living his sixth year with Simon. He lived as before. He went nowhere, only spoke when necessary, and had only smiled twice in all those years— once when Matryona gave him food, and a second time when the gentleman was in their hut. Simon was more than pleased with his workman. He never now asked him where he came from, and only feared lest Michael should go away.

They were all at home one day. Matryona was putting iron pots in the oven; the children were running along the benches and looking out of the window; Simon was sewing at one window, and Michael was fastening on a heel at the other.

One of the boys ran along the bench to Michael, leant on his shoulder, and looked out of the window.

"Look, Uncle Michael! There is a lady with little girls! She seems to be coming here. And one of the girls is lame."

When the boy said that, Michael dropped his work, turned to the window, and looked out into the street.

Simon was surprised. Michael never used to look out into the street, but now he pressed against the window, staring at something. Simon also looked out, and saw that a well-dressed woman was really coming to his hut, leading by the hand two little girls in fur coats and woolen shawls. The girls could hardly be told one from the other, except that one of them was crippled in her left leg and walked with a limp.

The woman stepped into the porch and entered the passage. Feeling about for the entrance she found the latch, which she lifted, and opened the door. She let the two girls go in first, and followed them into the hut.

"Good day, good folk!"

"Pray come in," said Simon. "What can we do for you?"

The woman sat down by the table. The two little girls pressed close to her knees, afraid of the people in the hut.

"I want leather shoes made for these two little girls for spring."

"We can do that. We never have made such small shoes, but we can make them; either welted or turnover shoes, linen lined. My man, Michael, is a master at the work."

Simon glanced at Michael and saw that he had left his work and was sitting with his eyes fixed on the little girls. Simon was surprised. It was true the girls were pretty, with black eyes, plump, and rosy-cheeked, and they wore nice kerchiefs and fur coats, but still Simon could not understand why Michael should look at them like that—

just as if he had known them before. He was puzzled, but went on talking with the woman, and arranging the price. Having fixed it, he prepared the measure. The woman lifted the lame girl on to her lap and said: "Take two measures from this little girl. Make one shoe for the lame foot and three for the sound one. They both have the same size feet. They are twins."

Simon took the measure and, speaking of the lame girl, said: "How did it happen to her? She is such a pretty girl. Was she born so?"

"No, her mother crushed her leg."

Then Matryona joined in. She wondered who this woman was, and whose the children were, so she said: "Are not you their mother then?"

"No, my good woman; I am neither their mother nor any relation to them. They were quite strangers to me, but I adopted them."

"They are not your children and yet you are so fond of them?"

"How can I help being fond of them? I fed them both at my own breasts. I had a child of my own, but God took him. I was not so fond of him as I now am of them."

"Then whose children are they?"

IX

The woman, having begun talking, told them the whole story.

"It is about six years since their parents died, both in one week: their father was buried on the Tuesday, and their mother died on the Friday. These orphans were born three days after their father's death, and their mother did not live another day. My husband and I were then living as peasants in the village. We were neighbors of theirs, our yard being next to theirs. Their father was a lonely man; a wood-cutter in the forest. When felling trees one day, they let one fall on him. It fell across his body and crushed his bowels out. They hardly got him home before his soul went to God; and that same week his wife gave birth to twins—these little girls. She was poor and alone; she had no one, young or old, with her. Alone she gave them birth, and alone she met her death.

"The next morning I went to see her, but when I entered the hut, she, poor thing, was already stark and cold. In dying she had rolled on to this child and crushed her leg. The village folk came to the hut, washed the body, laid her out, made a coffin, and buried her. They were good folk. The babies were left alone. What was to be done with them? I was the only woman there who had a baby at the time. I was nursing my first-born—eight weeks old. So I took them for a time. The peasants came together, and thought and thought what to do with them; and at last they said to me: "For the present, Mary, you had better keep the girls, and later on we will arrange what to do for them." So I nursed the sound one at my breast, but at first I did not feed this crippled one. I did not suppose she would live. But then I thought to myself, why should the poor innocent suffer? I pitied her, and began to feed her. And so I fed my own boy and these two—the three of them—at my own breast. I was young and strong, and had good food, and God gave me so much milk that at times it even overflowed. I used sometimes to feed two at a time, while the third was waiting. When one had enough I nursed the third. And God so ordered it that these grew up, while my own was buried before he was two years old. And I had no more children, though we prospered. Now my husband is working for the corn merchant at the mill. The pay is good, and we are well off. But I have no children of my own, and how lonely I should be without these little girls! How can I help loving them! They are the joy of my life!"

She pressed the lame little girl to her with one hand, while with the other she wiped the tears from her cheeks.

And Matryona sighed, and said: "The proverb is true that says, 'One may live without father or mother, but one cannot live without God.'"

So they talked together, when suddenly the whole hut was lighted up as though by summer lightning from the corner where Michael sat. They all looked towards him and saw him sitting, his hands folded on his knees, gazing upwards and smiling.

X

The woman went away with the girls. Michael rose from the bench, put down his work, and took off his apron. Then, bowing low to Simon and his wife, he said: "Farewell, masters. God has forgiven me. I ask your forgiveness, too, for anything done amiss."

And they saw that a light shone from Michael. And Simon rose, bowed down to Michael, and said: "I see, Michael, that you are no common man, and I can neither keep you nor question you. Only tell me this: how is it that when I found you and brought you home, you were gloomy, and when my wife gave you food you smiled at her and became brighter? Then when the gentleman came to order the boots, you smiled again and became brighter still? And now, when this woman brought the little girls, you smiled a third time, and have become as bright as day? Tell me, Michael, why does your face shine so, and why did you smile those three times?"

And Michael answered: "Light shines from me because I have been punished, but now God has pardoned me. And I smiled three times, because God sent me to learn three truths, and I have learnt them. One I learnt when your wife pitied me, and that is why I smiled the first time. The second I learnt when the rich man ordered the boots, and then I smiled again. And now, when I saw those little girls, I learnt the third and last, and I smiled the third time."

And Simon said, "Tell me, Michael, what did God punish you for? and what were the three truths? that I, too, may know them."

And Michael answered: "God punished me for disobeying Him. I was an angel in heaven and disobeyed God. God sent me to fetch a woman's soul. I flew to earth, and saw a sick woman lying alone, who had just given birth to twin girls. They moved feebly at their mother's side, but she could not lift them to her breast. When she saw me, she understood that God had sent me for her soul, and she wept and said: 'Angel of God! My husband has just been buried, killed by a falling tree. I have neither sister, nor aunt, nor mother: no one to care for my orphans. Do not take my soul! Let me nurse my babes, feed them, and set them on their feet before I die. Children cannot live without father or mother.' And I hearkened to her. I placed one child at her breast and gave the other into her arms, and returned to the Lord in heaven. I flew to the Lord, and said: 'I could not take the soul of the mother. Her husband was killed by a tree; the woman has twins, and prays that her soul may not be taken. She says: "Let me nurse and feed my children, and set them on their feet. Children cannot live without father or mother." I have not taken her soul.' And God said: 'Go—take the mother's soul, and learn three truths: Learn *What dwells in man*, *What is not given to man*, and *What men live by*. When thou hast learnt these things, thou shalt return to heaven.' So I flew again to earth and took the mother's soul. The babes dropped from her breasts. Her body rolled over on the bed and crushed one babe, twisting its leg. I rose above the village, wishing to take her soul to God; but a wind seized me, and my wings drooped and dropped off. Her soul rose alone to God, while I fell to earth by the roadside."

XI

And Simon and Matryona understood who it was that had lived with them, and whom they had clothed and fed. And they wept with awe and with joy. And the angel said: "I was alone in the field, naked. I had never known human needs, cold and hunger, till I became a man. I was famished, frozen, and did not know what to do. I saw, near the field I was in, a shrine built for God, and I went to it hoping to find shelter. But the shrine was locked, and I could not enter. So I sat down behind the shrine to shelter myself at least from the wind. Evening drew on. I was hungry, frozen, and in pain. Suddenly I heard a man coming along the road. He carried a pair of boots, and was talking to himself. For the first time since I became a man I saw the mortal face of a man, and his face seemed terrible to me and I turned from it. And I heard the man talking to himself of how to cover his body from the cold in winter, and how to feed wife and children. And I thought: "I am perishing of cold and hunger, and here is a man thinking only of how to clothe himself and his wife, and how to get bread for them-selves. He cannot help me. When the man saw me he frowned and became still more terrible, and passed me by on the other side. I despaired; but suddenly I heard him coming back. I looked up, and did not recognize the same man; before, I had seen death in his face; but now he was alive, and I recognized in him the presence of God. He came up to me, clothed me, took me with him, and brought me to his home. I entered the house; a woman came to meet us and began to speak. The woman was still more terrible than the man had been; the spirit of death came from her mouth; I could not breathe for the stench of death that spread around her. She wished to drive me out into the cold, and I knew that if she did so she would die. Suddenly her husband spoke to her of God, and the woman changed at once. And when she brought me food and looked at me, I glanced at her and saw that death no longer dwelt in her; she had become alive, and in her, too, I saw God.

"Then I remembered the first lesson God had set me: '*Learn what dwells in man.*' And I understood that in man dwells Love! I was glad that God had already begun to show me what He had promised, and I smiled for the first time. But I had not yet learnt all. I did not yet know *What is not given to man*, and *What men live by.*

"I lived with you and a year passed. A man came to order boots that should wear for a year without losing shape or cracking. I looked at him, and suddenly, behind his shoulder, I saw my comrade—the angel of death. None but me saw that angel; but I knew him, and knew that before the sun set he would take that rich man's soul. And I thought to myself, 'The man is making preparations for a year, and does not know that he will die before evening.' And I remembered God's second saying, 'Learn what is not given to man.'

"What dwells in man I already knew. Now I learnt what is not given him. It is not given to man to know his own needs. And I smiled for the second time. I was glad to have seen my comrade angel—glad also that God had revealed to me the second saying.

"But I still did not know all. I did not know *What men live by*. And I lived on, waiting till God should reveal to me the last lesson. In the sixth year came the girl-twins with the woman; and I recognized the girls, and heard how they had been kept alive. Having heard the story, I thought, 'Their mother besought me for the children's sake, and I believed her when she said that children cannot live without father or mother; but a stranger has nursed them, and has brought them up.' And when the woman showed her love for the children that were not her own, and wept over them, I saw in her the living God and understood *What men live by*. And I knew that God had revealed to me the last lesson, and had forgiven my sin. And then I smiled for the third time."

XII

And the angel's body was bared, and he was clothed in light so that eye could not look on him; and his voice grew louder, as though it came not from him but from heaven above. And the angel said:

"I have learnt that all men live not by care for themselves but by love.

"It was not given to the mother to know what her children needed for their life. Nor was it given to the rich man to know what he himself needed. Nor is it given to any man to know whether, when evening comes, he will need boots for his body or slippers for his corpse.

"I remained alive when I was a man, not by care of myself, but because love was present in a passer-by, and because he and his wife pitied and loved me. The orphans remained alive not because of their mother's care, but because there was love in the heart of a woman, a stranger to them, who pitied and loved them. And all men live not by the thought they spend on their own welfare, but because love exists in man.

"I knew before that God gave life to men and desires that they should live; now I understood more than that.

"I understood that God does not wish men to live apart, and therefore he does not reveal to them what each one needs for himself; but he wishes them to live united, and therefore reveals to each of them what is necessary for all.

"I have now understood that though it seems to men that they live by care for themselves, in truth it is love alone by which they live. He who has love, is in God, and God is in him, for God is love."

And the angel sang praise to God, so that the hut trembled at his voice. The roof opened, and a column of fire rose from earth to heaven. Simon and his wife and children fell to the ground. Wings appeared upon the angel's shoulders, and he rose into the heavens.

And when Simon came to himself the hut stood as before, and there was no one in it but his own family.

ANTHONY TROLLOPE

GEORGE ELIOT—ONE OF THE MOST SUCCESSFUL AND INFLU-
ential of the Victorian era's writers—once commented that she could not have
written *Middlemarch* without the precedent set by Anthony Trollope's novels.
Born in London in 1815, Trollope was the fifth of seven children. His father
was a failed barrister who, in 1834, fled with his family to Belgium in order to
avoid his increasing debts; while living there, Trollope became an usher at a
school in Brussels, hoping that while working there he might learn enough
French and German to be given a commission with an Austrian cavalry regiment. But this was not to be, as he took a position that fall as a junior clerk in
the General Post office in London. For seven years he lived and worked in
poverty, until in 1841 he was transferred to Ireland to serve as a deputy postal
surveyor; he married Rode Heseltine in 1844.

The new life and culture around him stirred his imagination, and it was
here that he began his most prolific writing career. Though he continued to
work for the postal service until 1867, rising in the ranks from junior clerk to
surveyor general, he also authored over 40 novels during his lifetime, among
them the much-loved Chronicles of Barsetshire series. Set in the imaginary
English countryside of Barset, these books include his most important volume, *Barchester Towers*, and relate primarily the life and times of the Victorian

countryside clergy. He is most noted for his ability to capture the joy and sorrow, delight and puzzlement and charm and reality of everyday English life. He died of a paralytic stroke in London in December of 1882.

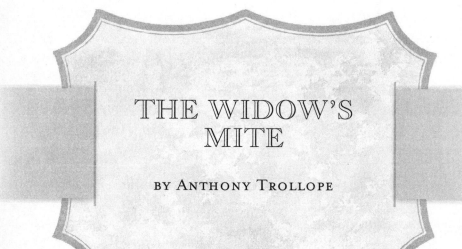

THE WIDOW'S MITE

BY ANTHONY TROLLOPE

B ut I'm not a widow, and I haven't got two mites."

"My dear, you are a widow, and you have got two mites."

"I'll tell both of you something that will astonish you. I've made a calculation, and I find that if everybody in England would give up their Christmas dinner—that is, in Scotland, and Ireland too—"

"They never have any in Ireland, Bob."

"Hold your tongue till I've done, Charley. They do have Christmas dinners in Ireland. It's pretty nearly the only day that they do, and I don't count much upon them either. But if everybody gave up his special Christmas dinner, and dined as he does on other days, the saving would amount to two millions and a half."

Charley whistled.

"Two millions and a half is a large sum of money," said Mrs Granger, the elder lady of the party.

"Those calculations never do any good," said the younger lady, who had declared herself not to be a widow.

"Those calculations do a great deal of good," continued Bob, carrying on his argument with continued warmth. "They show us what a great national effort would do."

"A little national effort, I should call that," said Mrs Granger. "But I should doubt the two millions and a half."

"Half-a-crown a-head on thirty million people would do it. You are to include all the beer, wine, and whisky. But suppose you take off one-fifth for the babies and young girls, who don't drink."

"Thank you, Bob," said the younger lady—Nora Field by name.

"And two more fifths for the poor, who haven't got the half-crown a-head," said the elder lady.

"And you'd ruin the grocer and butcher," said Charley.

"And never get your half-crown, after all," said Nora.

It need hardly be said that the subject under discussion was the best mode of abstracting from the pockets of the non-suffering British public a sufficiency of money to sustain the suffering portion during the period of the cotton famine.

Mr Granger was the rector of Plumstock, a parish in Cheshire, sufficiently near to the manufacturing districts to give to every incident of life at that time a colouring taken from the distress of the neighbourhood; which had not, however, itself ever depended on cotton,— for Plumstock boasted that it was purely agricultural. Mr Granger was the chairman of a branch relief committee, which had its centre in Liverpool; and the subject of the destitution, with the different modes by which it might be, should be, or should not be relieved, were constantly under discussion in the rectory. Mr Granger himself was a practical man, somewhat hard in his manners, but by no means hard in his heart, who had in these times taken upon himself the business of alms-begging on a large scale. He declined to look at the matter in a political, statistical, or economical point of view, and answered all questions as to rates, rates in aid, loans, and the Consolidated Fund, with a touch of sarcasm, which showed the bent of his own mind.

"I've no doubt you'll have settled all that in the wisest possible way by the time that the war is over, and the river full of cotton again."

"Father," Bob replied, pointing across the Cheshire flats to the Mersey, "that river will never again be full of American cotton."

"It will be all the same for the present purpose, if it comes from

India," said the rector declining to present argument on the great American question.

To collect alms was his immediate work, and he would do nothing else. Five-pound notes, sovereigns, half-crowns, shillings, and pence! In search of these he was urgent, we may almost say day and night, begging with a pertinacity which was disagreeable, but irresistible. The man who gave him five sovereigns instantly became the mark for another petition.

"When you have got your dinner, you have not done with the butcher for ever," he would say in answer to reproaches. "Of course, we must go on as long as this thing lasts."

Then his friends and neighbours buttoned up their pockets; but Mr Granger would extract coin from them even when buttoned.

The two younger men who had taken part in the above argument were his sons. The elder, Charles, was at Oxford, but now in these Christmas days—for Christmas was close at hand—had come home. Bob, the second son, was in a merchant's house in Liverpool, intending to become, in the fulness of time, a British merchant prince. It had been hinted to him, however, more than once, that if he would talk a little less and work a little harder, the path to his princedom would be quicker found than if his present habits were maintained. Nora Field was Mrs Granger's niece. She was Miss Field, and certainly not a widow in the literal sense of the word; but she was about to become a bride a few weeks after Christmas.

"It is spoil from the Amalekites," Mr Granger had said, when she had paid in some contribution from her slender private stores to his treasury:—"spoil from the Amalekites, and therefore the more precious."

He had called Nora Field's two sovereigns spoil from the Amalekites, because she was about to marry an American.

Frederic Frew, or Frederic F. Frew, as he delighted to hear himself called, for he had been christened Franklin as well as Frederic,—and to an American it is always a point of honour that, at any rate, the initial of his second Christian name should be remembered by all men,— was a Pennsylvanian from Philadelphia; a strong Democrat, according to the politics of his own country, hating the Republicans, as the Tories used to hate the Whigs among us before political feeling had become extinct, speaking against Lincoln the President, and Seward his minister, and the Fremonts, and Sumners, and Philipses, and Beechers of the Republican party, fine hard racy words of powerful condemnation, such as used to be spoken against Earl Grey and his followers, but nevertheless as steady for the war as Lincoln, or Seward, or any Republican of them all;—as steady for the war, and as keen in his bitterness against England.

His father had been a partner in a house of business, of which the chief station had been in Liverpool. That house had now closed its transactions, and young Frew was living and intended to live an easy idle life on the moderate fortune which had been left to him; but the circumstances of his family affairs had made it necessary for him to pass many months in Liverpool, and during that sojourn he had become engaged to Nora Field. He had traveled much, going everywhere with his eyes open, as Americans do. He knew many things, had read many books, and was decided in his opinion on most subjects. He was good-looking too, and well-mannered; was kindly-hearted, and capable of much generosity. But he was hard, keen in his intelligence, but not broad in genius, thin and meager in aspirations,—not looking to or even desirous of anything great, but indulging a profound contempt for all that is very small. He was a well-instructed, but by no means learned man, who greatly despised those who were ignorant. I fear that he hated England in his heart; but he did not hate Nora Field, and was about to make her his wife in three or four weeks from the present time.

When Nora declared to her aunt that she was not a widow, and that she possessed no two mites, and when her aunt flatly contradicted her, stating that she was a widow, and did possess two mites, they had not intended to be understood by each other literally. It was an old dispute between them.

"What the widow gave," said Nora, "she gave off her own poor back, and therefore was very cold. She gave it out of her own poor mouth, and was very hungry afterwards in consequence. I have given my two pounds, but I shall not be cold or hungry. I wish I was a widow with two mites; only, the question is whether I should not keep them for my own back after all, and thus gain nothing by the move."

"As to that," replied her aunt, "I cannot speak. But the widowhood and the two mites are there for us all, if we choose to make use of them."

"In these days," said Bob, "the widows with two mites should not be troubled at all. We can do it all without them, if we go to work properly."

"If you had read your Bible properly, sir," said Mrs Granger, "you would understand that the widows would not thank you for the exemption."

"I don't want the widows to thank me. I only want to live, and allow others to live according to the existing circumstances of the world." It was manifest from Bob's tone that he regarded his mother than little better than an old fogey.

In January, Nora was to become Mrs Frederic F. Frew, and be at once taken away to new worlds, new politics, and new loves and hatreds. Like a true, honest-hearted girl as she was, she had already become half an American in spirit. She was an old Union American, and as such was strong against the South; and in return for her fervour in that matter, her future husband consented to abstain from any present loud abuse of things English, and generously allowed her to defend her own country when it was abused. This was much as coming from an American. Let us hope that the same privilege may be accorded to her in her future home in Philadelphia. But in the meantime, during these last weeks of her girlhood, these cold, cruel weeks of desperate want, she strove vigorously to do what little might be in her power for the poor of the country she was leaving. All this want had been occasioned by the wretched rebels of the South.

This was her theory. And she was right in much of this. Whether the Americans of the South are wretched or are rebels we will not say here, but of this there can be no doubt, that they created all the misery which we then endured.

"But I have no way of making myself a widow," she said again. "Uncle Robert would not let me give away the cloak he gave me the other day."

"He would have to give you another," said Mrs Granger.

"Exactly. It is not so easy, after all, to be a widow with two mites!"

Nora Field had no fortune of her own, nor was her uncle in a position to give her any. He was not a poor man; but like many men who are not poor, he had hardly a pound of his own in the shape of ready money.

To Nora and to her cousins, and to certain other first cousins of the same family, had been left, some eighteen months since, by a grand-aunt, a hundred pounds a-piece, and with this hundred pounds Nora was providing for herself her wedding trousseau.

A hundred pounds do not go far in such provision, as some young married women who may read this will perhaps acknowledge; but Mr Frederic F. Frew had been told all about it, and he was contented. Miss Field was fond of nice clothes, and had been tempted more than once to wish that her great-aunt had left them all two hundred pounds a-piece instead of one.

"If I were to cast in my wedding veil?" said Nora.

"That will be your husband's property," said her aunt.

"Ah, but before I'm married."

"Then why have it at all?"

"It is ordered, you know."

"Couldn't you bedizen yourself with one made of false lace?" said her uncle. "Frew would never find it out, and that would be a most satisfactory spoiling of the Amalekite."

"He isn't an Amalekite, uncle Robert. Or if he is, I'm another."

"Just so; and therefore false lace will be quite good enough for you. Molly,"—Mrs Granger's name was Molly,—"I've promised to let them have the use of the great boiler in the back kitchen once a-week, and you are to furnish them with fuel."

"Oh, dear!" said Mrs Granger, upon whose active charity the loan of her own kitchen boiler made a strain that was almost too severe. But she recovered herself in half a minute. "Very well, my dear; but you won't expect any dinner on that day."

"No; I shall expect no dinner; only some food in the rough. You may boil that in the copper too if you like it."

"You know, my dear, that you don't like anything boiled."

"As for that, Molly, I don't suppose any of them like it. They'd all prefer roast mutton."

"The copper will be your two mites," whispered the niece.

"Only I have not thrown them in of my own accord," said Mrs Granger.

Mr Frew, who was living in Liverpool, always came over to Plumstock on Friday evening, and spent Saturday and Sunday with the rector and his family. For him those Saturdays were happy days, for Frederic F. Frew was a good lover. He liked to be with Nora, to walk with her, and to talk with her. He liked to show her that he loved her, and to make himself gracious and pleasant. I am not so sure that his coming was equally agreeable to Mr Granger. Mr Frew would talk about American politics, praising the feeling and spirit of his countrymen in the North; whereas Mr Granger, when driven into the subject, was constrained to make a battle for the South. All his prejudices, and what he would have called his judgment, went with the South, and he was not ashamed of his opinion; but he disliked arguing with Frederic F. Frew. I fear it must be confessed that Frederic F. Frew was too strong for him in such arguments. Why it should be so I cannot say; but an American argues more closely on politics than does an Englishman. His convictions are not the truer on that account; very often the less

true, as are the conclusions of a logician, because he trusts to syllo-
gisms which are often false, instead of to the experience of his life and
daily workings of his mind. But though not more true in his political convictions than an Englishman, he is more answerable, and therefore Mr
Granger did not care to discuss the subject of the American war with
Frederic F. Frew.

"It riles me," Frew said, as he sat after dinner in the Plumstock
drawing-room on the Friday evening before Christmas Day, "to hear
your folks talking of our elections. They think the war will come to an
end, and the rebels of the South have their own way, because the
Democrats have carried the ticket."

"It will have that tendency," said the parson.

"Not an inch; any more than your carrying the Reform Bill or
repealing the Corn Laws had a tendency to put down the throne. It's
the same sort of argument. Your two parties were at daggers drawn
about the Reform Bill; but that did not cause you to split on all other
matters."

"But the throne wasn't in question," said the parson.

"Nor is the war in question; not in that way. The most popular
Democrat in the States at this moment is M'Clellan."

"And they say no one is so anxious to see the war ended."

"Whoever says so slanders him. If you don't trust his deeds, look
at his words."

"I believe in neither," said the parson.

"Then put him aside as a nobody. But you can't do that, for he is
the man whom the largest party in the Northern States trusts most
implicitly. The fact is, sir," and Frederic F. Frew gave the proper twang

to the last letter of the last word, "you, none of you here, understand our politics. You can't realise the blessing of a—"

"Molly, give me some tea," said the rector, in a loud voice. When matters went as far as this he did not care by what means he stopped the voice of his future relative.

"All I say is this," continued Frew, "you will find out your mistake if you trust to the Democratic elections to put an end to the war, and bring cotton back to Liverpool."

"And what is to put an end to the war?" asked Nora.

"Victory and union," said Frederic F. Frew.

"Exhaustion," said Charley, from Oxford.

"Compromise," said Bobby, from Liverpool.

"The Lord Almighty, when He shall have done His work," said the parson. "And, in the meantime, Molly, do you keep plenty of fire under the kitchen boiler."

That was clearly the business of the present hour, for all in Mr Granger's part of the country;—we may say, indeed, for all on Mr Granger's side of the water. It mattered little, then, in Lancashire, whether New York might have a Democratic or a Republican governor. The old cotton had been burned; the present crop could not be garnered; the future crop—the crop which never would be future, could not get itself sown.

Mr Granger might be a slow politician, but he was a practical man, understanding the things immediately around him; and they all were aware, Frederic F. Frew with the rest of them, that he was right when he bade his wife keep the fire well hot beneath the kitchen boiler.

"Isn't it almost wicked to be married in such a time as this?" It was much later in the evening when Nora, still troubled in her mind about her widow's mite, whispered these words into her lover's ears. If she were to give up her lover for twelve months, would not that be a throwing in of something to the treasury from off her own back and out of her own mouth? But then this matter of her marriage had been so fully settled that she feared to think of disturbing it. He would never consent to such a postponement. And then the offering, to be of avail for her, must be taken from her own back, not from his; and Nora had an idea that in the making of such an offering as that suggested, Mr Frederic F. Frew would conceive he had contributed by far the greater part. Her uncle called him an Amalekite, and she doubted whether it would be just to spoil an Amalekite after such a fashion as that. Nevertheless, into his ears she whispered her little proposition.

"Wicked to get married!" said Frederic; "not according to my idea of the Christian religion."

"Oh! But you know what I mean," and she gave his arm a slight caressing pinch.

At this time her uncle had gone to his own room; her cousins had gone to their studies, by which I believe they intended to signify the proper smoking of a pipe of tobacco in the rectory kitchen; and Mrs Granger, seated in her easy chair, had gone to her slumbers, dreaming of the amount of fuel with which the kitchen boiler must be supplied.

"I shall bring a breach of promise against you," said Frederic, "if you don't appear in church with bridal array on Monday, the 12th of January, and pay the penalty into the war-treasury. That would be a spoiling of the Amalekite."

Then he got hold of the fingers which had pinched him.

"Of course I shan't put it off, unless you agree."

"Of course you won't."

"But, dear Fred, don't you think we ought?"

"No; certainly not. If I thought you were in earnest I would scold you."

"I am in earnest, quite. You need not look in that way, for you know very well how truly I love you. You know I want to be your wife above all things."

"Do you?"

And then he began to insinuate his arm around her waist; but she got up and moved away, not as in anger at his caress, but as showing that the present moment was unfit for it.

"I do," she said, "above all things. I love you so well that I could hardly bear to see you go away again without taking me with you. I could hardly bear it,—but I could bear it."

"Could you? Then I couldn't. I'm a weaker vessel than you, and your strength must give way to my weakness."

"I know I've no right to tax you, if you really care about it."

Frederic F. Frew made no answer to this in words, but pursued her in her retreat from the sofa on which they had sat.

"Don't, Fred. I am so much in earnest! I wish I knew what I ought to do to throw in my two mites."

"Not throw me over certainly, and break all the promises you have made for the last twelve months. You can't be in earnest. It's out of the question, you know."

"Oh! I am in earnest."

"I never heard of such a thing in my life. What good would it do?

It wouldn't bring the cotton in. It wouldn't feed the poor. It wouldn't keep your aunt's boiler hot."

"No; that it wouldn't," said Mrs Granger, starting up; "and coals are such a terrible price."

Then she went to sleep again, and ordered in large supplies in her dreams.

"But I should have done as much as the widow did. Indeed I should, Fred. Oh, dear! To have to give you up! But I only meant for a year."

"As you are so very fond of me—"

"Of course I'm fond of you. Should I let you do like that if I was not?"

At the moment of her speaking he had again got his arm round her waist.

"Then I'm too charitable to allow you to postpone your happiness for a day. We'll look at it that way."

"You won't understand me, or rather you do understand me, and pretend that you don't, which is very wrong."

"I always was very wicked."

"Then why don't you make yourself better? Do not you too wish to be a widow? You ought to wish it."

"I should like to have an opportunity of trying married life first."

"I won't stay any longer with you, sir, because you are scoffing. Aunt, I'm going to bed." Then she returned again across the room, and whispered to her lover, "I'll tell you what, sir, I'll marry you on Monday, the 12th of January, if you'll take me just as I am now; with a bonnet on, and a shawl over my dress, exactly as I walked out with you before dinner. When I made the promise, I never said anything about fine clothes."

"You may come in an old red cloak, if you like it."

"Very well; now mind I've got your consent. Good night, sir. After all it will only be half a mite."

She had turned towards the door, and had her hand upon the lock, but she came back into the room, close up to him.

"It will not be a quarter of a mite," she said. "How can it be anything if I get you?" Then she kissed him, and hurried away out of the room, before he could again speak to her.

"What, what, what!" said Mrs Granger, waking up. "So Nora has gone, has she?"

"Gone; yes, just this minute," said Frew, who had turned his face to the fire, so that the tear in his eyes might not be seen. As he took himself off to his bed, he swore to himself that Nora Field was a trump, and that he had done well in securing for himself such a wife; but it never occurred to him that she was in any way in earnest about her wedding dress. She was a trump because she was so expressive in her love to himself, and because her eyes shone so brightly when she spoke eagerly on any matter; but as to her appearing at the altar in a red cloak, or, as was more probable, in her own customary thick woollen shawl, he never thought about it. Of course she would be married as other girls are married.

Nor had Nora thought of it till that moment in which she made the proposition to her lover. As she had said before, her veil was ordered and so was her white silk dress. Her bonnet also had been ordered, with its bridal wreath, and the other things assorting therewith. A vast hole was to be made in her grand-aunt's legacy for the payment of all this finery; but, as Mrs Granger had said to her, in so spending it, she would best please her future husband. He had enough of his own, and would not care that she should provide herself with articles which he could afterwards give her, at the expense of that little smartness at his wedding which an American likes, at any rate, as well as an Englishman. Nora, with an honesty which some ladies may not admire, had asked her lover the question in the plainest language.

"You will have to buy my things so much the sooner," she had said.

"I'd buy them all to-morrw, only you'll not let me."

"I should rather think not, Master Fred."

Then she had gone off with her aunt, and ordered her wedding-clothes. But now as she prepared for bed, after the conversation which has just been recorded, she began to think in earnest whether it would not be well to dispense with white silk and orange-wreaths while so many were dispensing with—were forced to dispense with bread and fuel. Could she bedizen herself with finery from Liverpool, while her uncle was, as she well knew, refusing himself a set of new shirts which he wanted sorely, in order that he might send to the fund at Liverpool the money which they would cost him. He was throwing in his two mites daily, as was her aunt, who toiled unceasingly at woollen shawls and woollen stockings, so that she went on knitting even in her sleep. But she, Nora, since the earnestness of these bad days began, had done little or nothing. Her needle, indeed, had been very busy, but it had been busy in preparation for Mr Frederic F. Frew's nuptials. Even Bob and Charley worked for the relief committee; but she had done nothing,—nothing but given her two pounds. She had offered four, but her uncle, with a self-restraint never before or afterwards practised by him, had chucked her back two, saying that he would not be too hard even upon an Amalekite. As she thought of the word, she asked herself whether or not it was more incumbent on her, than on any one else, to do something in the way of self-sacrifice. She was now a Briton, but would shortly be an American. Should it be said of her that the distress of her own countrywomen,—the countrywomen whom she was leaving, did not wring her heart? It was not without a pang that she prepared to give up that nationality, which all its owners rank as the first in the world, and most of those who do not own it, rank, if not first, then as the second. Now it seemed to her as though she were deserting her own family in its distress, deserting her own ship in the time of its storm, and she was going over to those from whom this distress and this storm had come! Was it not needful that she should do something,—that she should satisfy herself that she had been willing to suffer in the cause?

She would throw in her two mites if she did but know where to find them.

"I could only do it, in truth," she said to herself, as she rose from her prayers, "by throwing in him. I have got over very great treasure, but I have not got anything else that I care about. After all, it isn't so easy to be a widow with two mites."

Then she sat down and thought about it. As to postponing her marriage, that she knew to be in truth quite out of the question. Even if she could bring herself to do it, everybody about her would say that she was mad, and Mr Frederic F. Frew might not impossibly destroy himself with one of those pretty revolvers which he sometimes brought out from Liverpool for her to play with. But was it not practicable for her to give up her wedding-clothes? There would be considerable difficulty even in this. As to their having been ordered, that might be overcome by the sacrifice of some portion of the price. But then her aunt, and even her uncle, would oppose her; her cousins would cover her with ridicule; in the latter matter she might, however, achieve something of her widowhood:—and, after all, the loss would fall more upon F. F. Frew than upon herself. She really did not care, for herself, in what clothes she was married, so that she was made his wife. But as regarded him, might it not be disagreeable to him to stand before the altar with a dowdy creature in an old gown? And then there was one other consideration. Would it not seem that she was throwing in her two mites publicly, before the eyes of all men, as a Pharisee might do it? Would there not be ostentation in her widowhood? But as she continued to reflect, she cast this last thought behind her. It might be so said of her, but if such a saying were untrue, if the offering were made in a widow's spirit, and not in the spirit of a Pharisee, would it not be cowardly to regard what men might say? Such false accusation would make some part of the two mites.

"I'll go into Liverpool about it on Monday," she said to herself as she finally tucked the clothes around her.

Early in the following morning she was up and out of her room, with the view of seeing her aunt before she came down to breakfast; but the first person she met was her uncle. He accosted her in one of the passages.

"What, Nora, this is early for you! Are you going to have a morning lovers' walk with Frederic Franklin?"

"Frederic Franklin, as you choose to call him, uncle," said Nora, "never comes out of his room much before breakfast time. And it's raining hard."

"Such a lover as he is ought not to mind rain."

"But I should mind it, very much. But, uncle, I want to speak to you, very seriously. I have been making up my mind about something."

"There's nothing wrong; is there, my dear?"

"No; there's nothing very wrong. It is not exactly about anything being wrong. I hardly know how to tell you what it is."

And then she paused, and he could see by the light of the candle in his hand that she blushed.

"Hadn't you better speak to your aunt?" said Mr Granger.

"That's what I meant to do when I got up," said Nora; "but as I have met you, if you don't mind—"

He assured her that he did not mind, and putting his hand upon her shoulder caressingly, promised her any assistance in his power.

"I'm not afraid that you will ask anything I ought not to do for you."

Then she revealed to him her scheme, turning her face away from him as she spoke. "It will be so horrid," she said, "to have a great box of finery coming home when you are all giving up everything for the poor people. And if you don't think it would be wrong—"

"It can't be wrong," said her uncle. "It may be a question whether it would be wise."

"I mean wrong to him. If it was to be any other clergyman, I should be ashamed of it. But as you are to marry us—"

"I don't think you need mind about the clergyman."

"And of course I should tell the Foster girls."

"The Foster girls?"

"Yes; they are to be my bridesmaids, and I am nearly sure they have not bought anything new yet. Of course they would think it all very dowdy, but I don't care a bit about that. I should just tell them that we had all made up our minds that we couldn't afford wedding-clothes. That would be true, wouldn't it?"

"But the question is about that wild American?"

"He isn't a wild American."

"Well, then, about that tamed American. What will he say?"

"He said I might come in an old cloak."

"You have told him, then?"

"But I am afraid he thought I was only joking. But, uncle, if you'll help me, I think I can bring him around."

"I daresay you can—to anything, just at present."

"I didn't at all mean that. Indeed, I'm sure I couldn't bring him round to putting off the marriage."

"No, no, no; not to that; to anything else."

"I know you are laughing at me, but I don't much mind being laughed at. I should save very nearly fifteen pounds, if not quite. Think of that!"

"And you'd give it all to the soup-kitchen?"

"I'd give it all to you for the distress."

Then her uncle spoke to her somewhat gravely.

"You're a good girl, Nora,—a dear good girl. I think I understand your thoughts on this matter, and I love you for them. But I doubt whether there be any necessity for you to make the sacrifice. A marriage should be a gala festival according to the means of the people married, and the bridegroom has a right to expect that his bride shall come to him fairly arrayed, and bright with wedding trappings. I think we can do, my pet, without robbing you of your little braveries."

"Oh, as for that, of course you can do without me."

There was a little soreness in her tone; not because she was feeling herself to be misunderstood, but because she knew that she could not explain herself further. She could not tell her uncle that the poor among the Jews might have been relieved without the contribution of those two mites, but that the widow would have lost all had she not so contributed. She had hardly arranged her thoughts as to the double blessing of charity, and certainly could not express them with reference to her own case; but she felt the need of giving in this time of trouble something that she herself valued. She was right when she had said that it was hard to be a widow. How many among us, when we give, give from off our own backs, and from out of our own mouths? Who can say that he has sacrificed a want of his own; that he has abandoned a comfort; that he has worn a thread-bare coat, with coats when their gloss on have been his customary wear; that he has fared roughly on cold scraps, whereas a well-spread board has been his usual daily practice? He who has done so has thrown in his two mites, and for him will Charity produce her double blessing.

Nora thought that it was not well in her uncle to tell her that he could do without her wedding-clothes. Of course he could do without them. But she soon threw those words behind her, and went back upon the words which had preceded them. "The bridegroom has a right to expect that the bride shall come to him fairly arrayed." After all, that must depend on circumstances. Suppose the bride had no means of arraying herself fairly without getting into debt; what would the bride-groom expect in that case?

"If he'll consent, you will?" she said, as she prepared to leave her uncle.

"You'll drive him to offer to pay for the thing himself."

"I daresay he will, and then he'll drive me to refuse. You may be quite sure of this, uncle, that whatever clothes I do wear, he will never see the bill of them"; and then that conference was ended.

"I've made that calculation again," said Bob at breakfast, "and I feel convinced that if an Act of Parliament could be passed restricting the consumption of food in Christmas week,—the entire week, mind,—to that of ordinary weeks, we should get two millions of money, and that those two millions would tide us over till the Indian cotton comes in. Of course I mean by food, butchers' meat, groceries, spirits, and wines. Only think, that by one measure, which would not entail any real disappointment on any one, the whole thing would be done."

"But the Act of Parliament wouldn't give us the money," said his father.

"Of course I don't really mean an Act of Parliament; that would be absurd. But the people might give up their Christmas dinners."

"A great many will, no doubt. Many of those most in earnest are pretty nearly giving up their daily dinners. Those who are indifferent will go on feasting the same as ever. You can't make a sacrifice obligatory."

"It would be no sacrifice if you did," said Nora, still thinking of her wedding-clothes.

"I doubt whether sacrifices ever do any real good," said Frederic F. Frew.

"Oh, Fred!" said Nora.

"We have rather high authority as to the benefit of self-denial," said the parson.

"A man who can't sacrifice himself must be selfish," said Bobby; "and we are all agreed to hate selfish people."

"And what about the widow's mite?" said Mrs Granger.

"That's all very well, and you may knock me down with the Bible if you like, as you might do also if I talked about pre-Adamite formations. I believe every word of the Bible, but I do not believe that I understand it all thoroughly."

"You might understand it better if you studied it more," said the parson.

"Very likely. I won't be so uncourteous as to say the same thing of my elders. But now, about these sacrifices. You wouldn't wish to keep people in distress that you might benefit yourself by releasing them?"

"But the people in distress are there," said Nora.

"They oughtn't to be there; and as your self-sacrifices, after all, are very insufficient to prevent distress, there certainly seems to be a question open whether some other mode should not be tried. Give me the country in which the humanitarian principle is so exercised that no one shall be degraded by the receipt of charity. It seems to me that you like poor people here in England that you may gratify yourselves by giving them, not as much to eat as they want, but just enough to keep their skins from falling off their bones. Charity may have its double blessing, but it may also have its double curse."

"Not charity, Mr Frew," said Mrs Granger.

"Look at your Lady Bountifuls."

"Of course it depends on the heart," continued the lady; "but charity, if it be charity—"

"I'll tell you what," said Frederic F. Frew, interrupting her. "In Philadelphia, which in some matters is the best organised city I know—"

"I'm going down to the village," said the parson, jumping up. "Who is to come with me?" and he escaped out of the room before Frew had had an opportunity of saying a word further about Philadelphia.

"That's the way with your uncle always," said he, turning to Nora, almost in anger. "It certainly is the most conclusive argument I know—that of running away."

"Mr Granger meant it to be conclusive," said the elder lady.

"But the pity is that it never convinces."

"Mr Granger probably had no desire of convincing."

"Ah! Well, it does not signify," said Frew. "When a man has a pulpit of his own, why should he trouble himself to argue in any place where counter arguments must be met and sustained?"

Nora was almost angry with her lover, whom she regarded as stronger and more clever than any of her uncle's family, but tyrannical and sometimes overbearing in the use of his strength. One by one her aunt and cousins left the room, and she was left alone with him. He had taken up a newspaper as a refuge in his wrath, for in truth he did not like the manner in which his allusions to his own country were generally treated at the Parsonage. There are Englishmen who think that every man differing with them is bound to bet with them on any point in dispute. "Then you decline to back your opinion," such men say when the bet is refused. The feeling of an American is the same as to those who are unwilling to argue with him. He considers that every intelligent being is bound to argue whenever matter of argument is offered to him; nor can he understand that any subject may be too sacred for argument. Frederic F. Frew, on the present occasion, was as a dog from whose very mouth a bone had been taken. He had given one or two loud, open growls, and now sat with his newspaper, showing his teeth as far as the spirit of the thing went. And it was in this humour that Nora found herself called upon to attack him on the question of her own proposed charity. She knew well that he could bark, even at her, if things went wrong with him. "But then he never bites," she said to herself. He had told her that she might come to her wedding in an old cloak if she pleased, but she has understood that there was nothing serious in this permission. Now, at this very moment, it was incumbent on her to open his eyes to the reality of her intention.

"Fred," she said, "are you reading that newspaper because you are angry with me?"

"I am reading the newspaper because I want to know what there is in it."

"You know all that now, just as well as if you had written it. Put it down, sir!" And she put her hand on to the top of the sheet. "If we are to be married in three weeks' time, I expect that you will be a little attentive to me now. You'll read as many papers as you like after that, no doubt."

"Upon my word, Nora, I think your uncle is the most unfair man I ever met in my life."

"Perhaps he thinks the same of you, and that will make it equal."

"He can't think the same of me. I defy him to think that I'm unfair. There's nothing so unfair as hitting a blow, and then running away when the time comes for receiving the counterblow. It's what your

Lord Chatham did, and he never ought to have been listened to in Parliament again."

"That's a long time ago," said Nora, who probably felt that her lover should not talk to her about Lord Chatham just three weeks before their marriage.

"I don't know that the time makes any difference."

"Ah! But I have got something else that I want to speak about. And, Fred, you mustn't turn up your nose at what we are all doing here,—as to giving away things, I mean."

"I don't turn up my nose at it. Haven't I been begging of every American in Liverpool till I'm ashamed of myself?"

"I know you have been very good, and now you must be more good still,—good to me specially, I mean. That isn't being good. That's only being foolish." What little ceremony had led to this last assertion I need not perhaps explain. "Fred, I'm an Englishwoman to-day, but in a month's time I shall be an American."

"I hope so, Nora,—heart and soul."

"Yes; that is what I mean. Whatever is my husband's country must be mine. And you know how well I love your country; do you not? I never run away when you talk to me about Philadelphia,—do I? And you know how I admire all your institutions,—my institutions, as they will be."

"Now I know you're going to ask some very great favour."

"Yes, I am; and I don't mean to be refused, Master Fred. I'm to be an American almost to-morrow, but as yet I am an Englishwoman, and I am bound to do what little I can before I leave my country. Don't you think so?"

"I don't quite understand."

"Well, it's about my wedding-clothes. It does seem stupid talking about them, I know. But I want you to let me do without them altogether. Now you've got the plain truth. I want to give uncle Robert the money for his soup-kitchen, and to be married just as I am now. I do not care one straw what any other creature in the world may say about it, so long as I do not displease you."

"I think it's nonsense, Nora."

"Oh, Fred, don't say so. I have set my heart upon it. I'll do anything for you afterwards. Indeed, for the matter of that, I'd do anything on earth for you, whether you agree or whether you do not. You know that."

"But, Nora, you wouldn't wish to make yourself appear foolish? How much money will you save?"

"Very nearly twenty pounds altogether."

"Let me give you twenty pounds, so that you may leave it with your uncle by way of your two mites, as you call it."

"No, no, certainly not. I might just as well send you the milliner's bill, might I not?"

"I don't see why you shouldn't do that."

"Ah, but I do. You wouldn't wish me to be guilty of the pretence of giving a thing away, and then doing it out of your pocket. I have no doubt that what you were saying about the evil of promiscuous charity is quite true." And then, as she flattered him with this wicked flattery, she looked up with her bright eyes into his face. "But now, as the things are, we must be charitable, or the people will die. I feel almost like a rat leaving a falling house, in going away at this time; and if you would postpone it—"

"Nora!"

"Then I must be like a rat; but I won't be a rat in a white silk gown. Come now, say that you agree. I never asked you for anything before."

"Everybody will think that you're mad, and that I'm mad, and that we are all mad together."

"Because I go to church in a merino dress? Well; if that makes madness, let us be mad. Oh, Fred, do not refuse me the first thing I've asked you! What difference will it make? Nobody will know it over in Philadelphia!"

"Then you are ashamed of it?"

"No, not ashamed. Why should I be ashamed? But one does not wish to have that sort of thing talked about by everybody."

"And you are so strong-minded, Nora, that you do not care about finery yourself?"

"Fred, that's ill-natured. You know very well what my feelings are. You are sharp enough to understand them without any further explanation. I do like finery, quite well enough, as you'll find out to your cost some day. And if ever you scold me for extravagance, I shall tell you about this."

"It's downright Quixotism."

"Quixotism leads to nothing, but this will lead to twenty pounds' worth of soup,—and to something else too."

When he pressed her to explain what that something else was, she declined to speak further on the subject. She could not tell him that the satisfaction she desired was that of giving up something,—of having made a sacrifice,—of having thrown into the treasury her two mites,—two mites off her own back, as she had said to her aunt, and out of her own mouth. He had taxed her with indifference to a woman's usual delight in gay plumage, and had taxed her most unjustly. "He ought to know," she said to herself, "that I should not take all this trouble about it, unless I did care for it." But, in truth, he did understand her motives thoroughly, and half approved them. He approved the spirit of self-abandonment, but disapproved the false political economy by which, according to his light, that spirit was accompanied. "After all," said he, "the widow would have done better to have invested her small capital in some useful trade."

"Oh, Fred;—but never mind now. I have your consent, and now I've only got to talk over my aunt." So saying, she left her lover to turn over in his mind the first principles of that large question of charity.

"The giving of pence and halfpence, of scraps of bread and sups of soup, is, after all, but the charity of a barbarous, half-civilised race. A dog would let another dog starve before he gave him a bone, and would see his starved fellow-dog die without a pang. We have just got beyond that, only beyond that, as long as we dole out cups of soup. But Charity, when it shall have made itself perfect, will have destroyed this little trade of giving, which makes the giver vain and the receiver humble. The Charity of the large-hearted is that which opens to every man the profit of his own industry; to every man and to every woman." Then having gratified himself with the enunciation of this fine theory, he allowed his mind to run away to a smaller subject, and began to think of his own wedding garments. If Nora insisted on carrying out this project of hers, in what guise must he appear on the occasion? He also had ordered new clothes. "It's just the sort of thing that they'll make a story of in Chestnut Street." Chestnut Street, as we all know, is the West End of Philadelphia.

When the morning came of the twelfth of January,—the morning that was to make Nora Field a married woman, she had carried her point; but she was not allowed to feel that she had carried it triumphantly. Her uncle had not forbidden her scheme, but had never encouraged it. Her lover had hardly spoken to her on the subject since the day on which she had explained to him her intention. "After all, it's a mere bagatelle," he had said; "I am not going to marry your clothes." One of her cousins, Bob, had approved; but he had coupled his approval with an intimation that something should be done to prevent any other woman from wearing bridal wreaths for the next three months. Charley had condemned her altogether, pointing out that it was bad policy to feed the cotton-spinners at the expense of the milliners. But the strongest opposition had come from her aunt and the Miss Fosters. Mrs Granger, though her heart was in the battle which her husband was fighting, could not endure to think that all the time-honoured ceremonies of her life should be abandoned. In spite of all that was going on around her, she had insisted on having mince-pies on the table on Christmas Day. True, there were not many of them, and they were small and flavourless. But the mince-pies were there, with whisky to burn with them instead of brandy, if any of the party chose to go through the ceremony. And to her the idea of a wedding without wedding-clothes was very grievous. It was she who had told Nora that she was a widow with two mites, or might make herself one, if she chose to encounter self-sacrifice. But in so saying she had by no means anticipated such a widowhood as this.

"I really think, Nora, you might have one of those thinner silks, and you might do without a wreath; but you should have a veil;—indeed you should."

But Nora was obstinate. Having overcome her future lord, and quieted her uncle, she was not at all prepared to yield to the mild remonstrances of her aunt. The two Miss Fosters were very much shocked, and for three days there was a disagreeable coolness between them and the Plumstock family. A friend's bridal is always an occasion for a new dress, and the Miss Fosters naturally felt that they were being robbed of their rights.

"Sensible girl," said old Foster, when he heard of it. "When you're married, if ever you are, I hope you'll do the same."

"Indeed we won't, papa," said the two Miss Fosters. But the coolness gradually subsided, and the two Miss Fosters consented to attend in their ordinary Sunday bonnets.

It had been decided that they should be married early, at eight o'clock; that they should then go to the parsonage for breakfast, and that the married couple should start off for London immediately afterwards. They were to remain there for a week, and then return to Liverpool for one other remaining week before their final departure for America.

"I should only have had them on for about an hour if I'd got them, and then it would have been almost dark," she said to her aunt.

"Perhaps it won't signify very much," her aunt replied. Then when the morning came, it seemed that the sacrifice had dwindled down to a very little thing. The two Miss Fosters had come to the Parsonage over night, and as they sat up with the bride over a bed-room fire, had been good-natured enough to declare that they thought it would be very good fun.

"You won't have to get up in the cold to dress me," said Nora, "because I can do it all myself; that will be a comfort."

"Oh, we shouldn't have minded that; and as it is, of course, we'll turn you out nice. You'll wear one of your other new dresses; won't you?"

"Oh, I don't know; just what I'm to travel in. It isn't very old. Do you know, after all, I'm not sure that it isn't a great deal better."

"I suppose it will be the same thing in the end," said the younger Miss Foster.

"Of course it will," said the elder.

"And there won't be all that bother of changing my dress," said Nora.

Frederic F. Frew came out to Plumstock by an early train from Liverpool, bringing with him a countryman of his own as his friend on the occasion. It had been explained to the friend that he was to come in his usual habiliments.

"Oh, nonsense!" said the friend, "I guess I'll see you turned off in a new waistcoat." But Frederic F. Frew had made it understood that an old waistcoat was imperative.

"It's something about the cotton, you know. They're all beside themselves here, as though there was never going to be a bit more in the country to eat. That's England all over. Never mind; do you come just as if you were going into your counting-house. Brown cotton gloves, with a hole in the thumbs, will be the thing, I should say."

There were candles on the table when they were all assembled in the Parsonage drawing-room previous to the marriage. The two gentlemen were there first. Then came Mrs Granger, who rather frightened Mr Frew by kissing him, and telling him that she should always regard him as a son-in-law.

"Nora has always been like one of ourselves, you know," she said, apologisingly.

"And let me tell you, Master Frew," said the parson, "that you're a very lucky fellow to get her."

"I say, isn't it cold?" said Bob, coming in—"where are the girls?"

"Here are the girls," said Miss Foster, heading the procession of three which now entered the room, Nora, of course, being the last. Then Nora was kissed by everybody, including the strange American gentleman, who seemed to have made some mistake as to his privilege in the matter. But it all passed off very well, and I doubt if Nora knew who kissed her. It was very cold, and they were all wrapped close in their brown shawls and greatcoats, and the women looked very snug and comfortable in their ordinary winter bonnets.

"Come," said the parson, "we mustn't wait for Charley; he'll follow us to church." So the uncle took his niece on his arm, and the two Americans took the two bridesmaids, and Bob took his mother, and went along the beaten path over the snow to the church, and, as they got to the door, Charley rushed after them quite out of breath.

"I haven't even got a pair of gloves at all," he whispered to his mother.

"It doesn't matter; nobody's to know," said Mrs Granger.

Nora by this time had forgotten the subject of her dress altogether, and it may be doubted if even the Misses Foster were as keenly alive to it as they thought they would have been. For myself, I think they all looked more comfortable on that cold winter morning without the finery which would have been customary than they could have done with it. It had seemed to them all beforehand that a marriage without veils and wreaths, without white gloves and new gay dresses, would be but a triste affair; but the idea passed away altogether when the occasion came. Mr Granger and his wife and the two lads clustered around Nora as they made themselves ready for the ceremony, uttering words of warm love, and it seemed as though even the clerk and the servants took nothing amiss. Frederic F. Frew had met with a rebuff in the hall of the Parsonage, in being forbidden to take his own bride under his own arm; but when the time for action came, he bore no malice, but went through his work manfully. On the whole, it was a pleasant wedding, homely, affectionate, full of much loving greeting; not without many sobs on the part of the bride and of Mrs Granger, and some slight suspicion of an eagerly-removed tear in the parson's eye; but this, at any rate, was certain, that the wedding-clothes were not missed. When they all sat down to their breakfast in the Parsonage dining-room, that little matter had come to be clean forgotten. No one knew, not even the Misses Foster, that there was anything extraordinary in their garb. Indeed, as to all gay apparel, we may say that we only miss it by comparison. It is very sad to be the wearer of the only frock-coat in company, to carry the one solitary black silk handerchief at a dinner-party. But I do not know but that a dozen men so arrayed do not seem to be as well dressed as though they had obeyed the latest rules of fashion as to their garments. One thing, however, had been made secure. That sum of twenty pounds, saved from the milliners, had been duly paid over into Mr Granger's hands. "It has been all very nice," said Mrs Granger, still sobbing, when Nora went upstairs to tie on her bonnet before she started. "Only you are going!"

"Yes, I'm going now, aunt. Dear aunt! But, aunt, I have failed in one thing—absolutely failed."

"Failed in what, my darling?"

"There has been no widow's mite. It is not easy to be a widow with two mites."

"What you have given will be blessed to you, and blessed to those who will receive it."

"I hope it may; but I almost feel that I have been wrong in thinking of it so much. It has cost me nothing. I tell you, aunt, that it is not easy to be a widow with two mites."

When Mrs Granger was alone with her husband after this, the two Miss Fosters having returned to Liverpool under the discreet protection of the two young Grangers, for they had positively refused to travel with no other companion than the strange American,—she told him all that Nora had said.

"And who can tell us," he replied, "that it was not the same with the widow herself? She threw in all that she had, but who can say that she suffered aught in consequence? It is my belief that all that is given in a right spirit comes back instantly, in this world, with interest."

"I wish my coals would come back," said Mrs Granger.

"Perhaps you have not given them in a right spirit, my dear."

HENRY VAN DYKE

HENRY JACKSON VAN DYKE WAS BORN THE SON OF A Presbyterian clergyman in 1852 in Germantown, Pennsylvania. He enrolled at the Brooklyn Polytechnic Institute and later attended Princeton Theological Seminary, although when he began classes in 1874 he wasn't certain he would enter the ministry, wanting instead to be a writer. But in 1879 he became the pastor of the famous Brick Presbyterian Church in New York City, gaining a national reputation for his preaching. Yet he was also able to follow his dream of being a writer, publishing *The Reality of Religion* in 1884 and *The Story of the Psalms* in 1887. Although his fame and influence as an important American scholar, pastor, and orator grew, it was his hugely popular "The Story of the Other Wise Man" that set him square in the eye of America's reading public. Originally read as a Christmas sermon in his church and published in the Christmas issue of *Harper's Monthly* in 1892, the story has continued in print to this day.

After his successful career as a minister, Van Dyke became the Murray Professor of English Literature at Princeton in 1900, and continued to write critical assessments of major literary figures, as well as serving as U.S. Ambassador to the Netherlands and Luxembourg, then serving as lieutenant commander for the Chaplain Corps of the U.S. Navy during World War I. Ever an outspoken advocate of the importance of the Christian life and the joys of literature, the man whom Helen Keller called "an architect of happiness" died in 1933 at his home in Princeton.

THE STORY
OF THE OTHER
WISE MAN

by Henry Van Dyke

Who seeks for heaven alone to save his soul,

May keep the path, but will not reach the goal;

While he who walks in love may wander far,

Yet God will bring him where the blessed are.

You know the story of the Three Wise Men of the East, and how they traveled from far away to offer their gifts at the manger-cradle in Bethlehem. But have you ever heard the story of the Other Wise Man, who also saw the star in its rising, and set out to follow it, yet did not arrive with his brethren in the presence of the young child Jesus? Of the great desire of this fourth pilgrim, and how it was denied, yet accomplished in the denial; of his many wanderings and the probations of his soul; of the long way of his seeking, and the strange way of his finding, the One whom he sought—I would tell the tale as I have heard fragments of it in the Hall of Dreams, in the palace of the Heart of Man.

THE SIGN IN THE SKY

In the days when Augustus Caesar was master of many kings and Herod reigned in Jerusalem, there lived in the city of Ecbatana, among the mountains of Persia, a certain man named Artaban, the Median. His house stood close to the outermost of the seven walls which encircled the royal treasury. From his roof he could look over the rising battlements of black and white and crimson and blue and red and silver and gold, to the hill where the summer palace of the Parthian emperors glittered like a jewel in a sevenfold crown.

Around the dwelling of Artaban spread a fair garden, a tangle of flowers and fruit-trees, watered by a score of streams descending from the slopes of Mount Orontes, and made musical by innumerable birds. But all colour was lost in the soft and odorous darkness of the late September night, and all sounds were hushed in the deep charm of its silence, save the plashing of the water, like a voice half sobbing and half laughing under the shadows. High above the trees a dim glow of light shone through the curtained arches of the upper chamber, where the master of the house was holding council with his friends.

He stood by the doorway to greet his guests—a tall, dark man of about forty years, with brilliant eyes set near together under his broad brow, and firm lines graven around his fine, thin lips; the brow of a dreamer and the mouth of a soldier, a man of sensitive feeling but inflexible will—one of those who, in whatever age they may live, are born for inward conflict and a life of quest.

His robe was of pure white wool, thrown over a tunic of silk; and a white, pointed cap, with long lapels at the sides, rested on his flowing black hair. It was the dress of the ancient priesthood of the Magi, called the fire-worshippers.

"Welcome!" he said, in his low, pleasant voice, as one after another entered the room—"welcome, Abdus; peace be with you, Rhodaspes and Tigranes, and with you my father, Abgarus. You are all welcome, and this house grows bright with the joy of your presence."

There were nine of the men, differing widely in age, but alike in the richness of their dress of many-coloured silks, and in the massive golden collars around their necks, marking them as Parthian nobles, and in the winged circles of gold resting upon their breasts, the sign of the followers of Zoroaster.

They took their places around a small black altar at the end of the room, where a tiny flame was burning. Artaban, standing beside it, and waving a barsom of thin tamarisk branches above the fire, fed it with dry sticks of pine and fragrant oils. Then he began the ancient chant of the Yasna, and the voices of his companions joined in the beautiful hymn to Ahura-Mazda:

> We worship the Spirit Divine,
> all wisdom and goodness possessing,
> Surrounded by Holy Immortals,
> the givers of bounty and blessing.
> We joy in the works of His hands,
> His truth and His power confessing.
> We praise all the things that are pure,
> for these are His only Creation;
> The thoughts that are true, and the words
> and deeds that have won approbation;
> These are supported by Him,
> and for these we make adoration.

> Hear us, O Mazda! Thou livest
> in truth and in heavenly gladness;
> Cleanse us from falsehood, and keep us
> from evil and bondage to badness;
> Pour out the light and the joy of Thy life
> on our darkness and sadness.
> Shine on our gardens and fields,

Shine on our working and weaving;
Shine on the whole race of man,
Believing and unbelieving;
Shine on us now through the night,
Shine on us now in Thy might,
The flame of our holy love
and the song of our worship receiving.

The fire rose with the chant, throbbing as if it were made of musical flame, until it cast a bright illumination through the whole apartment, revealing its simplicity and splendour.

The floor was laid with tiles of dark blue veined with white; pilasters of twisted silver stood out against the blue walls; the clearstory of round-arched windows above them was hung with azure silk; the vaulted ceiling was a pavement of sapphires, like the body of heaven in its clearness, sown with silver stars. From the four corners of the roof hung four golden magic-wheels, called the tongues of the gods. At the eastern end, behind the altar, there were two dark-red pillars of porphyry; above them a lintel of the same stone, on which was carved the figure of a winged archer, with his arrow set to the string and his bow drawn.

The doorway between the pillars, which opened upon the terrace of the roof, was covered with a heavy curtain of the colour of a ripe pome-granate, embroidered with innumerable golden rays shooting upward from the floor. In effect the room was like a quiet, starry night, all azure and silver, flushed in the East with rosy promise of the dawn. It was, as the house of a man should be, an expression of the character and spirit of the master.

He turned to his friends when the song was ended, and invited them to be seated on the divan at the western end of the room.

"You have come tonight," said he, looking around the circle, "at my call, as the faithful scholars of Zoroaster, to renew your worship and rekindle your faith in the God of Purity, even as this fire has been rekindled on the altar. We worship not the fire, but Him of whom it is the chosen symbol, because it is the purest of all created things. It speaks to us of one who is Light and Truth. Is it not so, my father?"

"It is well said, my son," answered the venerable Abgarus. "The enlightened are never idolaters. They lift the veil of the form and go in to the shrine of the reality, and new light and truth are coming to them continually through the old symbols."

"Hear me, then, my father and my friends," said Artaban, very quietly, "while I tell you of the new light and truth that have come to me through the most ancient of all signs. We have searched the secrets of nature together, and studied the healing virtues of water and fire and the plants. We have read also the books of prophecy in which the future is dimly foretold in words that are hard to understand. But the highest of all learning is the knowledge of the stars. To trace their courses is to untangle the threads of the mystery of life from the beginning to the end. If we could follow them perfectly, nothing would be hidden from us. But is not our knowledge of them still incomplete? Are there not many stars still beyond our horizon—lights that are known only to the dwellers in the far south-land, among the spice-trees of Punt and the gold mines of Ophir?"

There was a murmur of assent among the listeners.

"The stars," said Tigranes, "are the thoughts of the Eternal. They are numberless. But the thoughts of man can be counted, like the years of his life. The wisdom of the Magi is the greatest of all wisdoms on earth, because it knows its own ignorance. And that is the secret of power. We keep men always looking and waiting for a new sunrise. But we ourselves know that the darkness is equal to the light, and that the conflict between them will never be ended."

"That does not satisfy me," answered Artaban, "for, if the waiting must be endless, if there could be no fulfilment of it, then it would not be wisdom to look and wait. We should become like those new teachers of the Greeks, who say that there is no truth, and that the only wise men are those who spend their lives in discovering and exposing the lies that have been believed in the world. But the new sunrise will certainly dawn in the appointed time. Do not our own books tell us that this will come to pass, and that men will see the brightness of a great light?"

"That is true," said the voice of Abgarus; "every faithful disciple of Zoroaster knows the prophecy of the Avesta and carries the word in his heart. 'In that day Sosiosh the Victorious shall arise out of the number of the prophets in the east country. Around him shall shine a mighty brightness, and he shall make life everlasting, incorruptible, and immortal, and the dead shall rise again.'"

"This is a dark saying," said Tigranes, "and it may be that we shall never understand it. It is better to consider the things that are near at hand, and to increase the influence of the Magi in their own country, rather than to look for one who may be a stranger, and to whom we must resign our power."

The others seemed to approve these words. There was a silent feeling of agreement manifest among them; their looks responded with that indefinable expression which always follows when a speaker has uttered the thought that has been slumbering in the hearts of his listeners. But Artaban turned to Abgarus with a glow on his face, and said:

"My father, I have kept this prophecy in the secret place of my soul. Religion without a great hope would be like an altar without a living fire. And now the flame has burned more brightly, and by the light of it I have read other words which also have come from the fountain of Truth, and speak yet more clearly of the rising of the Victorious One in his brightness."

He drew from the breast of his tunic two small rolls of fine linen, with writing upon them, and unfolded them carefully upon his knee.

"In the years that are lost in the past, long before our fathers came into the land of Babylon, there were wise men in Chaldea, from whom the first of the Magi learned the secret of the heavens. And of these Balaam the son of Beor was one of the mightiest. Hear the words of his prophecy: 'There shall come a star out of Jacob, and a sceptre shall arise out of Israel.'"

The lips of Tigranes drew downward with contempt, as he said:

"Judah was a captive by the waters of Babylon, and the sons of Jacob were in bondage to our kings. The tribes of Israel are scattered through the mountains like lost sheep, and from the remnant that dwells in Judea under the yoke of Rome neither star nor sceptre shall arise."

"And yet," answered Artaban, "it was the Hebrew Daniel, the mighty searcher of dreams, the counselor of kings, the wise Belteshazzar, who was most honored and beloved of our great King Cyrus. A prophet of sure things and a reader of the thoughts of God, Daniel proved himself to our people. And these are the words that he wrote." (Artaban read from the second roll:) "'Know, therefore, and understand that from the going forth of the commandment to restore Jerusalem, unto the Anointed One, the Prince, the time shall be seven and threescore and two weeks.'"

"But, my son," said Abgarus, doubtfully, "these are mystical numbers. Who can interpret them, or who can find the key that shall unlock their meaning?"

Artaban answered: "It has been shown to me and to my three companions among the Magi—Caspar, Melchior, and Balthazar. We have searched the ancient tablets of Chaldea and computed the time. It falls in this year. We have studied the sky, and in the spring of the year we saw two of the greatest stars draw near together in the sign of the Fish, which is the house of the Hebrews. We also saw a new star there, which shone for one night and then vanished. Now again the two great planets are meeting. This night is their conjunction. My three brothers are watching at the ancient temple of the Seven Spheres, at Borsippa, in Babylonia, and I am watching here. If the star shines again, they will wait ten days for me at the temple, and then we will set out together for Jerusalem, to see and worship the promised one who shall be born King of Israel. I believe the sign will come. I have made ready for the journey. I have sold my house and my possessions, and bought these three jewels—a sapphire, a ruby, and a pearl—to carry them as tribute to the King. And I ask you to go with me on the pilgrimage, that we may have joy together in finding the Prince who is worthy to be served."

While he was speaking he thrust his hand into the inmost fold of his girdle and drew out three great gems—one blue as a fragment of the night sky, one redder than a ray of sunrise, and one as pure as the peak of a snow mountain at twilight—and laid them on the outspread linen scrolls before him.

But his friends looked on with strange and alien eyes. A veil of doubt and mistrust came over their faces, like a fog creeping up from the marshes to hide the hills. They glanced at each other with looks of wonder and pity, as those who have listened to incredible sayings, the story of a wild vision, or the proposal of an impossible enterprise.

At last Tigranes said: "Artaban, this is a vain dream. It comes from too much looking upon the stars and the cherishing of lofty thoughts. It would be wiser to spend the time in gathering money for the new fire-temple at Chala. No king will ever rise from the broken race of Israel, and no end will ever come to the eternal strife of light and darkness. He who looks for it is a chaser of shadows. Farewell."

And another said: "Artaban, I have no knowledge of these things, and my office as guardian of the royal treasure binds me here. The quest is not for me. But if thou must follow it, fare thee well."

And another said: "In my house there sleeps a new bride, and I cannot leave her nor take her with me on this strange journey. This quest is not for me. But may thy steps be prospered wherever thou goest. So, farewell."

And another said: "I am ill and unfit for hardship, but there is a man among my servants whom I will send with thee when thou goest, to bring me word how thou farest."

But Abgarus, the oldest and the one who loved Artaban the best, lingered after the others had gone, and said, gravely: "My son, it may be that the light of truth is in this sign that has appeared in the skies, and then it will surely lead to the Prince and the mighty brightness. Or it may be that it is only a shadow of the light, as Tigranes has said, and then he who follows it will have only a long pilgrimage and an empty search. But it is better to follow even the shadow of the best than to remain content with the worst. And those who would see wonderful things must often be ready to travel alone. I am too old for this journey, but my heart shall be a companion of the pilgrimage day and night, and I shall know the end of thy quest. Go in peace."

So one by one they went out of the azure chamber with its silver stars, and Artaban was left in solitude.

He gathered up the jewels and replaced them in his girdle. For a long time he stood and watched the flame that flickered and sank upon the altar. Then he crossed the hall, lifted the heavy curtain, and passed out between the dull red pillars of porphyry to the terrace on the roof.

The shiver that thrills through the earth ere she rouses from her night sleep had already begun, and the cool wind that heralds the daybreak was drawing downward from the lofty snow-traced ravines of Mount Orontes. Birds, half awakened, crept and chirped among the rustling leaves, and the smell of ripened grapes came in brief wafts from the arbours.

Far over the eastern plain a white mist stretched like a lake. But where the distant peak of Zagros serrated the western horizon the sky was clear. Jupiter and Saturn rolled together like drops of lambent flame about to blend in one.

As Artaban watched them, behold, an azure spark was born out of the darkness beneath, rounding itself with purple splendours to a crimson sphere, and spiring upward through rays of saffron and orange into a point of white radiance. Tiny and infinitely remote, yet perfect in every part, it pulsated in the enormous vault as if the three jewels in the Magian's breast had mingled and been transformed into a living heart of light. He bowed his head. He covered his brow with his hands.

"It is the sign," he said. "The King is coming, and I will go to meet him."

By the Waters of Babylon

All night long Vasda, the swiftest of Artaban's horses, had been waiting, saddled and bridled, in her stall, pawing the ground impatiently, and shaking her bit as if she shared the eagerness of her master's purpose, though she knew not its meaning.

Before the birds had fully roused to their strong, high, joyful chant of morning song, before the white mist had begun to lift lazily from the plain, the other wise man was in the saddle, riding swiftly along the high-road, which skirted the base of Mount Orontes, westward.

How close, how intimate is the comradeship between a man and his favourite horse on a long journey. It is a silent, comprehensive friendship, an intercourse beyond the need of words. They drink at the same wayside springs, and sleep under the same guardian stars. They are conscious together of the subduing spell of nightfall and the quickening joy of daybreak. The master shares his evening meal with his hungry companion, and feels the soft, moist lips caressing the palm of his hand as they close over the morsel of bread. In the gray dawn he is roused from his bivouac by the gentle stir of a warm, sweet breath over his sleeping face, and looks up into the eyes of his faithful fellow-traveler, ready and waiting for the toil of the day. Surely, unless he is a pagan and an unbeliever, by whatever name he calls upon his God, he will thank Him for this voiceless sympathy, this dumb affection, and his morning prayer will embrace a double blessing—God bless us both, and keep our feet from falling and our souls from death!

And then, through the keen morning air, the swift hoofs beat their spirited music along the road, keeping time to the pulsing of two hearts that are moved with the same eager desire—to conquer space, to devour the distance, to attain the goal of the journey.

ARTABAN MUST INDEED RIDE WISELY AND WELL IF HE would keep the appointed hour with the other Magi; for the route was a hundred and fifty parasangs, and fifteen was the utmost that he could travel in a day. But he knew Vasda's strength, and pushed forward without anxiety, making the fixed distance every day, though he must travel late into the night, and in the morning long before sunrise.

He passed along the brown slopes of Mount Orontes, furrowed by the rocky courses of a hundred torrents.

He crossed the level plains of the Nisaeans, where the famous herds of horses, feeding in the wide pastures, tossed their heads at Vasda's approach, and galloped away with a thunder of many hoofs, and flocks of wild birds rose suddenly from the swampy meadows, wheeling in great circles with a shining flutter of innumerable wings and shrill cries of surprise.

He traversed the fertile fields of Concabar, where the dust from the threshing-floors filled the air with a golden mist, half hiding the huge temple of Astarte with its four hundred pillars.

At Baghistan, among the rich gardens watered by fountains from the rock, he looked up at the mountain thrusting its immense rugged brow out over the road, and saw the figure of King Darius trampling upon his fallen foes, and the proud list of his wars and conquests graven high upon the face of the eternal cliff.

Over many a cold and desolate pass, crawling painfully across the wind-swept shoulders of the hills; down many a black mountain-gorge, where the river roared and raced before him like a savage guide; across many a smiling vale, with terraces of yellow limestone full of vines and fruit-trees; through the oak-groves of Carine and the dark Gates of Zagros, walled in by precipices; into the ancient city of Chala, where the people of Samaria had been kept in captivity long ago; and out again by the mighty portal, riven through the encircling hills, where he saw the image of the High Priest of the Magi sculptured on the wall of rock, with hand uplifted as if to bless the centuries of pilgrims; past the entrance of the narrow defile, filled from end to end with orchards of peaches and figs, through which the river Gyndes foamed down to meet him; over the broad rice-fields, where the autumnal vapours spread their deathly mists; following along the course of the river, under tremulous shadows of poplar and tamarind, among the lower hills; and out upon the flat plain, where the road ran straight as an arrow through the stubble-fields and parched meadows; past the city of Ctesiphon, where the Parthian emperors reigned, and the vast metropolis of Seleucia which Alexander built; across the swirling floods of Tigris and the many chan-nels of Euphrates, flowing yellow through the corn-lands—Artaban pressed onward until he arrived, at nightfall of the tenth day, beneath the shattered walls of populous Babylon.

Vasda was almost spent, and he would gladly have turned into the city to find rest and refreshment for himself and for her. But he knew that it was three hours' journey yet to the Temple of the Seven Spheres, and he must reach the place by midnight if he would find his comrades waiting. So he did not halt, but rode steadily across the stubble-fields.

A grove of date-palms made an island of gloom in the pale yellow sea. As she passed into the shadow Vasda slackened her pace, and began to pick her way more carefully.

Near the farther end of the darkness an access of caution seemed to fall upon her. She scented some danger or difficulty; it was not in her heart to fly from it—only to be prepared for it, and to meet it wisely, as a good horse should do. The grove was close and silent as the tomb; not a leaf rustled, not a bird sang.

She felt her steps before her delicately, carrying her head low, and sighing now and then with apprehension. At last she gave a quick breath of anxiety and dismay, and stood stock-still, quivering in every muscle, before a dark object in the shadow of the last palm-tree.

Artaban dismounted. The dim starlight revealed the form of a man lying across the road. His humble dress and the outline of his haggard face showed that he was probably one of the poor Hebrew exiles who still dwelt in great numbers in the vicinity. His pallid skin, dry and yellow as parchment, bore the mark of the deadly fever which ravaged the marsh-lands in autumn. The chill of death was in his lean hand, and, as Artaban released it, the arm fell back inertly upon the motionless breast.

He turned away with a thought of pity, consigning the body to that strange burial which the Magians deem most fitting—the funeral of the desert, from which the kites and vultures rise on dark wings, and the beasts of prey slink furtively away, leaving only a heap of white bones in the sand.

But, as he turned, a long, faint, ghostly sigh came from the man's lips. The brown, bony fingers closed convulsively on the hem of the Magian's robe and held him fast.

Artaban's heart leaped to his throat, not with fear, but with a dumb resentment at the importunity of this blind delay. How could he stay here in the darkness to minister to a dying stranger? What claim had this unknown fragment of human life upon his compassion or his service? If he lingered but for an hour he could hardly reach Borsippa at the appointed time. His companions would think he had given up the journey. They would go without him. He would lose his quest.

But if he went on now, the man would surely die. If he stayed, life might be restored. His spirit throbbed and fluttered with the urgency of the crisis. Should he risk the great reward of his divine faith for the sake of a single deed of human love? Should he turn aside, if only for a moment, from the following of the star, to give a cup of cold water to a poor, perishing Hebrew?

"God of truth and purity," he prayed, "direct me in the holy path, the way of wisdom which Thou only knowest."

Then he turned back to the sick man. Loosening the grasp of his hand, he carried him to a little mound at the foot of the palm-tree. He unbound the thick folds of the turban and opened the garment above the sunken breast. He brought water from one of the small canals near by, and moistened the sufferer's brow and mouth. He mingled a draught of one of those simple but potent remedies which he carried always in his girdle—for the Magians were physicians as well as astrologers—and poured it slowly between the colourless lips. Hour after hour he labored as only a skilful healer of disease can do; and, at last, the man's strength returned; he sat up and looked about him.

"Who art thou?" he said, in the rude dialect of the country, "and why hast thou sought me here to bring back my life?"

"I am Artaban the Magian, of the city of Ecbatana, and I am going to Jerusalem in search of one who is to be born King of the Jews, a great Prince and Deliverer for all men. I dare not delay any longer upon my journey, for the caravan that has waited for me may depart without me. But see, here is all that I have left of bread and wine, and here is a potion of healing herbs. When thy strength is restored thou can'st find the dwellings of the Hebrews among the houses of Babylon."

The Jew raised his trembling hands solemnly to heaven.

"Now may the God of Abraham and Isaac and Jacob bless and prosper the journey of the merciful, and bring him in peace to his desired haven. But stay; I have nothing to give thee in return—only this: that I can tell thee where the Messiah must be sought. For our prophets have said that he should be born not in Jerusalem, but in Bethlehem of Judah. May the Lord bring thee in safety to that place, because thou hast had pity upon the sick."

It was already long past midnight. Artaban rode in haste, and Vasda, restored by the brief rest, ran eagerly through the silent plain and swam the channels of the river. She put forth the remnant of her strength, and fled over the ground like a gazelle.

But the first beam of the sun sent her shadow before her as she entered upon the final stadium of the journey, and the eyes of Artaban, anxiously scanning the great mound of Nimrod and the Temple of the Seven Spheres, could discern no trace of his friends.

The many-coloured terraces of black and orange and red and yellow and green and blue and white, shattered by the convulsions of nature, and crumbling under the repeated blows of human violence, still glittered like a ruined rainbow in the morning light.

Artaban rode swiftly around the hill. He dismounted and climbed to the highest terrace, looking out towards the west.

The huge desolation of the marshes stretched away to the horizon and the border of the desert. Bitterns stood by the stagnant pools and jackals skulked through the low bushes; but there was no sign of the caravan of the wise men, far or near.

At the edge of the terrace he saw a little cairn of broken bricks, and under them a piece of parchment. He caught it up and read: "We have waited past the midnight, and can delay no longer. We go to find the King. Follow us across the desert." Artaban sat down upon the ground and covered his head in despair.

"How can I cross the desert," said he, "with no food and with a spent horse? I must return to Babylon, sell my sapphire, and buy a train of camels, and provision for the journey. I may never overtake my friends. Only God the merciful knows whether I shall not lose the sight of the King because I tarried to show mercy."

FOR THE SAKE OF A LITTLE CHILD

There was a silence in the Hall of Dreams, where I was listening to the story of the other wise man. And through this silence I saw, but very dimly, his figure passing over the dreary undulations of the desert, high upon the back of his camel, rocking steadily onward like a ship over the waves.

The land of death spread its cruel net around him. The stony wastes bore no fruit but briers and thorns. The dark ledges of rock thrust themselves above the surface here and there, like the bones of perished monsters. Arid and inhospitable mountain ranges rose before him, furrowed with dry channels of ancient torrents, white and ghastly as scars on the face of nature. Shifting hills of treacherous sand were heaped like tombs along the horizon. By day, the fierce heat pressed its intolerable burden on the quivering air; and no living creature moved, on the dumb, swooning earth, but tiny jerboas scuttling through the parched bushes, or lizards vanishing in the clefts of the rock. By night the jackals prowled and barked in the distance, and the lion made the black ravines echo with his hollow roaring, while a bitter, blighting chill followed the fever of the day. Through heat and cold, the Magian moved steadily onward.

Then I saw the gardens and orchards of Damascus, watered by the streams of Abana and Pharpar, with their sloping swards inlaid with bloom, and their thickets of myrrh and roses. I saw also the long, snowy ridge of Hermon, and the dark groves of cedars, and the valley of the Jordan, and the blue waters of the Lake of Galilee, and the fertile plain of Esdraelon, and the hills of Ephraim, and the highlands of Judah. Through all these I followed the figure of Artaban moving steadily onward, until he arrived at Bethlehem. And it was the third day after the three wise men had come to that place and had found Mary and Joseph, with the young child, Jesus, and had laid their gifts of gold and frankincense and myrrh at his feet.

Then the other wise man drew near, weary, but full of hope, bearing his ruby and his pearl to offer to the King. "For now at last," he said, "I shall surely find him, though it be alone, and later than my brethren. This is the place of which the Hebrew exile told me that the prophets had spoken, and here I shall behold the rising of the great light. But I must inquire about the visit of my brethren, and to what house the star directed them, and to whom they presented their tribute."

The streets of the village seemed to be deserted, and Artaban wondered whether the men had all gone up to the hill-pastures to bring down their sheep. From the open door of a low stone cottage he heard the sound of a woman's voice singing softly. He entered and found a young mother hushing her baby to rest. She told him of the strangers from the far East who had appeared in the village three days ago, and how they said that a star had guided them to the place where Joseph of Nazareth was lodging with his wife and her new-born child, and how they had paid reverence to the child and given him many rich gifts.

"But the travelers disappeared again," she continued, "as suddenly as they had come. We were afraid at the strangeness of their visit. We could not understand it. The man of Nazareth took the babe and his mother and fled away that same night secretly, and it was whispered that they were going far away to Egypt. Ever since, there has been a spell upon the village; something evil hangs over it. They say that the Roman soldiers are coming from Jerusalem to force a new tax from us, and the men have driven the flocks and herds far back among the hills, and hidden themselves to escape it."

Artaban listened to her gentle, timid speech, and the child in her arms looked up in his face and smiled, stretching out its rosy hands to grasp at the winged circle of gold on his breast. His heart warmed to the touch. It seemed like a greeting of love and trust to one who had journeyed long in loneliness and perplexity, fighting with his own doubts and fears, and following a light that was veiled in clouds.

"Might not this child have been the promised Prince?" he asked within himself, as he touched its soft cheek. "Kings have been born ere now in lowlier houses than this, and the favourite of the stars may rise even from a cottage. But it has not seemed good to the God of wisdom to reward my search so soon and so easily. The one whom I seek has gone before me; and now I must follow the King to Egypt."

The young mother laid the babe in its cradle, and rose to minister to the wants of the strange guest that fate had brought into her house. She set food before him, the plain fare of peasants, but willingly offered, and therefore full of refreshment for the soul as well as for the body. Artaban accepted it gratefully; and, as he ate, the child fell into a happy slumber, and murmured sweetly in its dreams, and a great peace filled the quiet room.

But suddenly there came the noise of a wild confusion and uproar in the streets of the village, a shrieking and wailing of women's voices, a clangor of brazen trumpets and a clashing of swords, and a desperate cry: "The soldiers! The soldiers of Herod! They are killing our children."

The young mother's face grew white with terror. She clasped her child to her bosom, and crouched motionless in the darkest corner of the room, covering him with the folds of her robe, lest he should wake and cry.

But Artaban went quickly and stood in the doorway of the house.

His broad shoulders filled the portal from side to side, and the peak of his white cap all but touched the lintel.

The soldiers came hurrying down the street with bloody hands and dripping swords. At the sight of the stranger in his imposing dress they hesitated with surprise. The captain of the band approached the threshold to thrust him aside. But Artaban did not stir. His face was as calm as though he were watching the stars, and in his eyes there burned that steady radiance before which even the half-tamed hunting leopard shrinks, and the fierce bloodhound pauses in his leap. He held the soldier silently for an instant, and then said in a low voice:

"There is no one in this place but me, and I am waiting to give this jewel to the prudent captain who will leave me in peace."

He showed the ruby, glistening in the hollow of his hand like a great drop of blood.

The captain was amazed at the splendour of the gem. The pupils of his eyes expanded with desire, and the hard lines of greed wrinkled around his lips. He stretched out his hand and took the ruby.

"March on!" he cried to his men, "there is no child here. The house is still."

The clamour and the clang of arms passed down the street as the headlong fury of the chase sweeps by the secret covert where the trembling deer is hidden. Artaban re-entered the cottage. He turned his face to the east and prayed:

"God of truth, forgive my sin! I have said the thing that is not, to save the life of a child. And two of my gifts are gone. I have spent for man that which was meant for God. Shall I ever be worthy to see the face of the King?"

But the voice of the woman, weeping for joy in the shadow behind him, said very gently:

"Because thou hast saved the life of my little one, may the Lord bless thee and keep thee; the Lord make His face to shine upon thee and be gracious unto thee; the Lord lift up His countenance upon thee and give thee peace."

In the Hidden Way of Sorrow

Then again there was a silence in the Hall of Dreams, deeper and more mysterious than the first interval, and I understood that the years of Artaban were flowing very swiftly under the stillness of that clinging fog, and I caught only a glimpse, here and there, of the river of his life shining through the shadows that concealed its course.

I saw him moving among the throngs of men in populous Egypt, seeking everywhere for traces of the household that had come down from Bethlehem, and finding them under the spreading sycamore-trees of Heliopolis, and beneath the walls of the Roman fortress of New Babylon beside the Nile—traces so faint and dim that they vanished before him continually, as footprints on the hard river-sand glisten for a moment with moisture and then disappear.

I saw him again at the foot of the pyramids, which lifted their sharp points into the intense saffron glow of the sunset sky, changeless monuments of the perishable glory and the imperishable hope of man. He looked up into the vast countenance of the crouching Sphinx and vainly tried to read the meaning of her calm eyes and smiling mouth. Was it, indeed, the mockery of all effort and all aspiration, as Tigranes had said—the cruel jest of a riddle that has no answer, a search that never can succeed? Or was there a touch of pity and encouragement in that inscrutable smile—a promise that even the defeated should attain a victory, and the disappointed should discover a prize, and the ignorant should be made wise, and the blind should see, and the wandering should come into the haven at last?

I saw him again in an obscure house of Alexandria, taking counsel with a Hebrew rabbi. The venerable man, bending over the rolls of parchment on which the prophecies of Israel were written, read aloud the pathetic words which foretold the sufferings of the promised Messiah—the despised and rejected of men, the man of sorrows and the acquaintance of grief.

"And remember, my son," said he, fixing his deep-set eyes upon the face of Artaban, "the King whom you are seeking is not to be found in a palace, nor among the rich and powerful. If the light of the world and the glory of Israel had been appointed to come with the greatness of earthly splendour, it must have appeared long ago. For no son of Abraham will ever again rival the power which Joseph had in the palaces of Egypt, or the magnificence of Solomon throned between the lions in Jerusalem. But the light for which the world is waiting is a new light, the glory that shall rise out of patient and triumphant suffering. And the kingdom which is to be established forever is a new kingdom, the royalty of perfect and unconquerable love. I do not know how this shall come to pass, nor how the turbulent kings and peoples of earth shall be brought to acknowledge the Messiah and pay homage to him. But this I know. Those who seek Him will do well to look among the poor and the lowly, the sorrowful and the oppressed."

So I saw the other wise man again and again, traveling from place to place, and searching among the people of the dispersion, with whom the little family from Bethlehem might, perhaps, have found a refuge. He passed through countries where famine lay heavy upon the land, and the poor were crying for bread. He made his dwelling in plague-stricken cities where the sick were languishing in the bitter companionship of helpless misery. He visited the oppressed and the afflicted in the gloom of subterranean prisons, and the crowded wretchedness of slave-markets, and the weary toil of galley-ships. In all this populous and intricate world of anguish, though he found none to worship, he found many to help. He fed the hungry, and clothed the naked, and healed the sick, and comforted the captive; and his years went by more swiftly than the weaver's shuttle that flashes back and forth through the loom while the web grows and the invisible pattern is completed.

It seemed almost as if he had forgotten his quest. But once I saw him for a moment as he stood alone at sunrise, waiting at the gate of a Roman prison. He had taken from a secret resting-place in his bosom the pearl, the last of his jewels. As he looked at it, a mellower lustre, a soft and iridescent light, full of shifting gleams of azure and rose, trembled upon its surface. It seemed to have absorbed some reflection of the colours of the lost sapphire and ruby. So the profound, secret purpose of a noble life draws into itself the memories of past joy and past sorrow. All that has helped it, all that has hindered it, is transfused by a subtle magic into its very essence. It becomes more luminous and precious the longer it is carried close to the warmth of the beating heart. Then, at last, while I was thinking of this pearl, and of its meaning, I heard the end of the story of the other wise man.

A Pearl of Great Price

Three-and-thirty years of the life of Artaban had passed away, and he was still a pilgrim and a seeker after light. His hair, once darker than the cliffs of Zagros, was now white as the wintry snow that covered them. His eyes, that once flashed like flames of fire, were dull as embers smouldering among the ashes.

Worn and weary and ready to die, but still looking for the King, he had come for the last time to Jerusalem. He had often visited the holy city before, and had searched through all its lanes and crowded hovels and black prisons without finding any trace of the family of Nazarenes who had fled from Bethlehem long ago. But now it seemed as if he must make one more effort, and something whispered in his heart that, at last, he might succeed. It was the season of the Passover. The city was thronged with strangers. The children of Israel, scattered in far lands all over the world, had returned to the Temple for the great feast, and there had been a confusion of tongues in the narrow streets for many days.

But on this day there was a singular agitation visible in the multitude. The sky was veiled with a portentous gloom, and currents of excitement seemed to flash through the crowd like the thrill which shakes the forest on the eve of a storm. A secret tide was sweeping them all one way. The clatter of sandals, and the soft, thick sound of thousands of bare feet shuffling over the stones, flowed unceasingly along the street that leads to the Damascus gate.

Artaban joined company with a group of people from his own country, Parthian Jews who had come up to keep the Passover, and inquired of them the cause of the tumult, and where they were going.

"We are going," they answered, "to the place called Golgotha, out-side the city walls, where there is to be an execution. Have you not heard what has happened? Two famous robbers are to be crucified, and with them another, called Jesus of Nazareth, a man who has done many wonderful works among the people, so that they love him greatly. But the priests and elders have said that he must die, because he gave himself out to be the Son of God. And Pilate has sent him to the cross because he said that he was the 'King of the Jews.'"

How strangely these familiar words fell upon the tired heart of Artaban! They had led him for a lifetime over land and sea. And now they came to him darkly and mysteriously like a message of despair. The King had arisen, but he had been denied and cast out. He was about to perish. Perhaps he was already dying. Could it be the same who had been born in Bethlehem, thirty-three years ago, at whose birth the star had appeared in heaven, and of whose coming the prophets had spoken?

Artaban's heart beat unsteadily with that troubled, doubtful appre-hension which is the excitement of old age. But he said within himself, "The ways of God are stranger than the thoughts of men, and it may be that I shall find the King, at last, in the hands of His enemies, and shall come in time to offer my pearl for His ransom before He dies."

So the old man followed the multitude with slow and painful steps towards the Damascus gate of the city. Just beyond the entrance of the guard-house a troop of Macedonian soldiers came down the street, dragging a young girl with torn dress and disheveled hair. As the Magian paused to look at her with compassion, she broke suddenly from the hands of her tormentors, and threw herself at his feet, clasping him around the knees. She had seen his white cap and the winged circle on his breast.

"Have pity on me," she cried, "and save me, for the sake of the God of Purity! I also am a daughter of the true religion which is taught by the Magi. My father was a merchant of Parthia, but he is dead, and I am seized for his debts to be sold as a slave. Save me from worse than death!"

Artaban trembled.

It was the old conflict in his soul, which had come to him in the palm-grove of Babylon and in the cottage at Bethlehem—the conflict between the expectation of faith and the impulse of love. Twice the gift which he had consecrated to the worship of religion had been drawn from his hand to the service of humanity. This was the third trial, the ultimate probation, the final and irrevocable choice.

Was it his great opportunity, or his last temptation? He could not tell. One thing only was clear in the darkness of his mind—it was inevitable. And does not the inevitable come from God?

One thing only was sure to his divided heart—to rescue this help-less girl would be a true deed of love. And is not love the light of the soul?

He took the pearl from his bosom. Never had it seemed so lumi-nous, so radiant, so full of tender, living lustre. He laid it in the hand of the slave.

"This is thy ransom, daughter! It is the last of my treasures which I kept for the King."

While he spoke the darkness of the sky thickened, and shuddering tremors ran through the earth, heaving convulsively like the breast of one who struggles with mighty grief.

The walls of the houses rocked to and fro. Stones were loosened and crashed into the street. Dust clouds filled the air. The soldiers fled in terror, reeling like drunken men. But Artaban and the girl whom he had ransomed crouched helpless beneath the wall of the Praetorium.

What had he to fear? What had he to live for? He had given away the last remnant of his tribute for the King. He had parted with the last hope of finding Him. The quest was over, and it had failed. But, even in that thought, accepted and embraced, there was peace. It was not resignation. It was not submission. It was something more profound and searching. He knew that all was well, because he had done the best that he could, from day to day. He had been true to the light that had been given to him. He had looked for more. And if he had not found it, if a failure was all that came out of his life, doubtless that was the best that was possible. He had not seen the revelation of "life everlasting, incorruptible and immortal." But he knew that even if he could live his earthly life over again, it could not be otherwise than it had been.

One more lingering pulsation of the earthquake quivered through the ground. A heavy tile, shaken from the roof, fell and struck the old man on the temple. He lay breathless and pale, with his gray head resting on the young girl's shoulder, and the blood trickling from the wound. As she bent over him, fearing that he was dead, there came a voice through the twilight, very small and still, like music sounding from a distance, in which the notes are clear but the words are lost. The girl turned to see if some one had spoken from the window above them, but she saw no one.

Then the old man's lips began to move, as if in answer, and she heard him say in the Parthian tongue:

"Not so, my Lord! For when saw I thee hungered, and fed thee? Or thirsty, and gave thee drink? When saw I thee a stranger, and took thee in? Or naked, and clothed thee? When saw I thee sick or in prison, and came unto thee? Three-and-thirty years have I looked for thee; but I have never seen thy face, nor ministered to thee, my King."

He ceased, and the sweet voice came again. And again the maid heard it, very faintly and far away. But now it seemed as though she understood the words:

"Verily I say unto thee, inasmuch as thou hast done it unto one of the least of these my brethren, thou hast done it unto me."

A calm radiance of wonder and joy lighted the pale face of Artaban like the first ray of dawn on a snowy mountain-peak. One long, last breath of relief exhaled gently from his lips.

His journey was ended. His treasures were accepted. The other Wise Man had found the King.

LARRY WOIWODE

ONE OF AMERICA'S MOST RESPECTED WRITERS, LARRY Woiwode was born in Sykeston, North Dakota, in 1941, and at age eight his family moved to Illinois. His writing career began when he was in high school, and continued at the University of Illinois, Urbana, where he also pursued a career in acting. Later he moved to New York City, where he saw his first stories appear in *The New Yorker* (over two dozen of his stories have appeared there), as well as in *The Atlantic, Harper's, Paris Review,* and other publications. He has received a fellowship from the Guggenheim Foundation, and the Award of Merit Medal from the American Academy of Arts and Letters for "Distinction in the Art of the Short Story," and his stories have appeared in four volumes of *Best American Short Stories.* In 1995 he was named poet laureate of North Dakota.

His books include *What I'm Going To Do, I Think,* which received the William Faulkner Foundation Award; *Beyond the Bedroom Wall, Indian Affairs, Silent Passengers, Eventide, Neumiller Stories, Poppa John, Born Brothers;* and the memoir *What I Think I Did,* named a Notable Book of the Year by the *New York Times Book Review.*

Woiwode's nonfiction book *Acts* is the novelist's meditation on the lives of the apostles as rendered in the Book of Acts, and is an intensely moving exploration of what it means to live today as a follower of Christ. He and his wife, Carole, live in North Dakota on their 160-acre farm near Mott, in the southwestern corner of the state.

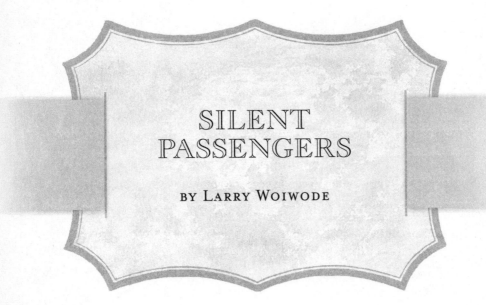

SILENT PASSENGERS

BY LARRY WOIWODE

Shut it off, Steiner told himself, and the station wagon was silent. He had pulled into the drive and up to the Chinese elm at the house without the reality of any of it registering, and now he turned to his nine-year-old, James, in the seat beside him, and saw the boy's face take on the expression of sly imbalance that Steiner had first noticed this afternoon.

Steiner got out, and James bucked against his seat belt, holding up a hand, so Steiner eased back in, shoving his unruly hair off his forehead, and took hold of the wheel. He was so used to James being out of the car and headed across the yard the moment after they stopped that he felt dazed. His white-blond twin daughters, seven, who were in the rear with his wife, Jen, were whispering, and Steiner turned to them with a look that meant *Silence*. He got out again with a heaviness that made him feel that his age, forty-five, was the beginning of old age, and the remorse that he'd been undergoing now had a focus: it was that he and Jen hadn't had more children.

As he was driving home, a twin had pulled herself forward from the backseat and whispered that James had reached over and honked the horn while Steiner was in the department store, where he had gone to look for a shatterproof full-length mirror and an exercise mat of the kind the physical therapist had recommended. And since James hadn't spoken for two weeks, the incident had set them to whispering about James, in speculative and hopeful terms (with James sitting right there), for most of the trip home.

"I'm sorry," Steiner said, seeing he was still the only one outside the car, as if he had to apologize for being on his feet. He slid back in, brushing aside his hair again, and began to unbuckle James's seat belt.

The boy stared out the windshield with an intensity Steiner couldn't translate and, once free, tried to scoot over to the passenger door by bending his torso forward and back.

"Take it easy, honey," Steiner said, and then added for the boy and the others, in the phrase he'd used since James was an infant, "Here we are, home." Silence. Steiner turned to Jen, who was leaning close, her pretty lips set, and said, "Do you have his other belt?" She gave a nod.

Steiner got out and looked across the top of the station wagon, through the leaves of the four-trunked elm, at their aging farmhouse. He hadn't seen it in two weeks. He'd spent that time at the hospital with James, first in intensive care, then in a private room, where physical therapists came and went, and at the sight of the white siding that he and James and Jen had scraped and repainted at the beginning of summer, he had to swallow down the loss he had started to feel when he realized he was grieving for a son he might never see again.

He looked up at a second-story window and remembered waking, sweaty, from a nap on the day that this began, on the floor of the twins' upstairs room, where he'd gone to be alone, and hearing James say, "Dad, do you still need me to help, or can I go to Billy Allen's with Mom and the girls and go riding?"

"They're going now?" Steiner had asked, feeling dislocated at finding himself on the floor of a room he usually visited only at the twins' bedtime. He had climbed up there after downing two beers in the August heat, and since he drank so seldom lately, he had almost passed out. He and the family were back at their high-plains ranch for the summer, to get away from the silicon-chip firm on the Coast which Steiner partly owned, and he and James and a neighbor had been trying to start a tractor that Steiner wanted to use to cultivate trees—"to play farmer," as the neighbor said. Steiner and the neighbor had spent most of that hot August morning pulling the diesel tractor in ovals around the drive with a second tractor, getting it going for a while and then listening to it die, with James hooking and unhooking the draw-bar chain and having to jump aside once in his nimble way when the neighbor missed the clutch and struck Steiner's big rear tires and merely bounced backward as the tractor stalled again.

Now Steiner strained to hear James's voice from that afternoon—the last time he'd heard him speak—and sensed that James had been at a distance, perhaps already heading downstairs, aware that Steiner was angry at the tractor and might be short-tempered after the beer. James would sometimes come up to Steiner, take his hand, and say, "Dad, I forgive you," before Steiner realized he'd been harsh or unfair, but James wasn't a do-gooder or tattletale; more a conscience.

Steiner had hoped to establish their home on this ranch and run his business from here, in order to spend more time with the children, as Jen had said he should. This last year he had been out of the office every month, traveling on consulting trips to Europe, and at the thought of all those jet-fuel-smelling 747s, Steiner was back on the floor of the twins' bedroom that August afternoon, reeking of the tractor fuel on his hands and clothes and the beer on his breath, caught off guard, laid low by drinking, and then he heard, as if James were standing above the spot where he lay: "I'll stay and help with the tractor if you want, Dad."

The memory of Steiner's response went through him so wildly he felt as dislocated as after an electrical shock. What was it he'd said? "I don't care."

He realized Jen had spoken, and saw James rubbing the window on his side, impatient to get out. Steiner hurried over and opened the door, and James grabbed at the dash and the seat, trying to propel himself from the car. Steiner squatted at the boy's level and took his hands in his. "Be patient a minute, honey," he said. "Remember your belt?"

The boy's hair was as unruly as his, and the sandy-colored curl at its edges needed trimming. James's eyes were nearly covered by it, Steiner saw, and then they rested on him in a dull love. Steiner coughed and felt a hand on his shoulder. Jen was standing above him, smiling—wisps of hair lifting from her forehead in a wind Steiner hadn't noticed until now—and the sight of her somehow enabled him to understand that he could endure handling James in the condition he was in on home ground. The boy loved the ranch so much that his usual good health appeared to get even better once they were here; he seemed to grow an inch his first week back, each time. Steiner lifted James from the seat, turning him so his back rested on Steiner's stomach, careful of the boy's ribs, and the heated weight of James against him had the effect of blocking the blood to his brain. His mind went blank, and he couldn't think who he was.

James started pedaling his feet in a spinning run in place, and Jen laughed and shook her head. Then she glanced around the yard and off to a blue-shaded butte, as if to make the landscape hers again, and looked buoyant with the breath she took, then wiped at the corner of an eye. "You're so dear," she said to James, smiling down at him.

Steiner had spent the last week trying to decide if James's sense of humor was returning, as when a therapist had helped the boy down a ramp into the hospital pool for the first attempt at one of the forms of therapy a pediatrician had prescribed and James, a natural swimmer, had become so excited at the sensation of water that he tried to run and fell with a splash. When the therapist and Jen, who got her skirt soaked, pulled him from the pool, James mimicked a hangdog look, and then, for the first time since the accident, contrived a smile, wry and lopsided, that caused Steiner to laugh.

James produced the same smile when he was on his next instrument of therapy—a stainless-steel tricycle—every time the therapist relaxed her control over the handlebars and he rammed it into a wall, reminding Steiner of the time a colleague from the East, a designer whose chips were as intricate as a gridwork of Manhattan, with each cornice and window in place in every building, was scheduled to arrive at the ranch and Steiner was on the phone, trying to contend with a local plumber who had promised to check their failing sewage systems but now was pretending he hadn't promised *when* he would, and Steiner tried to say, "But we must have a bathroom," and was only able to get out "But . . . But . . ." And when he hung up, James came hurrying past—nearly impossible now to recapture this dancing half run the boy performed with such agility—and said from the side of his mouth, "Is your butt broke, Dad?" Once Steiner had begun to grieve for the James he had known, the grief grew worse when he realized that in the last year or so it had been James, as much as anyone, who had been able to cheer him.

Now Jen slid an arm between Steiner's stomach and James, passing the padded canvas belt around the boy's waist. She drew it snug and then buckled him in. James's closed-head injury, as the doctors called it, was in the rear-left quadrant, so his right limbs weren't responding as they should, and the physical therapist had demonstrated to Steiner and Jen how to grip the belt from behind in order to support James in his walking, which kept improving with his visits to the pool.

"Do you want to—" Steiner began, but Jen already had the belt, and James went teetering off, with her in tow, past the front of the car, as if on a beeline toward the last moment he might remember—the tractor. Steiner's daughters went past with their hair streaming back, laughing at the speed of James's walk and Jen's attempts to keep up. James was enamored of farm equipment, and the connection he might make to the person he had been before, Steiner had thought through the hospital stay, was the tractor. Their neighbor had fixed it—a plugged fuel filter, he discovered—and had driven to the hospital to tell them when James was still in the state the doctors called comatose, and Steiner was sure he'd seen James respond.

So all through the hospital stay, Steiner kept telling James they would get the tractor song as soon as they returned home. He was grateful to Jen now, though, that she had taken him away. Steiner tried again to hear James's voice asking to go to Billy Allen's that afternoon, and then he remembered waking a second time, after the family was gone from the house, to somebody calling his name—the neighbor who had been helping with the tractor. "Billy Allen's on the line," the man had said, and Steiner's first thought was *Something's happened to James*. The neighbor was in the kitchen, staring out at the tractor, Steiner saw as he went by, noticing the broken-open six-pack on the table.

"Yes?" he said into the receiver.

"Steiner," Billy Allen said. "Bad news. The kids was back from riding, unsaddling the horses—your wife was there, I wasn't—when my gelding, Apache, spooked, I guess, and went over the top of James. He's hurt. I don't know how bad, Steiner, but he ain't conscious yet." Allen's voice parted with fear at this. "I called the ambulance. We'll meet you at the hospital," Billy said, and hung up.

Steiner called right back, but the phone kept ringing. Billy Allen lived on a river-bottom ranch thirty miles off and all summer he had been asking the twins to come and ride, and Steiner's response had been, "What's wrong with our horses?" until Jen said, "Surely you know that poor lonely old bachelor dotes on girls." So why did James go? Steiner almost yelled into the phone that kept on ringing.

He drove to the hospital at a speed his pickup probably wouldn't recover from, trying not to picture the ways James could be injured. He had bought the six-pack on an errand to town, for his neighbor to enjoy in the heat, he told himself, but back home he cracked a can himself, irritated at that damn tractor that had already cost him enough, and then looked down to see James staring up in sadness, prepared to forgive him. Then he recalled that he had told James on the trip to the ranch that he wasn't going to drink this summer, not even a beer— since lately drinking made Steiner unpredictable. The image of James staring up, with Jen's beauty in his features, stayed in Steiner's mind throughout the twenty-some miles to the hospital, while he kept saying, "Please, please," meaning, Don't let his face be disfigured.

He beat the ambulance in. The nurse at the emergency desk, wearing an orange stopwatch on a cord around her neck, seemed the bulky focus of a world that was still stable. She said the ambulance had called in, and from somewhere under the counter between them a radio crackled on, and an amplified voice said something Steiner couldn't catch. Before he was able to ask the nurse anything, she picked up a microphone from under the counter and said, "How is he?" A wash of static went through Steiner like anxiety, and again he couldn't make out a word.

The nurse studied him with set lips, appraising him, and said, "There are no marks on him, they say"—as if she knew what he needed to hear—"but he isn't conscious yet."

NOW STEINER SAW JAMES SWERVE TOWARD THE GRANARY near the drive, with Jen keeping up and with one daughter holding James's hand and the other grabbing at her mother's skirt. The tractor sat in the unmowed grass ahead. Steiner turned from them into a flash like a press camera's—the mirror in the rear of the station wagon reflecting sun into his eyes. He leaned against the automobile, unable to stop this sequence that kept returning: the stretcher tilting from the ambulance, James's blue face against sheets, Jen squalling up in the station wagon and running over in riding denims, the girls running after her, and then the glass doors to the hospital springing open with a hiss; hearing this and the clattering of the footsteps but no sound of a voice. Then the stretcher rolled closed, and he could hear James going, "Ohhh, ohh," in shallow sighs. Jen embraced Steiner with an impact that set him off balance and cried, "It's my fault!"

"No," Steiner said, holding her so hard that the snaps of her jacket dug into his chest. The stretcher paused, as if the ambulance attendants were waiting for a command, and Steiner turned, one arm still around Jen, and tried to locate James's hand under the blanket and discovered that he was strapped to some sort of hard-plastic carrier. Two swelling, padded curves gripped his jaw on each side, and straps were buckled across his forehead and near his neck.

"It's Dad, I'm here," Steiner said, and thought he heard a catch in James's breathing. Good God, he thought, and closed his eyes and understood that each "Oh" from James was an attempt to cry out in pain and felt that if he could enter James and bear this moment for him, his son would rise from the stretcher and walk away. Then the doctor, a French Vietnamese who had taken over a local quarter-horse ranch, was in the midst of them, looking like a jockey in a torn red T-shirt, saying to an ambulance attendant, "You thought a spinal injury?"

He quickly undid the buckles near James's neck to help him breathe more freely, and the attendant said, "In case."

"Here," the doctor said, and grabbed the head of the stretcher and pulled it into a side room himself—as if to be free of the attendants— and over to an examining table. "Dad and Mom, here," he said, and when an attendant with a full beard attempted to block the door, he called, "No! I want them in here to help—answer questions! What's his name?"

"James."

"James! Can you hear me?"

James lay inert, expressionless, ivory, and beneath the overhead lights Steiner saw the boy's lips tug and quiver with inner pain, as if bearing it took his entire concentration. The nurse helped the doctor slide James and the board onto the examining table, and the doctor probed his neck and skull and took a flashlight from the nurse and looked into James's eyes, drawing his lids high with a thumb, and then, with a look, scraped the soles of both feet, hammered at James's knees and elbows, drew the tool up his sternum, and said, "Get upper X-rays, quick."

To Steiner he said, "I'm going to give him some oxygen through a nasal cannula here," already tearing open a sack. A coil of blue-tinted plastic fell from it over the boy's bare legs, pale and dirt-smeared. Why was he wearing shorts to ride? Steiner almost shouted, and felt a hand on his back. Billy Allen stood with a hat over his chest, chin trembling, and said, "I should have been there to help. Call my insurance company. Sue me." The elderly man looked almost in tears, and one of the ambulance attendants led him away into the hall.

"That's all I can do," the doctor said. "I see head injury but no sign of it. He's not posing or putting on displays of extensive damage, but is comatose, you see. I'm running quick X-rays"—the machine above them clicked on, humming, and the doctor glanced at it and shrugged. "I'm sending him to the city hospital. You'll want all the attention he can—"

Steiner swooped for James, who had grabbed the side of the table to pull himself over, about to fall as Steiner got to him, and then, in a spasm that drew James's knees near his chest, he gagged up watery stuff, then groaned and gagged up a dark spoonful the nurse caught in a stainless-steel bowl.

"Last meal?" the doctor asked.

"Lunch," Jen whispered, hoarse, and Steiner saw her on the other side, ducking the X-ray machine a technician was running on an overhead track, holding James's hand.

"Goodness," the doctor said, "look at him empty his stomach—good response. We'll have to keep his lungs clear. I'm putting in a stomach tube. Catheter, too," he said to the nurse, already through a leg of James's shorts with glittering shears and clipping off his stained T-shirt.

"Test that," he said to the nurse, nodding at the bowl. "Could be bloody tinged. Maybe internal injuries," he whispered to Steiner. "I'm telling you straight. You see he doesn't respond in any normal way. Oh—a hoof got him." A curved ridge of torn skin lay under the stained T-shirt, and James's high arch of ribs was dented in. "Ribs," the doctor said to the technician. "Poor kid." Then to Steiner, "He'll be prepped for the ambulance."

"Let's call a helicopter," Steiner said, and everybody looked up, as if the shout he'd subdued had come out. He'd heard that helicopters were being used in this sparsely populated territory to ferry people to city hospitals, and the thought of this had arrived with a jolt: *critical accident victim.*

"The ambulance is as fast, I bet," the doctor said. "And about as smooth a ride. I don't want him jarred too much till we get a CAT scan. His spine's okay, I think. I'll get him ready and can just about guarantee he'll get to the hospital fine."

A silence came, and as Steiner waited for further reassurance, he looked across at Jen and saw her head bowed over James's hand, which she held to her lips. "James!" she cried, "I know you can hear me!"

The boy writhed: tubes were in his nostrils, and one was in his mouth—hurriedly taped to his sleep-struck face—and he seemed to be writhing in resistance to the catheter the nurse was trying to insert; his hand swung at her.

"Good!" the doctor said, and took the tube from the nurse and tried himself, sweat running beneath his glasses until he whispered, "This is so hard with little boys," nearly in tears. "It's just that we got to have access to his functions. Oh, little boy. His heart is steady, good." A black-and-gray negative clopped into a white-lit frame. "Oh," the doctor said, "four ribs, at least, in this first X-ray, but no lung puncture that I see. I can say for sure they'll get him there without a change."

"I'll ride in the ambulance!" Jen declared.

There were looks all around, and the doctor said, "I'm sorry—I think they have regulations. Is the driver here?"

"Me." A young fellow at the door in a baseball cap.

"Follow right behind," the doctor told Steiner, tucking a blanket around James. To an elderly nurse who was looking in from the hall, he said, "Ride along and keep him warm. And you," he said to the ambulance driver, "take it slow, easy over bumps, no use exceeding, play it safe."

It was the longest trip Steiner had endured, it felt, following at the ambulance's back, separated from James. But during it he heard the story from Jen. Billy Allen had been busy moving irrigation pipes, so he got the horses saddled and went back to work, and when they were done and had started to unsaddle, the horse that James was riding, Apache, went wild, Jen said—all of this happening so fast she hardly had a chance to get the girls out of the way as Apache charged. She was sure James was safe, because he had been standing farther back, and then the horse spun, its saddle swinging to one side, and she heard a sound like a post struck and came around the corner where she'd taken cover and saw James, a ways from Apache, hit down.

"I knew right away he was terribly hurt. The horse sent off to a fence, kicking at the saddle, and the worst part of it, I mean now, is that James was on his back trying to push himself up. He's that strong. His head came up, he tried to open his eyes, and then he sank back, and I caught his head. I didn't think he'd breathe, I waited so long, I don't know how long, rubbing him and asking him to breathe—I knew I had to support his head—and finally he gasped."

Steiner saw that James had traveled past the tractor with his mother and was heading toward the pasture at the northern corner of the yard. The twins were going ahead, through shaggy grass that hadn't been mowed in weeks and reached to their hips, toward a garage that stood alone at the corner of the two-acre farmyard, the peak of its roof like a parody of the tepee buttes that rose above it—so hazy in the late-summer heat that they seemed to simmer on the horizon like a mirage. Then Steiner saw where James was headed. At the end of the garage, on the other side of the pasture fence that from his distance was invisible, three of their quarter horses—a stately bay the size of a cavalry mount and a buckskin mare who seemed on a constant nervous search for the colt nudging up behind her—came ambling forward, all of them at attention, their heads and ears up. Then the bay whinnied in acknowledgement of the family he knew.

James was heading toward him.

He remembers, Steiner thought, his hair going back in the wind, and sat down in the seat where James had been sitting. Steiner had imagined taking a 30.30 to Allen's and dropping the rogue Apache. I still might, he thought, once James is—

The second night at the hospital, while he stood watch in the intensive-care ward as Jen slept, he heard the beeps of James's heart monitor start to slow, and when he checked the digital display that printed out every half minute, he saw it read forty-six. At forty an alarm went off, and the nurse on duty, who was at a desk behind glass, looked up. It was a large ward, but James's bed was the only one in it, and the nurse glanced at the monitor on her desk and then shook her head as if to clear it. She was Steiner's age, responsible for supervising the student nurses, beside her ICU duties, and Steiner understood by her response that she was overworked.

She came through the door into the ward, which was dimly lit by baseboard lights, and stood at the other side of James's bed. "Is our boy tired?" she whispered, and with the second sense Steiner was developing, he realized that her concern for James exceeded medical limits; she had become personally involved. She was wearing slacks and a turtleneck—the informality on pediatrics disturbed Steiner; nobody wore white—and he could picture her standing like this with her husband, the baseboard lights projecting their shadows on the ceiling above a son's bed. "Should his heartbeat be so slow?" he whispered, imagining James heard every word.

"Oh, he's a child," she said, recovering from whatever state she had slipped into. "It's surprising how low it can go in one. Did he use to run a lot?"

"Yes."

"If it was you or me, I'd be concerned."

But when she went back to her desk, he saw her turn aside to make a phone call. The next digital printout read thirty-five. At thirty Steiner saw her go to a refrigerator and prepare a syringe, and then he had to blink against the overhead lights she suddenly switched on. She walked in and looked down at James, her hands on her hips, detached and angry, a nurse again, then strode back to her station.

Steiner put a hand on the far side of James and leaned over him. "James," he said, and couldn't say any more. Without a sign of injury, James looked more beautiful than ever, and all Steiner could do was stare down at him and take in every feature and inch of skin in case he never saw him alive again. He felt he could see into James to the place where he had retreated, where his real self rested, hidden, and should call to him there. Then this seemed presumptuous, grandiose—as if it were in his power to call James back! His lips felt sealed. But if he, the boy's father, wouldn't make the effort, who would? "James," he said firmly, more severely than he'd intended, and with a skip the boy's heart rate on the monitor picked up again.

The neurologist was noncommittal, one neurosurgeon was hopeful, many of the physical therapists were encouraged, but the pediatrician overseeing James was pessimistic, given to scowling, and when James didn't fully awaken from the coma after forty-eight hours, and seventy-two, and then four days, his scowl deepened. Wriggling a toothbrush mustache as he pursed and compressed his lips, he asked Steiner and Jen "to step with" him from James's bed, where they were sharing a shift. He sat them down in a lounge and said that since they hadn't seen any of the signs in James they were looking for, all of them had to face the worst: that James might not recover, or if he did, he would have to undergo the most comprehensive therapy merely to restore his basic functions, which did not mean—his mustache wriggled—vocal speech.

They tried to convince him that they had seen a change, that

James's eyes were open more often, that he seemed to respond to his name, that the head nurse had said she was sure he was following along when she read from a children's book she held in front of him, and Jen brought up a theory she'd mentioned to Steiner—that James was such a perfectionist, he wouldn't speak until he could speak as he used to. No, the doctor insisted, they must not get their hopes up; that was why they were having this "counseling session."

So Steiner got up and took Jen's hand and walked off with her to a room the head nurse was letting them use for naps, and in a rawness of intimacy he wanted to have her on the spot, but knew they must do something as parents. Without a word to one another, they went down on their knees. Steiner wasn't sure what he said but felt they were on an ascending elevator and when they stood had reached another plane. Then Jen said, "I want to hold him."

They went into the hall hand in hand and hurried to the boy's bed, like youngsters escaping the pediatrician. Steiner helped Jen draw James from the bed, moving tubes and an IV stand, and into a rocker with her. James's head dropped back, his lips apart and his eyes open, and he stared up at her with the distant look Steiner had seen in him when he rested in the crook of her arm like this as a nursing infant. Then James struggled to rise and put his arms around Jen's neck.

The next morning, as the pediatrician was doing his daily tests and called, "James, squeeze my finger!" he glanced at Steiner and Jen, eyes wide, and said, "Some grip!" Later that day, James opened his mouth to speak and looked puzzled, then tried again, shifting his lips, and finally gave up. But from then his progress was fast. The next day, he was transferred from intensive care and put on his course of physical therapy, and then Jen said it was time to go home. The pediatrician, who by now was less pessimistic, went so far as to say that Jen was doing more for James than most of the—there was a twist of his mustache—"care professionals."

So they left, and now, away from that institution and under this expanse of sky, Steiner understood that though he may have thought the worst at times, and didn't always know how to handle what was happening, there was a part of him that never doubted that James would recover. Which was what allowed him to stay sane enough to help the boy. James's recovery seemed an internal process, nearly separate from him and Jen, and they had been borne along by it, silent passengers, aware of the movement of time overhead, until it had brought them home.

So now Steiner drew himself from the seat and walked around the station wagon to watch James and Jen and his daughters at the fence. The horses were arching their necks down to them, and James leaned forward from the belt, his left hand up, and stroked the nose of the bay, then the skittish buckskin, who jerked back at his touch, checked for her colt, then came forward and nodded her head at him. His hand traveled over her face and muzzle, unsteadily at first, and then he assumed a courtly stance that he used to favor, and Steiner had a glimpse of the son who had always had a way with pardon. That's enough, he thought. He had always wondered how parents with injured or diminished children were able to bear it. He pitied their patience and calm, but now he understood; it was enough to have the child with them, alive.

James turned, sensing Steiner's eyes on him, and brought Jen swinging around as she held to his belt, and the horses wheeled away, heading down the hill toward the pasture. *Get back*, Steiner cried to himself. He could feel the battering of hooves from where he stood and imagined the weighty charge of Apache toward James, and then a gust of wind took his hair straight up, and he saw James's and Jen's and the twins' hair climb the air also, the girls' high above their heads, streaming back like banners against the sky. And over the days and months afterward, when James had started talking and traveling everywhere on a run, the sensation of that moment kept returning to Steiner—all of them suspended for a second against the horizon, silent in the wind.

ACKNOWLEDGMENTS

THE EDITOR WOULD LIKE TO THANK THE FOLLOWING FOR their help in bringing together this collection:

John Specht for the legwork involved

Greg Wolfe for his blessed advice

Melanie Lott for her enduring faith and typing skills

Amanda Bostic and Allen Arnold for their patience, patience, patience, and their vision for the role of literature and art in the lives of believing Christians everywhere